Big Beaver Road

By
Michael Ripinski

MARSHALL - MICHIGAN
800PUBLISHING.COM

Thanks for READING!

Mike Ripple

For Mrs. B

1

Between 1962 and 1965, the Burnstek Chemical Company used area landfills to dispose of waste from its processing plants located in Southeast Michigan. Public records showed that owner Stanley Burns had been routinely cited by local municipalities for illegal dumping and improper handling of hazardous waste. One such landfill was owned by the Norris family and was located on a two- lane road in Troy Michigan.

An excavation, fifty-yards in diameter, had left a large hole, a mound of dirt and rock piles around the edge of the crater. On a cloudy, damp, late October night, a large unidentified truck containing unmarked barrels, disposed of its cargo into the twenty-foot deep hole followed by a crew with a backhoe filling in with sand and dirt. By morning the entire area was filled, leveled and clear of vehicles. The entry gate on Big Beaver Road had been padlocked and a rust edged white sign with red letters announced KEEP OUT. For the next thirty years the area was left unattended, to be reclaimed by the weeds and grasses that covered the adjacent land.

Walt Jacob had discovered the problem while digging through the files of the property owner, just the normal due diligence. Now he regretted ever agreeing to be a partner with the other three investors who had hired these so-called consultants, but he was doing it as a favor to his wife and for Charles B. Vandenberg, Governor of the State of Michigan; Charlie V to his friends and the press. It wasn't enough that the Jacobs were among the biggest private donors to The Governor and had hosted fund raising parties in order to help stuff the coffers of the Friends of Charlie V, but now he was mixed up in this deal that was sure to collapse due to a fraudulent environmental report. It could get very expensive for the investors. Millions were at stake. He was assured that everything would be taken care of by some friend of the Governor but he still didn't like it. In his mind it was just plain wrong. The Oakland County property was one of the most attractive parcels not yet developed along Big Beaver Road. Once the site of a private landfill, it was used primarily as an overflow parking lot for the nearby hotel and convention center. Not many recalled that the now defunct chemical company had once used the site to dispose of waste. PCB's, mercury and cyanide by- products were among the highly dangerous and deadly contents of the barrels that were lying twenty feet below the surface. Walt and his partners were planning to develop the land as a new retail and office complex and had already lined up major tenants including a prominent accounting firm and two national retailers. With close to thirty acres total and a thousand feet of frontage along Big Beaver Road, it was a prime piece of real estate. The most recent owner was the seventy-year old daughter of the original landfill operator and she had decided to finally sell after turning down many lucrative offers over the years. Edna Biddle Norris was also the widow of David Norris, second cousin to one Charlie Vandenberg. Realizing that she could get a lot more for the land, nevertheless she agreeably sold it to Charlie's friends for a fraction of its worth, unaware of the hazardous material buried deep in the ground. But Walt Jacob knew. He found the old records in a file belonging to David Norris that was stored in Edna's basement showing that the land was once leased to Burnstek and he made the mistake of turning over the files to one of his partners.

2

The new truck, a deep forest green color, with only two thousand miles on the odometer rolled slowly to a stop in the horseshoe driveway near the overgrown thirty-foot spruce. Extended boughs and branches obstructed any view from the stately home on Blissfield Drive. Wearing jeans, green tee shirt and cap, the slender young man quickly opened the door on his new Ford 150, leaving the motor running as he hurried to the side of the four-bedroom, white frame colonial in the affluent Detroit suburb of Birmingham. Having left this same location earlier in the day after completing his weekly landscaping job, Tom Hodges was a little embarrassed to admit that he had forgotten his expensive hedge trimmers near the row of cedars at the north side of the house. Also worried that his new clients might think he was careless, he avoided being seen; stealthily moving around the property, stepping carefully around a rock garden and a Chinese maple that he had planted just last week.

Tom was conscious about his image. He graduated from high school in nearby Madison Heights in spite of a severe speech defect. He stuttered. Always feeling a little left out in groups, he concentrated instead on solo activities. While in school he had few friends but those who knew him realized he was quite intelligent and appreciated him as good listener. It came with the territory. Becoming more observant, he formed a keen awareness of speaking habits and personalities.

Starting when he was just fifteen, mowing lawns in his neighborhood, Tom found the solitary work very rewarding and his extreme attention to detail brought many referrals. To compensate for his lack of verbal skill, he learned to create impressive flyers and advertisements, which he distributed himself. There were usually few words spoken as he pointed to the type of services each new customer desired. Mowing, Tree Trimming, Sod Replacement, Fertilizing, Hedge Trimming, and Irrigation were item on his menu of offerings. Below was a standard hourly labor rate and he offered bids on regular contracts. These new clients in Birmingham had recently signed a seasonal contract for weekly lawn care with an additional fee for designing and planting that had included the Chinese maple as well as two large perennial gardens along either side of the main entrance. This job alone would make his summer very profitable and he hoped to impress them enough to be renewed for the following year. The more his business grew the more he dreamed about how he could make a better life for himself and his single mother who raised him while barely making ends meet on a small disability pension from an automotive supplier in Pontiac.

The mid summer evening brought some cooling relief after a hot and humid day, in the high eighties, one of those Michigan, July dog-days. The sweat stains remained on his tee shirt and around the edges of his Detroit Tigers cap. He was tired but he decided to just get the trimmers and leave quickly.

Approaching the north side of the house, he noticed the silver Mercedes C-280 with Illinois plates parked in the driveway in front of the attached garage. It wasn't there earlier in the day and he knew that the couple both drove black BMW's. Spotting the trimmers at the base of a large rose bush just below a window, he quickly reached to retrieve them when he heard the shouting inside. At first he couldn't make out the words but he could identify at least three different voices and one belonged to his client Mr. Jacob. He only wanted to get his trimmers and get the hell out of there but something else caught his attention. More shouting followed by a thumping noise, which he was certain was caused by a struggle. Whatever was going on inside was none of his business, however Tom felt concern for Mr. Jacob. The noises stopped and he could faintly hear more voices as he cowered beneath the window remaining out of sight for the moment. Deciding that he better make a run for his truck he clutched the trimmers in his left hand and, staying low to the ground, sprinted away from the building toward the big spruce tree, looking back only after he ducked around the branches hiding his truck.

Inside, the two men who arrived in the Mercedes stood over the unconscious form of Walt Jacob. Dressed in gray wool slacks and a black collarless shirt, thick biceps and forearms extending from the sleeves, the driver spoke to his companion. "We can't let him talk to anyone after this. I have orders. "

"I Know. I know. Do you think we should take care of this right now? He's just passed out from your choke hold."The second man, wearing tan slacks and a Navy blue golf shirt moved toward the window. "Hey come here. Look at this."Pointing toward the truck as it pulled forward in the circular driveway beyond the spruce, turning in a tight radius, tires tracking over the edge of freshly mowed lawn, heading toward the street.

"Damn."The driver ran to the front door and with one swift motion opened it, leaped to the brick paved walkway, skipping the four steps altogether and began sprinting toward the entry to the driveway, arriving just in time to see the truck speeding away. As it swerved to avoid another car approaching, the Mercedes driver was able to make out the name stenciled on the back hatch, *Tommy's Landscape Services*.

After grabbing a black duffel bag from the back seat of his car, he entered the house to find his partner dragging the motionless body of Walt Jacob toward the door leading to the basement. Without speaking, the driver opened the door, tossed the bag down the stairs, grabbed the legs of their victim and assisted in lifting him down to the lower level where they sat him in a leather chair his arms hanging over the sides and his legs stretched straight out in front on the carpet.

The driver spoke first. "I got the name on the truck. It must have been the lawn guy who we saw here last week. I kinda remembered the green truck. We'll have to deal with him later. Right now we got to take care of this. Wake him up Tony."

Tony Parnelli walked to the bar in the corner of the finished basement and ran water over a hand towel then returned to the leather chair. "I think this will do it."Wiping the cold, wet towel over Walt Jacob's face and head made him moan and come around. Tony slapped him across the cheeks a couple of times as he opened his eyes to see the driver pointing a 38 Smith and Wesson at his head.

Coughing and grabbing his throat at the same time, Walt tried to speak but couldn't. The last thing he remembered before passing out was the hand around his throat as they fell backwards against the dining room wall. He also recalled the argument over his intention to warn the other investors on the dangers of proceeding with the deal and if they wouldn't agree, he would go public and give the information to some friends in the press. They could not change his mind and it would cost him.

It became apparent that his two visitors had no intention of listening and were there to get his agreement. The driver lowered the gun for a moment as he reached into his pocket for a pen. Placing it on the table he again raised the gun toward Walt and asked; "Where's your computer? "

Walt pointed toward a door at the opposite end of the room and replied in a raspy whisper. "I have an office in there."

The driver said to Tony. "Get me a plain piece of computer paper and bring it here."

As directed, Tony opened the door, turned on the light switch and located the printer on the corner desk. After taking a sheet of paper from the tray, he returned to the table and placed it in front of Walt Jacob.

"Now you're gonna do as I tell you or your wife is going to find a bloody mess here with your brains all over this table. Sign your name on the bottom of the page as if you were signing a birthday card to your wife. You know. Love Walt. Or something like that."

Not knowing why they were asking him to do this, he felt that he'd better go along and with the pen provided by the driver he signed the blank piece of paper. *Love Always, Walter*. Placing the pen back onto the table he looked at each of his captors and tried to search their eyes for some sign of what they were planning.

Taking the paper in his gloved hand the driver said. "Good. Good. This will work fine."Motioning with the gun "Now get up and stand against the wall."

"Don't. Don't shoot me. Please. I'll keep my mouth shut."Getting up and doing as he was told.

"We ain't gonna shoot you. Are we Tony?"Handing the gun over to his partner, the driver pushed Walt Jacobs against the wall.

"No we ain't gonna shoot you Walt."Tony placed the barrel next to Walt's cheek reminding him that they could change their minds.

The driver opened the duffel and extracted a white rope. The type that was sometimes used for sash cords in windows found in older homes. Unwinding the rope he stretched a length about two feet apart and held the ends in either hand as he approached his unsuspecting victim. With a startling quick motion he placed the cord around his victim's neck and crossing his hands, tightened the slack so fast that Walt immediately lost consciousness for the last time – his body slumping to the floor as the driver held tight to the rope. After shaping the rope to form a rough noose the driver and Tony carefully carried him to a closet located next to the stairwell. Wrapping the long end of the rope around the metal bar which stretched along the back of the closet they lifted the lifeless body until the feet were about six inches above the floor and tightened the slack tying it off to the bar. Finally, they left an overturned empty wash pail a few feet from the body.

After cleaning up the house, eliminating any trace of their visit, the driver went to the computer, erased some document files and grabbed a disc that was labeled simply -Big Beaver Project. There was one last thing to do. He put the paper with Walt's signature in the computer tray and typed out the suicide note, printed it, then placed it on the table along with the pen before they left the house.

Michael Ripinski

3

Dick Hagan retired from The Detroit Police Department as a homicide detective and had recently moved to the spacious two bedroom detached condo just off Long Lake Road in the northern part of Troy. After thirty years he had enough of the nasty, often frustrating business of investigating murders in the violent areas of this notorious city. Times had changed dramatically over the years especially with the severe impact of the economy and on-going, local government corruption investigations. It was dangerous work with the occasional success story mixed in with the mostly futile attempts at solving cases, which were frequently connected to the rampant illegal drug trade and lucrative car theft business. About the only thing he missed was the friendship of his fellow detectives and the times they spent at the Old Shillelagh Bar on Monroe near Greektown, about a block from the Beaubien Street Police Headquarters. He rarely went downtown any more and mostly kept busy reading and playing golf, which he found to be a whole new kind of challenge. Occasionally finding a partner at the local municipal course, he enjoyed meeting new people who were much different from the tough guy cops he worked with or the thugs and gang members who made up the usual list of suspects in his old line of work. The real bright spot in his transition was meeting Melissa Connolly at the local upscale health and fitness club. They were exclusive since the third date when she took him back to her apartment on a Friday night and he didn't leave until Sunday.

It was just after eight PM on a Thursday as he was about to pour himself a glass of scotch. The bottle of Glenlivet was a gift from a Greektown restaurant owner. After the first sip he heard the familiar sound. At first thinking he was hearing fireworks, actually hoping it was, Dick instinctively knew the sound of small arms gunfire. *Not here. Not in this part of town. Not in my new neighborhood.* Hurrying to the front door he waited a moment before carefully opening it. After crouching to a near kneeling position he peaked out to the grassy square, common to the row of buildings that made up the Oak Woods Estates Condominium complex. He scanned the area - four buildings on each side of a three-sided courtyard- with the center lawn highlighted by a natural pine gazebo, which was part of the curb appeal of the development. Laying partially on the paved brick walkway leading to the gazebo was a lifeless body and even from where he was, some fifty yards away, he could tell that the man was probably dead. Taking care to visually examine the area before heading out of his condo, he pulled his cell phone from his pants pocket and called 911.

The voice answered "Troy Police Emergency. "

In his practiced detective procedural voice. "We have a shooting at 2016 Red Oak Lane." giving his own address. "One man down. Send EMS."

"Yes sir. Let me make sure I understand. You are reporting a shooting. The victim is in your house? Is the shooter still in the area? "

"Negative. The victim is lying near the gazebo in the middle of our courtyard. I am a resident here. No sign of the shooter. You should send detectives as well."

"Are you a police officer sir?"

"Uh yeah. Sort of. I'm retired DPD."

"I am sending a car right now. Could you stay on the line sir? "

"Just send the car. I will be in the area. My name is Hagan. I will be here when they arrive." Folding the phone to its compact position he placed it back in his right front pocket and after scanning the area again he eased out on the front steps of his condo. A few other residents had come out onto their steps as well and he proceeded cautiously toward the gazebo. Approaching the body he noticed the blue Detroit Tigers cap lying on the ground. As he reached along the side of the man's neck to determine a pulse he already knew there was no hope. Two crimson stained entry wounds marked the back of the white cotton tee shirt and a third had entered at the base of his left ear.

Now noticing about five or six other residents approaching,

he abruptly stood which made them halt about twenty feet from the body. Holding his left hand out flat, fingers pointing up, he motioned for them to stay back before speaking. "The police are on their way."Not recognizing any of these neighbors among the few he had met, he felt that he should identify himself. "I'm Dick Hagan. I live over there."Pointing to his new condo. "I am a retired cop. Did anyone see anything? "Looking at them one at a time, as they each nodded no.

An older, balding man wearing tan shorts and a yellow golf shirt spoke up. "I heard the shots as I was getting in my car in the garage. Heard someone running past my place. I live in the end unit there by the entrance. There's a sidewalk that goes along the fence on the other side. Didn't see nothing though. By the time I came back through my house and out the front door I saw you approaching here. Name's Purdy. Al Purdy."

Dick was about to respond as a siren and flashing lights announced the arrival of the first black police squad car. Soon a second and a third entered the area with one of them riding over the lawn all the way to the scene where Dick was now standing over the body.

"Everyone stay back. You there, move away from the body."A young uniformed police officer announced as he exited the squad car, motioned to Dick to step back, his right hand on his weapon attached to the utility belt around his waist. His partner, standing behind the driver's side door his hand also on his weapon held the radio mic near his face.

Soon the other officers exited their cars and were immediately upon the scene. An older officer with the rank of sergeant took control of the situation while the first one stooped over the victim and repeated the same actions that Dick had done only a few moments before. Looking back at the sergeant without speaking he nodded negatively to confirm that the wounds were fatal.

During this routine Dick stayed silent allowing these men to do their job but now he decided to offer his assistance. "My name's Hagan. Retired Detroit Homicide. Live in the second building over there"Pointing again to his condo. "I heard the shots while I was inside and when I opened my door, saw the victim here. Didn't see anything else. Man over there, Mister Purdy says he heard someone running along the side of his house right after the shots. Don't think any of these other folks saw anything."

One of the other officers approached Al Purdy and began interviewing him as the sergeant turned to Dick. "Do you have some ID sir?"

"Sure, no problem."Reaching for his wallet from his rear pants pocket he produced the plastic folder with his driver's license and a gun permit with his name and former police rank.

"Homicide, huh? You're used to this kind of thing then. We don't get too much of this here in Troy."

"Yeah. I moved here for the peace and quiet. "

As he smiled sarcastically, Dick noticed an EMS unit along with another vehicle entering the complex and immediately identified the unmarked police car common to most investigative units. A female with short dark hair wearing a dark pinstriped pantsuit accompanied by her partner, a taller man wearing a tan sport coat and black crew neck shirt approached the scene. After surveying the area, the detective in the tan coat looked toward the small group where Dick now stood and cocked his head to one side grinning as he squinted in their direction

Returning the same gesture Dick now recognized the tall guy in the tan coat as an old acquaintance from Detroit. "Sean? Carson? You out here now? I didn't know."

"Dick Hagan. I'll be damned. Heard you retired. What're you doing here? "Extending his hand as he moved closer to the group who along with the police officers were all now watching these two former co-workers get reacquainted.

"Just moved into my condo about a month ago. Moved here for the peace and quiet."Repeating the comment made earlier.

As their conversation continued with Dick explaining how he spends his retirement playing golf and trying to keep busy, the other officers and rescue attendants handled the crime scene, examining the body carefully so as not to disturb any evidence and interviewing the other residents, confirming Dick's assumption that none of them saw anything that was helpful to the investigation. The female detective, Mary Beth Wisner, extracted a wallet from the victim's jean pocket examining the driver's license, making an entry on a notepad. Thomas Alan Hodges. 119 Palmer. Madison Heights, MI. Date of Birth 9-19-1980. Placing the wallet into a plastic evidence bag she continued to scan the area reaching to pick up the sweat stained Detroit Tigers cap in the grass nearby.

Motioning to his old friend to join him off to the other side of the gazebo about twenty yards from the body, Carson waited until they both were away from the others. "This ain't random. No robbery that I can see. Probably knew the shooter. "

"Looks like he was being chased. You might want to see if there's a vehicle out there on the main entrance road."Dick replied pointing toward the entrance to the condo complex and the main access leading in off of Long Lake Road.

"I'll get someone on it."Waving to a uniformed cop, he directed the officer to search the area for vehicles that looked like they didn't belong. Continuing his conversation with his former co-worker. "So you retired huh? What are you fifty something? "

"Fifty one last January. It was time. Especially with all the cutbacks and federal investigations and all that shit. I guess the final straw was when Levon Jefferson got blown away by that crazy woman who killed her kids."referring to another homicide detective who was killed as he was attempting to interview a suspect about the murder of her two children. She initially told the police that she left the boys at home while she went to buy cigarettes and found them shot dead when she returned. She blamed her ex-boyfriend. After he suspected that she was lying about the cigarettes, Detective Jefferson went to her house to ask more questions and when he knocked on the door she opened it while firing three rounds from a 22 pistol into his face and then put one in her mouth.

"Yeah that one shook us all up. I knew Levon from our days as uniformed cops in the twelfth. I left to come out here just before that happened. Glad I did. Stuff we get into out here is nothing compared to the D. My only other case this year was the one with the Serbian who killed his ex-girlfriend because she wanted to date an Irish guy. Strange bunch those Serbs. Albanians too. Always wanting to shoot each other."

Dick remembered the incident well. "Did you know he took my place on that one? I was tied up in court as a witness in a different case and Levon took that one for me. It coulda been me ya know? "

"Don't beat yourself man. You might a' handled that differently. Levon was just unlucky."

"Tell that to his wife and kids."

As they continued talking, Mary Beth joined them and provided more information about the victim. "I found some business cards in his other pocket. Looks like he was in the landscape business. We should be looking for a truck or something."

"Already on it. Radio the uniform guy I sent out that he's looking for a truck. Maybe we'll find some connection in it."

Dick stepped back as the two detectives continued discussing the crime scene and what evidence they had so far. Slowly retreating back to where the other residents were gathered he knew that there was much work to be done yet he felt like he should be part of it. This was the stuff he did for almost twenty years in Detroit and he found that in this moment he missed it. There was a familiar feeling in his gut that he always felt when introduced to a new case. Connecting with the victim and quite often the grieving families, he found purpose in seeking the often times elusive criminals and bringing them to justice. He wanted to offer his help but decided against it. This was not his territory and Carson was a capable cop. He thought about calling Melissa at that moment but decided to wait. She was working late at the club and he didn't want to upset her while she was with her clients.

"Listen Sean, I'll be in my condo if you want to talk some more before you leave."

"Thanks. I probably will."

Before wrapping up the crime scene, long after the body was removed, Carson walked over to Hagan's front door and knocked. A voice from inside announced, "It's open."

Entering through the foyer he found his old friend sitting in a recliner sipping his third glass of scotch. "I'd offer but I know you're on the clock."Pointing to the bottle on the table.

"We found the guy's truck down the street. We're asking around if anyone else saw him talking to another person before he ran into the courtyard."

"Keep digging for this one Sean. I'm pissed that this happened right here."Taking another sip.

"You can count on it. Doesn't seem random. I want to check on Hodges. See if was involved in anything other than cutting grass, know what I mean."

"Can you keep me posted? As one old cop to another."

Extending his hand to say good-bye Carson offered an invitation. "If you're interested, I could maybe use some of your expertise on this one. Off the record of course. How about a couple of beers at the Wagon Wheel? "

"Yeah. If you think I can help. It's the least I can do. How about tomorrow night after your shift?"The offer surprised him but he could not resist. He had seen too many of these crimes and this one was certainly looking like a hit. Professional job. There were dozens of men in prison today because of his expert crime solving skills. They always thought they were smarter than him but he was good at his job. Sooner or later they'd make a mistake and he was right there to get his man. He had the best success rate in the department when he retired and he knew he could help in this case.

"I'll meet ya there, say six o'clock."

"Good. See ya."

Carson found Mary Beth near the gazebo and they returned to their car leaving Dick standing on the front porch of his condo as they pulled away. Peace and quiet was going to be put off for a while.

Michael Ripinski

4

Rita Jacob drove her BMW into the semi circle driveway past the familiar spruce tree stopping at the apron in front of the two-car garage. As she pressed the remote opener, the separate door for the left slot began to open revealing her husband's almost identical car in its right side adjoining space. Surprised that it was still there, she entered and looked around for a moment. Walt was supposed to be in Farmington Hills meeting with lawyers regarding a deal they were putting together on a warehouse and retail strip center. She talked to him last night while she was in Lansing supposedly attending a conference on School reforms, which was a favorite political cause. What Walt didn't know, nor did he suspect, she had spent the night like so many others, with Charlie Vandenberg at his condo in Okemos near the Michigan State Campus. She and Charlie had been carrying on for a few years now and managed to keep the affair mostly discreet in spite of the Governor's high profile life.

Her marriage with Walt had deteriorated to more of a co-existence, with each of them pursuing their interests. He was more married to his career as a prominent land developer and she was involved in various political causes serving on several committees and task forces, often appointed by her good friend The Governor. In public they gave the appearance of the perfect- couple, with mentions in The Detroit Free Press society page or local magazine stories showing them attending all the major charitable functions. The Detroit Symphony. United Way Campaign. The Detroit Institute of Arts. Privately the love had ceased for quite a few years. The few times they were even home together they spoke only of business deals and social-political causes. Wisely, they elected to stay childless and had come to the current living arrangement without actually discussing the details. It was just an understanding.

As a young girl in Royal Oak Public Schools, Rita dreamed of this life. Well not exactly the whole thing with the Charlie V. affair, but being part of society, being important, being somebody. Her parents, father was a union carpenter and mom a registered nurse, raised four girls in a three-bedroom bungalow which was always crowded and noisy and being the youngest, Rita often felt like she had to prove herself, be better than the rest. An all- state swimmer, she attended Michigan State University on a sports scholarship where a shoulder injury ended her career after her sophomore year giving her time to pursue other interests, like Walt Jacob the son of Judge William Jacob of Bloomfield Hills, who she met in a business law class and dated through out her remaining college years. They were married in nineteen eighty-three in a lavish ceremony held at the Orchard Lake Country Club and mentioned in all the local papers. One of the guests at the wedding was a young State Representative from Birmingham, Charles B.Vandenberg.

Charlie and the Jacobs became close friends as he rose through the ranks of state government from the State House, to State Senator and eventually the top spot. During this time his marriage was falling apart. Shortly after being sworn in for his first four-year team, Susan Vandenberg filed for divorce and moved to Chicago to pursue her own career in business with a major venture capital firm. His constituents were not surprised as the troubled relationship of their new governor was well documented and, being his first year in office, he was able to quickly get over any political fallout. He was arguably the most popular governor in the history of the state in spite of tough economic conditions and a declining automotive industry. Charlie was the people's choice as he managed to push through legislation that lowered taxes while enticing new business in the form of high tech development companies. Bringing together a coalition of Detroit and out-state legislators his aid package for the troubled city was hailed as nothing less than a miracle. Young and handsome -six feet three, two hundred twenty pounds, light brown curly hair, Hollywood good looks and only forty when he took office, he was famous for using his charm and wit to persuade his adversaries and friends alike to see his point of view. Charlie was on a roll and he was not aware of the impending crisis.

Her first suspicion came when Rita turned the handle to the entry door leading from the garage to the kitchen area and found it locked. Walt always forgot to lock this door, which annoyed her even though the entry to the garage was secure. It was one of many little things that annoyed her but she had come to accept the arrangement and learned to live with it. Fumbling for her keys she shouted toward the door. "Hey! Hello! It's me. Ya wanna open up the door please? "

No reply.

Retrieving her keys from the black leather Gucci bag in her left hand she opened the door with her right while poking her head inside the kitchen. "Walt. Are you here? "She shouted as she entered. *Must be in the basement office. If he's on the computer he might be on another phone as well.* Thinking that her husband must be working and not paying attention she decided to go to the second floor bedroom where she kept her lavish wardrobe in a separate walk-in closet.

Rita glanced at the king size bed beneath the framed replica Picasso and had a brief reflective moment about the last time they slept in that bed at the same time. It was nearly two weeks ago after another Charlie V fundraiser at the Townsend Hotel, just a short drive from home. They both had too much to drink and maybe that was why she was able to tolerate the amorous overtures from her husband. Actually she recalled that the sex was not that bad. Better than the act of going through the motions which always ended much too soon with both of them sleeping apart at the very edge of their large mattress. No talking. No touching afterwards. It was a sham and they both knew it but still they hung on to the relationship for their own selfish reasons: Walt for the appearance of a stable home life, which served him in business dealings; she for the political connections. It allowed her to see Charlie in public settings without causing suspicion. Or so she had convinced herself to believe. Truth was that Walt was about the only one in their close circle of friends that did not know or suspect Rita and Charlie were involved.

After changing into a pair of jeans with a pink Ralph Lauren cotton tee, she paused at the floor to ceiling mirror to admire her figure. Five foot three, dark brown hair and bright green eyes, she looked good for forty-one and the frequent workouts at The Tone House Gym were well worth the effort. It sure kept Charlie's attention. And that was the most important part of her life in this fast paced world of politics, civic duty and business. She loved Charlie and was sure that the feeling was mutual. Her future was sure to play out the way she always dreamed when the right opportunity presented itself and she would be able to leave Walt Jacob and become Mrs. Charles Vandenberg. Maybe as first lady of the State of Michigan or perhaps as the wife of an ambassador to a significant foreign ally. It was possible that they would end up in Washington D.C. if the Governor were to accept an oft rumored cabinet position. She could see herself and Charlie as significant players in the Beltway, where the stakes were much higher and the politics dirtier. She would be right in the middle of it. Till then she'd bide her time and be satisfied with her current arrangement.

Descending to the first floor once again, Rita paused at the door leading to the basement and decided to let her husband know that she just stopped home for a change of clothes before meeting a few friends at J Alexander's in the Somerset Mall. "Walt. Are you here? "Not hearing a response she wondered if maybe he wasn't even home. *But his car's here and he always takes his own car.* Pushing the switch to turn on the lights she slowly stepped down the flight of stairs to the finished basement. This was Walt's space and she seldom ventured here when he was working or watching sports on his new high def TV with the forty-inch screen. Stopping in her tracks she spotted the paper and pen laying on the square table in the middle of the room. Without reading the typed note her eyes moved to the signature at the bottom of the page. She knew immediately that something was not right. He never signed his whole name on any note or letter that he ever wrote to her. Her worry was soon to be confirmed as she moved to the open door to the closet just a few feet from where she was standing. Her screams echoed throughout the otherwise empty house and Rita Jacob no longer cared about her appearance or Charlie V or any of it.

She now faced a new problem after reading the rest of the note. Should the police see this she would no longer be secure in her relationship with Charlie. Walt had left a letter citing his recent discovery of the affair as the reason for his self inflicted demise. Rushing back up to the kitchen she fumbled through her purse once again, locating her cell phone and punched in the speed dial number connecting her to the private number for the Governor of the State of Michigan.

Michael Ripinski

4

The driver steered the silver Mercedes through the traffic on I-75 exiting at the Rochester Road ramp and turned right heading north toward Long Lake Road. Ahead, the green F-150 moved along at the posted speed. Still wearing his gray slacks and black shirt, he had earlier called information to obtain the address for *Tommy's Landscape Services* learning that he might find him at the Madison Heights address and sure enough as he rounded the corner of Palmer Street there was the green truck in the driveway next to a large white trailer. He decided to wait in the parking lot of the 7-11 at the corner on 12 Mile Road before following Tom as he left for his next appointment.

After returning home to empty his truck Tom had one more call for the day. A potential new client, Mister Dickson, requested to meet with him this evening in Troy and it sounded like a good deal – cutting a couple of vacant lots as needed to keep the weeds and scrub grass from being overgrown. Most cities had an ordinance requiring this sort of thing and Troy was no exception. It would be an easy job and would not take too much time. Unaware that he was being followed, he thought about the Jacobs and what he had heard inside the house.

Using his cell phone Tom called his girlfriend Jennifer as he headed toward his meeting in Troy. "Hhhhhi it's me."

"What's up?"

"I hhhhhave a mmmmeeting in Troy. New client. Shouldn't take too long."Using the short clipped speech that seemed to work for him. Since meeting Jennifer Statler he discovered that he could communicate with her and usually his speech impediment diminished when they talked. Tom felt this was a good sign and really was felling positive about this relationship-the only one that has lasted more than a few dates. It had been six months now.

"Will you be able to stop by after?"she inquired hopefully.

"Yeah. 'bout nnnnnnine o'clock. I hhhhhhhave something ttttoooo tell you. At the Jacob's house. I hhhheard something."

"Like what?"

"A fight."Pausing to get the words out slowly. "A car was there. Silver Mmmmmmercedes.

Yelling inside. Sssssssssounded bad."

"Do you think somebody got hurt or something?"

"Maybe."

"Why don't you call them just to make sure they are all right?"

"Tttttttttttttomorrow. Okkkkkay?"

Jennifer waited to hear any further words from her boyfriend and finally asked him to come right over after his meeting. "See you 'bout nine then. It's probably nothing babe. A family argument or something. Come over and I'll fix you a late dinner."

"Okay. Love you."He folded the phone and placed it on the seat next to his clipboard without looking. He didn't often use the cell phone while driving being careful to keep his attention on the road.

Approaching Long Lake Road the Mercedes kept a safe distance with a few cars between him and the green truck. The driver observed Tom make a right turn onto Long Lake and sped up to make sure he did not catch the light following his potential victim into a new subdivision, a combination of new homes on one side and condos on the other. The truck slowed to a stop at the subdivision entrance near a mature maple, one of the few trees spared when the bulldozers and construction trucks first descended upon the vacant tract of land, before anything was built. As Tom Hodges sorted through the papers in his briefcase preparing for his meeting he didn't notice the Mercedes parked about a half block behind him and he didn't notice the man in the gray slacks until he was standing next to his truck. After Tom exited the truck the Mercedes driver came around the rear tailgate as Tom approached from the driver's side.

"Excuse me."Said the driver to a startled Tom.

"Uh. Uh. Uh. Can I Hhhhhhhhelp you?"

"Yeah. I saw your truck here and thought it looked familiar. Do you do some work over in Birmingham?"

Clearly unsettled by this man who he noticed was carrying a small black duffel bag and his reference to the area where he had been earlier this evening, Tom could barely get the words out. "Uh. Uh. Uh. Uh. Yeah. I I I I I dddddddo."

"For Mister Jacob?"

Now he was really nervous and wondered if this man was there when he heard the noises in the house as he retrieved his clippers. What did he want? Then he noticed it – the silver car parked up the street from where they stood. "Is he Okkkkkkkkay?"

"Now why would you ask a question like that? Did you see something there today? I'm gonna guess that you did because you sure drove outa there like a bat outa hell didn't ya?" As he spoke the driver reached into the bag extracting a handgun. But before he could point it in his direction, Tom turned and began running across the street toward the entrance to the condo sub. The driver immediately followed in pursuit of his prey. Passing the sign with the raised red letters against the forest green background, Oak Woods Estates Condominiums, Tom ran toward the gazebo in the center of the courtyard, tripping over a sprinkler head protruding from the freshly mowed lawn. This gave the driver just enough time to catch up and without hesitation he fired three shots from the Smith and Wesson at the stumbling man who immediately dropped to the ground his Tigers cap landing in the grass.

Certain of his result, the driver continued running along the side of the condo closest to the five-foot high brick wall near the main road and out to the street after hurdling a short fence. He couldn't believe his good fortune that no one was outside but he figured he had better get out of there in a hurry in case any one was looking out a window. Now that he was out on the main street he ran to the Mercedes tossing the bag into the backseat before starting the vehicle, turning around in a driveway then speeding back out to Long Lake Road. The entire incident lasted less than three minutes and before anyone could figure out what had occurred he was well on his way out of the City of Troy. The time was eight PM. By eight-thirty he was well on his way down I-75 and out of the Detroit area entirely.

Michael Ripinski

5

16 Mile Road is also known as Quarton Road in part of Birmingham and it's named Walnut Lake Road in West Bloomfield. To the east it is called Metro Parkway leading out to Lake Saint Clair and the entrance to the popular Metro Park with its beach and marina. But in the City of Troy, 16 Mile is Big Beaver Road.

The mile roads in Oakland County are an extension of the grid system, which begins in Detroit in Wayne County and was created by the Public Land Survey System as part of The Land Ordinance of 1785. The legendary 8 Mile Road separates the two counties as well as the racial population of the entire area - Oakland County being mostly white and Wayne County mostly African American. At 15 mile, also known as Maple Road, the name game begins. 17 Mile Rd is Wattles followed by Long Lake and Square Lake roads – the latter two named after area bodies of water that most residents couldn't locate if they tried. Further north is Auburn Road or 21 mile and Avon Road in the City of Rochester Hills. If a newcomer could figure out the mile road names it was easy to get around and acclimate to the area.

The twenty-eight acre site was located just west of I-75 and included the frontage along Big Beaver adjacent to a fifteen-story office building owned and anchored by a large regional bank. On the other adjacent side was the Troy Wilmont Hotel, with adjoining convention center. The front ten-acre parcel along Big Beaver was asphalt paved at the city's expense and used for parking during major events at the convention center. No one in the recent administrations could recall the exact arrangement with the owner but it was understood that the land was used for the city's needs without compensation; part of a long ago deal in exchange for some minor tax breaks. As far as anyone knew it was a verbal arrangement and self renewed each year as part of the city budget. Rubber stamped by politicians knowing that they had a sweet deal to utilize the property for the economic benefit of the area.

The back parcel, away from the road, remained undeveloped and overgrown with scrub grass as well as few small trees and there were splotchy areas scattered about that remained barren of any vegetation. Despite the numerous PRIVATE - KEEP OUT signs, children could often be seen playing in the area and even carved out a crude soccer field with home made wooden goals. Once in awhile, when things were slow or they were bored, the Troy Police would drive up and tell the kids to get off the land knowing they would be right back the next day. Unless the owner complained, there was no reason to enforce the law and Edna Biddle Norris never complained. She seldom remembered that she even owned the land until the day that Charlie V called to ask a favor. Would she consider selling the property to some friends of his? After he convinced her that the city was taking advantage of her by not paying to use the parking area and explaining that his friends would name the development after her, she agreed to Charlie's request, selling the land for a fraction of its real worth. The Norris Center had a nice ring to it.

William Greening was sitting at his desk in his windowless office on the second floor of the State Office building in Lansing. As part of the Department of Environmental Quality, a.k.a. the DEQ, his responsibilities included recommending approval or rejection of land development requests after the required studies, soil testing and surveys. A short man, twenty pounds overweight with gray-flecked brown hair, he was a geologist by his education and training. He had also become an accomplished bureaucrat, seasoned in the ways of government red tape and political influence. After twenty-one years he was now near the top of the ladder in his department and had learned to use his position for personal gain as well as political favor.

It was all working out well for William except for the one little issue. He loved to gamble. Betting on everything, football, basketball, horse racing, baseball, and now the new rage, Texas Hold-em poker which he could play every weekend at the many Indian casinos or one of the Detroit casinos. He could play on-line as well but he liked the live action. Sometimes he would go to Detroit during the week, driving the ninety miles one-way after work returning to Lansing at three in the morning to an empty apartment. His wife took the kids and left three years ago because of his problem and his refusal to seek help. Heavily in debt and constantly looking for the next big win to get out of the hole, he was the typical addict. Lose a bet and double up on the next one. Always looking for the one time he could beat the system. Then he'd quit. It would never happen and he knew it – unless someone could bail him out.

The phone call came on a Friday morning as he was thinking about plans to make the trip to Detroit for the weekend. He picked up the phone on the second ring. "Greening. DEQ. "

"Mister Greening, I have the governor's office on the line. Could you please hold?"the polite female voice announced the call.

Adjusting his posture to a straight up position he reacted as if the Governor was in the room. "Yes. Sure I'll hold."Wondering what the heck the man would be calling him for. He had met Charlie V, having worked on his campaign, a wise move he reminded himself often, but the Governor never called and he wasn't even sure he knew his name.

After a minute the unmistakable deep baritone of Charles Vandenberg was on the other end. "Bill? Bill Greening? This is Charlie."As if they were long time pals.

"Yes sir. How can I help you?"A little surprised that he called him Bill. No one did. It was always William. He preferred it that way.

"Bill, could you make some time for me this afternoon here in my office? Say one o'clock? There is a matter I need your help with."

"Why yes sir. Certainly. Anything I should bring?"Nervously waiting for a response he glanced at his watch. Twelve fifteen. He hoped this was not some special project that would tie up his weekend.

"No. Just yourself. My secretary will tell me when you arrive. And Bill. This is a confidential meeting okay? Keep this between us for now."

"Sure. Sure. Okay then I'll be there at one."

"Good. Thank you Bill."

Well now that was a strange call wasn't it? Whatever the governor wanted seemed important enough for a personal call. He called himself *Charlie* like they were old buddies and he didn't even mind being called *Bill*. There must be some kind of state project that needed his personal involvement. A project that needed to have the red tape kept to minimum. It wasn't unusual for him to handle these things but it was certainly unusual for the Governor to ask himself. Maybe there'd be a benefit in this one for him. A little quiet kickback from a contractor or even a trip. Vegas maybe? He could go for that one. Bill Greening had almost forgotten about his planned trip to the casino.

In the dark paneled office with the round seal of The State of Michigan on the wall behind his desk, Charlie Vandenberg rose from the leather chair and walked to the window looking at the skyline of downtown Lansing, such as it was. Turning to his three guests he placed his hands in his pockets. "Well I think that this Greening guy will give you what you need. You received the information about his little problem I hope? Use it if you have to but keep my name out of it."

"Thanks Charlie. We knew we could count on you."said the mostly bald man in the pinstriped suit. Bob Banker was his name and in fact he was a principal investor in Michigan Global Bank. Everyone called him Bob THE Banker and laughter ensued with all of the accompanied jokes and sarcasm. Making millions during the mortgage boom from the late 90's through 2004, he was smart enough to get out before the bubble burst. Behind the scenes he was known as a ruthless bully and it was rumored that he was not afraid to use force if necessary. A former associate with the bank called him the Godfather of the local financial markets.

Reminding himself that there was someone missing from this meeting the governor inquired. "By the way, where's Walt? I thought he was coming today."

The tall, slender man with thinning blonde hair spoke next. "Walt said he had to be in Detroit. He's got a deal downtown he's working on with a couple of minority investors He said he'd join us later. Are we going to meet with this Greening fellow right here? "

Taking his seat behind the oversized oak desk while rolling up the sleeves on his white shirt, Charlie replied. "No. Not a good idea. I'll make the introductions and make sure he knows what to do. You guys take him someplace else to talk. Maybe the Spartan Grille or someplace like that."

Sam Ford was no relation to the car clan but he didn't mind if people made that assumption. Rising from the leather sofa he towered over his companions and looked very much the casual yachtsman with his navy blazer, tan slacks, powder blue button down shirt and yellow tie with tiny blue sails. Sam was old money from Grosse Pointe, his mother was a cousin of the Crowley Department Store family, and his reputation as a ladies man was legend. Just ask his three former wives. Each one cast adrift as he moved on to the next newer model – meaning a younger more active woman whom he usually met during one of the many regattas on the Great Lakes. His current girlfriend was a twenty- five year old who he met on Mackinac Island. Sam was forty-eight but acted like thirty.

"I know a place near here on Saginaw."The third man said as all heads turned his way. Paul Lapone was new to their group. Dark hair, combed back with just a slight wave and a thick dark mustache made him look very Italian and reminded Charlie very much of one of the Soprano characters. Sam met him during the annual Chicago to Mackinac race. A mutual friend from the Windy City introduced them. To their collective surprise their new partner was familiar with the Lansing restaurant scene and the Governor was the most curious.

"I didn't know you were an expert on Lansing cuisine, Paul? Please share with us this hot spot of yours."Laughter filled the room as the tension eased for the moment. They all knew the stakes were high in the deal that they were putting together. Failure was not acceptable, mostly for financial reasons but pride and reputation came into play as well. "I know of the famous Chez Wendy's but that's about it."Charlie's remark brought more laughter and a smile from Paul.

"Actually it's a little Italian place that just opened this week. I ate there last night and the veal was excellent. Great wine list too. Name of the place is Georgio's. You should try it Governor."

"I did read about that place in the paper yesterday. Good review. My apologies. I should have known a Chicago guy would find the good Italian spot. "Folding his hands in mock prayer and gesturing like the characters he observed in the show on HBO. "Now if you'll excuse me gentlemen I have a call to make in private. You can wait in our conference room till he gets here."

The three men moved to the entry door with the governor showing them the way while pointing to the door across the hall from his secretary's desk. The attractive thirty –something African American woman smiled as she rose to open the door for them.

"Tonya. Give these men anything they need in the way of computer access and phones."Speaking as he turned to re-enter his office, closing the heavy door behind him. Inside he used his cell phone to call Rita Jacob.

Tonya Washington was secretary to the Governor of the State of Michigan and she was proud of her position. Coming from inner city Pontiac she managed to escape a home life dominated by a welfare dependant mother and 3 brothers who all had different fathers. She met Charlie Vandenberg at a political event while she was a student at Oakland Community College and he was a young State Senator. He hired her as a part time staff assistant and they worked well together with her gaining more responsibility as he moved up the political mountain. Trusting her more than anyone else on his staff, she was the first to know about his affair with Rita and it was often up to Tonya to suppress the rumors.

Pointing to the bi-fold door at the opposite end of the room dominated by a long mahogany table, she smiled again and said: "You'll find beverages and snacks in there. There is a fridge with pop and ice and fruit in the basket. Dial nine for an outside line and the computer is over there."Directing their attention to a desk in the corner. "I'll be out here if you need anything."

Sam immediately opened the bi-fold doors revealing a stainless steel GE refrigerator and a basket of apples, bananas and pears. Taking a can of Diet Pepsi he glanced toward his partners. "Anyone else?"

Bob the Banker and Paul from Chicago both now sitting at the long table nodded to indicate they were not interested. After taking his seat next to these two, Sam sipped his drink from the can and the three of them waited.

6

After checking his watch for the fourth time in the past ten minutes, William Greening decided to walk across Capitol Avenue to his meeting with Charlie V. No longer considering his trip to Detroit, he planned on working overtime if necessary to accommodate the forthcoming request – whatever it might be. He had heard about a big road project over in Grand Rapids that might involve some site excavation near an old fertilizer plant. Usually this involved soil testing and some remediation, which added to the overall cost of the project, sometimes well in to the six figure range. Contractors, and in this case the Department of Transportation, would want to avoid any extra cost and he would be the one to make any potential problems go away. He had done this kind of thing before, like the time he was asked to sign off on a building project for a new high school in Ann Arbor. Once used as a gas station and car repair business the site contained old tanks and holding drums that were suspected of seepage into the ground water. Greening did a personal site inspection at the request of a friend in DOT and signed off without doing the normal detailed soil testing. The building contractor rewarded him with much coveted 50 yard-line tickets to the Ohio State – Michigan football game and dinner at Win Schulers, a premier area restaurant. It was no big deal he remembered, as the land in question was only a small part of the overall campus and was designated as an access road and parking lot anyway. There was to be no building on the actual site. This, he figured, was to be something similar yet the Governor himself had called. The significance of a personal call from Charlie V was enough to make him anxious and excited. His mind raced with the possibilities as he entered the executive office area of the state capitol building, a magnificent domed structure that dominated the central downtown Lansing district.

After passing through security, which announced his arrival to Tonya via speakerphone, he entered the outer lobby of the governor's suite of offices and took a seat. He wasn't there very long.

"Mister Greening? My name is Tonya. The Governor is expecting you. Right this way please."With a swift, professional and friendly gesture, Tonya had opened the door to the inner offices and waved him in while leading him directly to the Governors private office. One knock and she opened the door announcing, "Sir. Mister Greening is here."

"Yes Please. Thank you Tonya."Charlie came around from the desk, flashing his best campaign honed smile, extending his hand as Bill Greening entered the office. "Bill. It's good of you to come. Thank you. Thank you. Please sit. Can I get you anything? Coffee? Pop? Water?"It was hard not to be overwhelmed by the famous Charlie V charm.

Indeed he was a little intimidated by it all. "No thank you sir. I'm okay."Sitting in the same leather chair recently occupied by Bob the Banker.

"It's Charlie. Call me Charlie, Bill."He sat in one of the leather chairs almost directly opposite his guest. Close enough to whisper if needed. "I believe we have met before haven't we? You worked on the campaign with my team here in Lansing and helped out at the big fund raiser at the University Club."Obviously doing his homework, Charlie had made sure he could establish his relationship with this bureaucrat who had indeed been a low level volunteer in his campaign. But he had absolutely no recollection of ever meeting him before this moment.

Impressed by the Governor's memory and sucking it all in, Bill was starting to feel like he was an important part of the political machine called Charlie V, Governor of The Great State of Michigan. Whatever the Gov was selling he had already bought in and he still didn't know why he was asked to be here. "Yes. Yes. I did some work with Karen Bastow and the folks here during the election."Referring to one of the assistant campaign managers who in fact had given Charlie the background information on Mister Greening. Karen was now his Chief of Staff and one of his closest confidants.

"I can't thank you all enough,"still flashing the Charlie V smile. "Karen reminded me that you were over in DEQ and I thought of you when something came up recently."Pausing to lower his voice and lean toward his guest while rubbing his hands together. "Bill, I know some people who are doing a development down in Troy and they are really gonna make a huge impact on the economy of that area. Big development. Lots of jobs. First in construction, then in retail and other businesses. This is a really big deal and we can really help the people who want this thing to happen. We are talking millions of dollars at stake here Bill."His piercing blue eyes focus directly on his guest in the manner, which made him famous as a communicator. Often compared to Bill Clinton with his charm and appeal he could make anyone feel like a close personal friend on their first meeting. Bill Greening was enrolled. There was just the matter of explaining his part in this project without being specific. In a way that could be denied if the thing somehow backfired. Reaganesque in his ability to avoid controversy, Charlie did not get to this level in politics by having anything in the way of scandal that could stick to his reputation. Even his divorce was handled in a way that made people think that Susan and he were remaining friends. Only three people knew that she was paid off. Susan, Charlie and Bob the Banker who sent her packing to Chicago with a nice chunk of cash to get her through till she settled in. Three hundred grand and a promise to keep it quiet was all it took and Susan felt like a lottery winner because she planned to leave him anyway.

"Sounds like this project is real important to you Charlie."Hesitating. It was the first time he had actually called the Governor by his popular name.

"Not to me Bill."Holding his right hand against his chest. "To the people of the State of Michigan. To those people in Troy, who are going to have jobs, Bill. To those citizens who are going to be able to contribute to their communities because we made this thing happen. Because progress, Bill, is what's important here. Building things. Selling things. It all comes back to the economic impact, which is good for all the people. All government has to do is get out of the way so that this thing gets done. Do you understand Bill?"Reaching across the space separating them, Charlie gently touched him on the arm and once again lowered his voice. "If somehow this deal falls through people will be hurt by the loss of their potential prosperity. It's up to us Bill. It's up to you."Bill Greening had just heard the famous Charlie V compassionate leader speech. Using this same approach in different situations over the years had enabled The Governor to get things done. Government getting out of the way. Progress is Important. Prosperity for the people. Themes that got him elected again and again and usually resulted in standing ovations at rallies and banquets. Bill Greening had just received his own private campaign speech and at that moment, he would have jumped out the window for Charlie V if it would help the people of the Great State of Michigan.

Knowing that he had the authority to rubber stamp any environmental paperwork that could potentially disturb the project in Troy, Bill understood the nature of the request. Make sure nothing comes up. Don't necessarily cover up anything, just don't look for it. In any proposed project like the one in Troy on Big Beaver Road, that involved a former landfill, there were several soil and ground water tests required to receive approval from DEQ. After all the tests were complete and results verified either one of two events followed. Approval with no conditions or cleanup and removal required before approval would be given. The latter obviously causing added expense, sometimes millions of dollars, and construction delays, also an adverse and expensive development.

"I will handle the situation personally. I can recall a project in Ann Arbor a few years ago with similar background details and I know how to handle this one."He said confidently, smiling back at the governor.

"Okay now. Just so we are clear on this Bill. I am not asking you do to anything except what you feel is the right thing to do. Within your authority at DEQ. Agreed?"

"As I said, I'll handle it."He was feeling important now. Finally. After all these years he was a player on the big stage. The man himself, asking for a favor. Nothing specific he concluded, but he understood what was necessary. "…. It's up to you."He knew what that meant and he would not let Charlie down. His new friend Charlie V.

"Good. Good. Now I want to introduce you to some friends of

mine in the conference room across the hall. I'd like you to hear about the details of this project. I think you'll be impressed."Charlie stood and before Bill could join him the governor had the door open and was waiting for his guest to accompany him. Noticing her boss as he emerged from his office, Tonya had dutifully risen from her desk and preceded the two men by opening the conference room doors getting the attention of the other three.

"Gentlemen, I want you to meet Bill Greening our main guy at DEQ."The governor began. After introducing each man to the government employee, Charlie quickly retreated from the room closing the door behind him.

Bob the Banker reached for a chair and motioned to Bill. "Please join us Mister Greening"

"Bill is okay with me."

"Well then Bill, I'd like to explain our exciting project in Troy to you."

As had been previously planned, Paul offered an alternative. "Gentlemen. I have a suggestion. Why don't we head out from here and find a more relaxing spot. Anybody hungry? There is a place not far from here that's quiet and the food is very good. Do ya like Italian Bill?"

"Uh Yeah. Sure."Not expecting this change of venues and for the first time noticing that Charlie had left the room, he agreed to the offer. Heck, he was a bit hungry anyway.

After spending an hour hearing about the Big Beaver project and enjoying a fabulous lunch including a couple bottles of wine, Bill was feeling light headed but still impressed with his new found importance. These guys were players in the world of big business and things were said. Things were implied. We'll take care of you Bill. Do you like to travel Bill? Do you like sports Bill? Red Wings. Lions. Michigan State basketball, his favorite team. You name it and we can hook you up. Of course they had investigated his background and knew about his gambling habit and financial distress. They alluded to the casinos and some inside info on sports betting. The guy named Paul, he remembered, said he would take him to Vegas on a private jet. Make sure he had a good time. It had not yet sunk in but he was looking forward to reaping the rewards. He had finally hit the big time and it never bothered him that he might be asked to do anything illegal. Just make sure government got out of the way. There was nothing wrong with that. Progress was a good thing. Charlie V had said so himself. For one brief moment he wondered why all of a sudden his services might be needed. Weren't deals like this done all the time without including a special meeting with DEQ? The thought was fleeting as he once again looked forward to enjoying all of the perks and benefits of associating with these people. His new associates. That was the term used by one of them when describing their relationship. Was it Sam? No the quiet one Paul. He said they were associates. "You will have to meet one of our other associates. A friend of mine from Chicago. Joey. He knows how to treat my friends." He was referring to the Mercedes driver, Joey Palzonian.

7

The Wagon Wheel bar and restaurant on the corner of Big Beaver and Rochester Roads had survived the tremendous growth and development in the area over the past few years. What was once a congested intersection of two and four lane roads surrounded by some commercial and residential property had been transformed into a combination of four and five lane convergences, just off the I-75 exit ramp. Directly west, across Rochester Road, was a new major shopping center where once there was just a lot of vacant land and few residential homes. To say that this intersection was bustling was an understatement. But the Wagon Wheel retained its neighborhood bar charm and was still a popular gathering place for factory and construction workers, dark suited business types and off-duty cops.

Sitting at the end of the bar with an empty stool next to him, Sean Carson did not notice Hagan had entered while squinting to adjust from the bright sunlight to the dark interior of the Wagon Wheel. Finally spotting his friend at the bar he sat in the vacant stool without speaking.

"Thanks for coming. What'll ya have?" Carson greeted his former Detroit PD friend.

"Bud Light."

The bartender, a young man in his twenties wearing a Wagon Wheel tee shirt, was anticipating the order and quickly delivered the cold beer with a frosted glass in one hand. "Glass?"

"Yeah. That'll be fine." Dick poured the beer while slightly tilting the glass leaving frothy foam about one inch beneath the rim. Again without speaking he touched his glass to the bottle of Heineken being held by Carson before bringing the liquid to his lips and taking a slow sip.

"How's the golf game?"

"Shot an 88 at Sylvan Glen. Broke 90. It was a good day."

"I don't get to play often but I can see how you enjoy it. Once in awhile, me and a few guys from the force play on Sunday afternoon. We hack it up pretty good. One guy, Ed Domanski, shoots in the eighties all the time. I shoot ninety something but I cheat."Laughing as he confessed his tactic. "But so do the other guys."

Both men sipped their beers and almost simultaneously placed their respective beverages on the bar. Dick took in a breath before bringing up the subject. "Any news?"

"Yeah. Something interesting that we are trying to make sense out of right now. The guy in your courtyard, Thomas Hodges, had a girlfriend who gave us something. She says he was worried about something that happened in Birmingham earlier in the day. He did landscaping ya know."

"I remember your partner mentioning that the other night. His card said Tommy's or something. Right? "

"Right. Tommy's Landscape Services. Young guy like that owned his company and was doing well from what we can tell. Worked his way up from mowing lawns as a kid and had just bought the new truck. He was supposed to meet a man in the housing sub across the road from your condos. We talked to him. No connection. Hodges never made the appointment and the guy, named Dickson, got his name from a direct mail piece the kid sent out. Too bad. Seems like he was an honest hard working kid. "

"Damn. That pisses me off even more. Why would somebody pop him just like that? "Wondering about the girlfriend and what she had told them, Dick's old investigative instincts were starting to kick in. "This girlfriend. What did she give ya? "

"Not much up till now. Too upset last night. She agreed to come in to talk to us though. Mary Beth is going to do the interview. I figure she'll feel more comfortable with another chic. You Know. A girl-to-girl thing. "

"When she comin' in?"

"Actually she's there right now. Mary Beth is going to call me if she gets anything. I did not want to skip our meeting here."Carson raised the Heineken to his lips and sipped a few gulps before placing the bottle back on the bar.

"You said something about Birmingham. Did ya call them to see if anything unusual was going down in their city? I'd start looking at the kid's client list to find any connection."Dick was getting into it now. The old juices were flowing and he was feeling the thrill of the chase. All of his background and training coming into play. He didn't want to admit that he really missed it; in spite of the bullshit and the politics of working for the Detroit PD he really did miss the work.

Carson knew exactly what he was doing too. There was going to be an opening in the Troy Department for an experienced investigator and there was no one promotable from within. He and the chief had talked about it and decided they would have to go outside just like when they had hired him. Unfortunately as the city grew in population so did the crime rate. Dick Hagan was right for the job but Carson wanted to feel him out first. This was the perfect situation with the crime scene right in his front yard. He knew that his old friend would have to get involved. "Only thing they had was a suicide that they could not share with us right now. Said it was a prominent citizen whose family asked for confidentiality."

"I'd follow up on that one if I was you. Maybe I can help. I know a guy in Birmingham who used to be in the violent crimes unit in Detroit. Those guys that would bust a door down put a shotgun in a perp's face then yell 'knock knock'. Got burned out like the rest of us and went to the suburbs for less pay but lower stress level. His name is Abernathy. I can call him for you. We worked together on the Whitey Worthington case back in ninety -five. You remember the Nice Boys Gang? "Referring to a notorious drug ring whose leader was a white guy that was finally convicted of murdering two of his own dealers who were plotting to kill him first. Whitey eventually rolled over on a number of other gang members in exchange for a possible parole after a minimum sentence of thirty years. They had to ship him out of state because he would have never lasted in Jackson Prison for more than a month once word got around of his deal. Not that anyone would have cared.

"Yeah. I remember. What an asshole. And dumb too. It was a wonder he lasted as long as he did. Driving around in a pimped out white Caddy Deville. Had two black girlfriends. The one I remember, Watonda, was his baby's momma."Shaking his head at the story that in reality had a tragic ending. Watonda and the baby were killed in a drive-by a few months after Whitey went to prison. That one remained unsolved.

They could have traded stories for another hour but Dick knew that Carson had work to do. As he was about to excuse himself to go to the john, he saw his friend reach for his buzzing cell phone in his coat pocket.

"Carson."He answered. "Yeah. Go ahead."Pausing to listen to the person on the phone. Dick assumed it was Mary Beth. "Really. We were just talking about that."Listening again for a few seconds. "I'll be right over. Keep her there if you can. I would like to ask a few questions myself."He folded the sliver cell phone and returned it to his pocket as he started to get up from the barstool. "Well that Birmingham thing is panning out."

Dick was holding it in. He could wait to pee. "What do ya have?"

"The girlfriend told Mary Beth that the Hodges kid phoned her on his way to his meeting last night and said something about a problem with one of his clients in Birmingham. He was worried about somebody getting hurt. He heard something. Maybe he heard too much. Can you get a hold of your friend Abernathy? We need some info on this suicide. Let's assume that this is the client that our victim was talking about."

"No problem. I think he still lives in Ferndale. I went to his house a few times to watch the Super Bowl. Great Party. I'll look him up. And call you as soon as I get anything."

Carson pulled a card from his wallet with his cell number and the Troy Police Desk number. He scribbled his home number on the back before giving it to Dick as he turned to leave. Extending his hand he said: "Thanks man. This one is heating up. I appreciate the help."

"No problem. You'd better go. I'll call ya as soon as I talk to my friend in Ferndale. Don't worry I'll get the bar tab."As he spoke Carson was already on his way toward the front door and Dick headed to the men's john after letting the bartender know that he'd be right back. When he returned, he guzzled the remaining beer in his glass, paid the tab and headed for Ferndale to see if he could find his old buddy James "Rambo" Abernathy. He remembered a case they worked on together back in ninety-nine. Rambo got his nickname on that one. Wrestled a suspect to the ground who had put an 8-inch Buck hunting knife to the throat of his girlfriend. He took 20 stitches to his leg but managed to break the guy's arm in three places.

Once again thoughts of his days in Detroit came flooding back like a stuck sewer in summer a rainstorm. You couldn't stop it once the water came through the grate and Dick Hagan was standing knee deep in memories of his old job.

Michael Ripinski

8

Charlie Vandenberg was about to leave the Governors residence to meet with a few supporters at The University Club in East Lansing near the Michigan State University campus. He really hated the old house, a sprawling four-bedroom ranch that was more suited to a family with kids than a bachelor like himself. He had lived alone in the place inside a sprawling compound near The Lansing Country Club since he took office. Susan never moved in since the relationship was already on the rocks and she elected to stay in the condo they owned in Okemos until the divorce was final. Charlie usually had one of the bodyguards from the State Police protection unit stay in one of the guest rooms. Sometimes he made them stay up late with him watching a Red Wings game or an old movie on TV. A few of the men became good friends and all of them knew about Rita Jacob. It was impossible not to.

His cell phone was lying on top of the kitchen island near a bowl of fruit. Charlie had the ringer tone set to Hail to The Chief which he always made sure that everyone knew was just a joke. He professed his decision not to seek national office many times but no one was absolutely sure of his real intentions. As the notes sounded out the familiar tune he reached for the phone and identified the caller as Rita Jacob, RJ on the screen.

"Governor Vandenberg here."He always answered the same just in case there was ever a mistake and someone else was using her phone.

The hysterical, sobbing voice on the other end was unmistakable however and he was taken by surprise. "Charlie. Charlie. Oh my God.

Walt's dead. He's in the basement hanging in a closet. Oh my god. Charlie. Help me. What am I going to do?"

"What? Calm down. What happened?"He felt the blood rush to his face as he heard the news.

"I came home about thirty minutes ago and I thought he was working in his office downstairs."More sobs and gasping for breath. "When I went down to check on him I found him. Oh my God. He's dead Charlie. He's dead. And he left a note."

"Jesus, Rita. Did you call the police or anybody yet?"

Hesitating because she didn't know quite what to say. "Charlie, something's not right here. He said he killed himself because he found about us."

"What? Holy shit Rita. Get rid of that note. We can't have that. Uh.Uh. You know. If it gets out we got a problem. I've got a problem. Uh. Uh. You know what I mean. I'm sorry Baby."He knew he was being selfish at this moment but the problem was obvious. He had to think quickly and tell her how to handle this.

But before he could say anything else, Rita responded. "There's a bigger problem than you think."Sounding more composed now; she spoke softly even though there was no one else in the house. "I'm not sure it was suicide."

As those words sunk in, Charlie stood in disbelief. Could they really have done this? He knew there was a problem with Walt over the Big Beaver project and he was threatening to pull out and expose some details of what was in the landfill. He didn't know and didn't want to know those details but he did bring Greening into the deal. "Listen to me. First of all where is the note?"

"I have it right here in my hand. He signed it Walter. It's his handwriting but the note is typed and he never signed anything to me in his life with his full name. It's as if he did it on purpose. Oh my God Charlie. I'm scared."

"Are you sure there is no one else in the house? Did you look around? Is there anything out of place?"He had to think fast. Had to get a handle on this. "Rita. Listen to me. Read me what the note says. Okay."

She had placed the note on the table and picked it up as he

requested. She noticed that her hand was shaking. "It says; *Dearest Rita, Today I have learned about you and Charlie and it has broken my heart. I cannot live with the thought that you love another and I have nothing left to live for. I hope you two are happy together.* That part is typed then he signed. *Love Always, Walter.* He would not have signed his name like that and the note doesn't make sense. I know that we had grown apart but he would not have handled it this way. Walt was a businessman. He would have negotiated a settlement with me. I know him. You know him Charlie. Do you think he did this to himself?"

"No. No. You are right. Walt was a good businessman and I don't think he was depressed, at least not about you and me."Right now he had to act as though nothing was wrong and he had to be someplace very soon. Charlie V was very good about damage control but he usually had help, Either Tonya or someone else on his staff like his communications director Will Balanger and of course, Karen Bastow. But he couldn't call any of them right now. He and Rita would have to handle this. "Look babe. Are you okay right now? Talk to me."

She was still holding the note but also thinking about the consequences. All of her dream and plans were at stake. Her husband was hanging in a closet in her basement but the man she loved and the one who held the ticket to her future was on the phone. "I'm gonna be okay. Tell me what to do Charlie."

"First of all you need to destroy that note. Don't use a shredder. Burn it. Take it outside and burn it where no one can see you do it. Then get rid of the ashes. Scatter them someplace away from the house. Then you need to call 911 and be sure to act upset when you call. Like when you first called me. The police are going to ask you questions Rita. Like why you think he did this. You don't know and you are very upset. They may ask if you and Walt were having problems. Don't lie. Tell them you two were not as close as you used to be but that you never talked about divorce or anything. That's true isn't it?"

Again she had to keep her composure. She had not thought about having to answer questions from the police. "Yes. Yes of course. You know how it was with us. All business."

His driver had entered the kitchen and waved to his boss that they had to go. Charlie held up one finger and motioned for him to go out to the car. "I wish I could be with you right now but we have to handle this the right way. We will figure out what happened and who did this if he didn't. Make sure somebody is asked to call me to give me the news. It would be obvious if you didn't because everyone knows you and Walt were good friends of mine. I will be sure to act shocked. I'll call Slattery and give him the news. I'll ask him to go right over there and handle things."Mike Slattery, the Chief of the Birmingham Police Department, was an old friend and confidant of Charlie V and he was aware of the relationship between Charlie and Rita. "And Rita, one more thing. Delete all of your recent calls from your cell phone. Now I have to go. Remember. I love you. I will call you tomorrow morning."

"I love you too Charlie."She folded the phone and stood alone in the kitchen for a moment before going back to the basement to use the phone near Charlie's desk to call 911. That was the closest phone to the closet and was the obvious choice if she had just discovered his body. She dialed the numbers and repeated her call of distress at finding her husband's body. After returning to the kitchen she took the note and folded it in half but instead of following Charlie's instructions, she took the note up to her bedroom closet looking around before deciding to place the paper inside the pocket of a new black Saint John's suit. Insurance she thought. She loved Charlie and trusted him. But right now she believed that her husband's death was not self-inflicted and she wanted some answers before she discarded this note. Returning to the main level of the house she decided to wait in the foyer sitting on a parson's bench adjacent to a narrow beveled glass window. It wasn't long before the fire and rescue vehicle, red and blue lights flashing, entered the curved driveway passing the dominant spruce tree and stopped at the base of the steps. Shortly thereafter a Birmingham police car rolled to a stop directly behind her BMW. Rita Jacob was surprised that the tears came easily and wondered if it was a real sadness at the loss of her poor husband Walt – after all they were still friends and they had shared the past twenty years together. Or was it fear. What was happening here? Charlie seemed to know something that he wasn't telling her. Distressed, angry and confused she practically collapsed in the arms of the first cop on the scene as she directed them to the stairwell and told them to open the basement closet. She did not want to go down there again. Ten minutes later Chief Slattery arrived, taking charge of the scene and comforted Rita until her oldest sister arrived.

Michael Ripinski

9

He purchased the new Escape soon after he retired because Dick always drove Ford products when he worked in Detroit. Usually the deluxe, cop ready, plain black Crown Victoria with black rims and no hubcaps. The things literally shouted "Cop"and were noticeable anywhere in the city by the criminals and lowlifes he was trying to track down. Sometimes it was an advantage because the damn things were a symbol of authority and regardless of the common perception that Detroit was filled with thugs and thieves, many of the citizens were really trying to make it a better place and they appreciated the police presence. Dick checked his cell phone and saw that there was a message from Melissa and punched in her auto dial number.

As she walked out of the Tone House Health Club, Melissa Connolly pulled the vibrating cell phone from her purse, noticing the familiar caller. "Hi. I was hoping you'd call. How is it going? Did you meet with your friend?"

He had called her earlier in the day to tell her about the incident the night before and of his planned meeting with Carson. "I met with him and he asked for some help. I'm on my way to visit an old friend in Ferndale who works for Birmingham PD."

"You sound like you're really into this. I thought you said you liked retirement?"

"I do but this thing happened right in front of my place. I don't like having my privacy disturbed."Annoyed that she suggested that he missed the police work he had to remember that when they first met she was skeptical about dating an ex cop. She had even told him about one failed relationship with another cop who tried to physically abuse her. Fortunately her training made her strong enough to fend him off and she thought she had sworn off cops for good. He was different and she liked his sensitivity and he respected her choices. They hit it off from the beginning.

"When will I see you?"She inquired hopefully.

"I'm not sure. It depends on what I find out from Abernathy. He's the guy I'm going to see. I'll call you when I'm done and maybe we can meet for a drink later. Okay?"

Disappointed that he seemed to be preoccupied and not interested in her, she reluctantly agreed. "Sure. Okay. But not too late. I had busy day at the club."

"If I am running late I'll just call you tomorrow. Bye."Abruptly ending the call he felt like she was going to be annoyed anyway. He'd have to make it up to her and he knew how to do just that. A nice dinner at her favorite Sushi restaurant and a nice back rub. If they had sex that would be a bonus.

Heading down Woodward Avenue past the Zoo, Dick recalled the last time he visited Rambo Abernathy. Last year's Super Bowl party and there were several old friends from Detroit and some guys from Birmingham. Not everyone was getting along. A Detroit cop called one of the Birmingham guys a pussy. He complained that they didn't have the rough stuff out in the suburbs like in Detroit. Words were exchanged and macho challenges were offered to ' take it outside' before cooler heads prevailed.

This part of Ferndale was lined with older pre WW II two bungalows, colonials and craftsman style homes and the streets were narrow, not designed for the bigger cars and SUV's of today. As he eased the Ford into a space directly in front of a two story brick colonial he noticed a few kids playing soccer in the yard next door. Thinking back to his own childhood in Detroit he remembered playing baseball in the yards and parks near his home. Soccer was something they played in Europe and was a game for sissies. Times had changed. The ball got away from the boy nearest to him as he walked toward the steps to the house and he picked it up, dribbled it like a basketball and tossed to the boy who played it off his head and directed it to his friends without even a *thanks*. Stepping onto the porch he hoped that his friend was home as he rang the doorbell. It didn't take long to find out.

As the inner door opened a familiar face filled the frame of the outer screen door. "Hey Dick. What're you doing here?"The muscular figure in sweat pants and a Laker's jersey tank top stepped out onto the porch to join him. Rambo Abernathy, his short dark hair barely an inch with a Marine Corps emblem tattooed on his right forearm, extended his hand.

"Hey. How ya doin? I was hoping you'd be home. You still working in Birmingham right?"As he shook hands Dick noticed the calloused scars on his friend's fingers the result of numerous fist fights – some in the line of duty and some not.

"Yeah. Yeah. It's good. What're you looking for a job or something?"Not waiting for an answer he pointed to the pair of plastic chairs on the porch. "Have a seat. Can I get ya a beer?"

"No. I'm good. Actually I came by to ask you something."

"Well if ya don't mind, I'm gonna get me one."He entered the house and returned in less than a minute carrying two cans of Bud Light placing one on the floor next to his chair. "In case ya change yer mind."

The soccer ball rolled out into the street and just missed a speeding car as Rambo yelled at the kids. "Hey Nicky. Be careful. You kids should go to the park and play soccer."

The boy who had headed the ball from Dick yelled back. "Okay dad. But remember mom grounded me for beatin up that shithead Timmy Womack."

"Don't worry about it. Just go. I'll cover for you."Turning to his former colleague with a wide grin. "Like father like son. Hey?"

Shaking his head and laughing, Dick agreed. "Does he want to be a cop too?"

"No. Hell no. Kid's smart like his mother. He's already interested in engineering. Computers and stuff. I won't let him get into this bullshit job."After a short pause. "So you wanted to ask me something."

Leaning forward and lowering his voice Dick replied. "Yeah. First I should tell you that there was a guy shot right near my place out in Troy. I called 911. When the boys come to investigate, who shows up but Sean Carson? He works out in Troy now. So we get caught up on old times and the next thing, I'm helping him with the case. Off the record of course."

With a snap of the pull-tab, Rambo popped a can of beer and said. "Carson hey? Don't know him. Not like friends anyway. I know he was with you in homicide wasn't he? Good cop?"

"Yeah he is. Knows what he's doin. I'm kinda glad he's on this case. I don't mind helping him either. I'm sure his people in Troy PD don't have the experience that we had in Detroit. I get the feeling he needs someone to partner up with like we used to do. Which brings me to why I'm here."

Taking a long sip from the can, Rambo eyed his old friend and waited a few seconds. Wiping his mouth with his hand he replied. "Go ahead. Anything I can help you guys with."

Dick explained the background of the case so far and how the victim had been in Birmingham earlier in the day. "Carson says that there was a VIP in your town who committed suicide and that our victim did some work for him. The girlfriend says he was upset about one of his clients maybe having some kind of trouble."

"I heard about it as we were changing shifts. Captain comes in and tells everyone to keep this low-key 'cuz this guy was a leading citizen. Good friend of the Governor I'm told. Says the wife is all shook up and wants to keep it private. Says she doesn't know why he'd do this. "

Both men sat quietly as they contemplated what each other had shared. Going over the possibilities and the possible connection to Charlie V – Governor of the State of Michigan. Things could get interesting. Very interesting.

"Suppose this kid, Hodges was his name by the way, suppose he knows why this guy killed himself. Suppose he heard or saw something. Scared. Somebody finds out he knows somethin'. Somebody who doesn't want him talking about it."Dick reached down and grabbed the can of Bud Light and received the OK from his friend.

"You mean like he hears the wife and the guy arguing?"

"Yeah"Dick took a long sip from the Bud Light "Maybe she's a real ball buster. Pushes the guy too far. We seen this kinda shit before."

"Don't make sense."Standing now and scratching his head,

Rambo looks out toward the street. "Okay. How about this? Hodges sees or hears something and freaks out. Somebody who doesn't want him to talk sees his truck and follows him until he gets out to your neck of the woods and confronts the kid. He whacks him because the kid figures it out."

Dick took a sip of the beer and replied. "It's a possibility and we need to explore that angle don't you think? Can you call someone in your department to check this out? It seems that if wasn't a suicide they would be able to tell."

"I can find out but not tonight. I'm not scheduled again til Monday. I'll go in tomorrow and say I forgot something in my locker. I'll nose around. It's different in Birmingham ya know. The chief is friends with a lot of these people. They have some loyalty. I'll call ya with what I can find out."

They exchange cell phone numbers and Dick finished his beer. As the two former Detroit Cops walk toward the car they stop and shake hands. Rambo says, "Ya know if this somehow connects to Charlie V, this thing could blow up big time."

"Let's not go there just yet. We got a lot of dots to connect first and right now I want to know if someone who also knew your VIP did this Hodges kid. The big question is was it made to look like a suicide? See if you can get the name and call me tomorrow. Thanks man."

After pulling on the seat belt and starting the car, he waved to Rambo who was looking over his shoulder on his walk back up to his porch. Dick was feeling the old rush again. There was more to this story and he could feel it, sense it, and taste it.

As he drove back to the condo in Troy he went over the events of the past twenty-four hours and finally had a chance to think about other things. He told Melissa that he'd call her and he grabbed the cell phone from the front seat where he had placed it when he climbed into the car. Waiting until he stopped for a red light he punched in her speed dial number.

She answered on the second ring. "Hey baby."Recognizing his number from her phone screen.

Glancing at his watch and noticing that it was only eight thirty he was hoping she'd be up for a few drinks with him. He needed her company right now. He needed to step away from the case. In his mind he called it *The Case*. Just like back in his old job. "How about a drink at Champs? I can pick you up in ten minutes."

Even though she really thought Champs was too noisy, she knew that Dick liked the bar and they had big screens all over the place with all the games on. The Tigers were playing the Yankees tonight and she was a big baseball fan. If there wasn't much to talk about they could at least watch the game. "Okay. I'm just about ready. I'll come out when I see you in the driveway."

"I'll be right over"The light turned green and he pressed on the gas pedal. He was hoping he could spend the night at Melissa's. It was looking good so far.

10

Bob the Banker was sitting at his computer desk in his corner office of the three-story building he owned in Farmington Hills, nervously awaiting the phone call from Paul Lapone. They last spoke earlier on this Thursday after Bob left a meeting with Walt Jacob that didn't go well as they argued about the contaminated property. Why couldn't Walt just go-along with the rest of them? Why couldn't he see that they were going to lose millions of dollars if they aborted this deal? Walt didn't care about the money and he said they had to do the right thing. There was no way they should build on this site unless a very expensive and potentially obstructing process of testing and abatement was implemented and it still was no guarantee. Bob had told him that some of the tenants were already committed and would probably back out if they found out about the old landfill contamination. Bob and Sam were looking at bankruptcy if this went south. He was not about to let that happen. Walt would just have to agree. Paul had told him about his consultant friends who would persuade Walt to go along and Bob didn't want to know the details. He would patch things up with Walt later. He did not realize that there would be no *later*.

His cell phone startled him as it buzzed on his glass desktop. "Hello. This is Bob."

The familiar voice on the other end announced, "It's all taken care of. Walt won't be a problem any more."

"You mean he agreed to go along?"Hopefully.

"No. I mean he is not a problem any more. It seems our partner was planning on screwing us by going public. He wouldn't listen. Joey had no choice but to make sure he couldn't do anything. The rest of us will have to pick up his share. Is that a problem?"The message was clear and Paul Lapone was making sure that his partners were on board.

"Are you telling me that Walt is dead? You're kidding me, right?"His face turned ashen and his hand was trembling as held the cell phone. It wasn't supposed to get this far. He was sure they could reason with Walt. This whole thing was spinning out of control and he had to get a handle on things.

"You'll hear all about it shortly. Our partner was despondent after he found out about his wife's affair. I am sad to inform you that Walt Jacob took his own life."Hearing no reply, he continued. "After things settle down we'll proceed as before with one less partner."

"Shit Paul. I didn't want this to happen. Walt was a friend of mine. There had to be another way."His plea was obviously futile and he knew that he could not let Paul see his distress. Yet he could understand from a purely business point of view that Walt was going to be a major obstacle and in his world major obstacles had to be eliminated. There was too much at stake. His fortune and his reputation were on the line. *Damn you Walt. Why couldn't you just go along?*

"You okay there man?"Paul was fishing for a reaction. He really didn't want to lose any more partners.

"Yeah. I'm okay. Walt's stubbornness was his downfall. It had to be done. What about his wife, Rita? She could be a problem."

Paul had thought this whole thing through and now it was time to inform his partner of his assignment. "You have to deal with her Bob. You're Charlie's friend and you know that they will have to cover it up. I don't think she's gonna miss old Walt do you? "

"It's not like he moved out and asked for a divorce, ya know. Jesus Christ Paul, what if she decides to go public about her and Charlie and decides to look into Walt's business? It'll lead right to us."Bob had to stop and think for a moment. What would he say to Rita to make sure she kept quiet? "I better go meet with her. To console her ya know. I'll get a feeling for where she's at and of course Charlie will be all pissed off. But he'll do as I say."Bob the Banker knew that he had Charlie V in his back pocket. Ever since his run for State Senate, Bob was his chief moneyman. Charlie would not be where he was today without his friends and of course it was Bob who arranged for Susan to leave quietly. There were few decisions Charlie made without consulting with him in order to insure all the real constituents were considered. Bob was confident about his influence over the governor. Rita was another matter.

"Okay man. Listen I have to go back to Chicago tonight but I'll be back in a few days. You have my cell number. Keep me posted." said Paul.

"Right"

"And Bob, sorry about Walt. It was a problem that had to be handled."

"Yeah. I know..."

After setting the phone back on the table, Bob the Banker collected his thoughts. He was used to being a tough guy in business deals and he was known to screw a friend or two to get his way. Recalling that he once blackmailed a local judge, he knew how to make things happen outside the legal and ethical arena. The judge, a middle age conservative, Catholic, with a drinking problem was set to rule against him in a civil lawsuit costing him a couple of hundred thousand. Bob set the judge up with a prostitute and pictures were taken that would have been more than a little embarrassing. The judge changed his mind. Another time he was about to lose out on a prime piece of real estate in Southfield to a slick talking Armenian that underbid the deal. Bob had this guy's Cadillac blown up right in his driveway as the guy was about to leave his house. The Armenian was eager to withdraw his bid when he received the message that the next time he might actually be in the car. These we examples of his methods that always worked but he never before resorted to murder. No matter how hard he tried to block it out he realized that he had crossed a line that he never thought would be necessary, especially with a friend like Walt Jacob.

Deciding that he should get to Rita as soon as possible he placed the cell phone in the pocket of his Kenneth Cole blazer, grabbed his briefcase and left the building. Before starting the engine in his black Lexus ZX, Bob planned his next move. He drove across Maple Road toward Birmingham and the home of Walt and Rita Jacob.

Michael Ripinski

11

At seven AM, Dick sat at Melissa's kitchen table with a yellow legal pad making notations about the murder of Tom Hodges. All of his police training and experience told him this was no random shooting and had to be a planned hit. But why? What was the connection between Hodges and the shooter? Did this all connect to the VIP suicide? He needed to call Carson and bring him up to date about his meeting with Abernathy. As he sat there his cell phone buzzed on the table. He didn't recognize the number at first. "Hagan here."

"Hey buddy, it's me Rambo. Sorry for the early call but I got a name for ya on the VIP. Jacob. Walt Jacob. I've heard his name around town before. He is definitely connected to the governor. Big money guy. Him and the wife. Her name is Rita. There is definitely something fishy. Some of the guys here in Birmingham said the Chief is keeping the lid on this. They say he took charge of the investigation and next thing anyone knew the body was removed and sent to the funeral home. Not normal procedure for sure."

"You say the chief in Birmingham okay'd the body to be removed before any forensics made it to the scene."

"Well sort of. They came but only stayed for a short time. It was a quick once over and they left. I am sure there's a valid report with a suicide ruling on it. "

"See if you can get us anything on the wife. Did you say her name was Rita?"

"Yeah. I'll see what I can get but you know I got to be careful. Some people in this town can screw ya big time if you know what I mean. Money can buy a lot of things and there are many deep pockets in Birmingham. I gotta go now but I'll call ya later."

Dick heard the line click off and as he pondered the information he just received from Rambo, he had that old feeling that he just knew they were on to something. He had to call Carson right away. He didn't care if was early on a Saturday morning.

Standing in the hallway leading to the bedroom, Melissa emerged after hearing him speaking on the phone. She was wearing an oversized white tee shirt with a sixties peace symbol in pink on the front. She had managed to make a quick stop in the bathroom to splash water on her face and run a brush through her medium length auburn hair. Even at this early hour, Melissa Connolly looked gorgeous; her well-toned body not at all concealed by the tee shirt. Almost forty, looking much younger with natural proportioned breasts and sculpted legs and butt, she could turn heads whenever she entered a room. There had been a few serious relationships over the years but she never could take the next step. Marriage wasn't for her, she was certain, but still there was a need for the company of men. A relationship. Usually lasting a few months to a year and then she'd move on when the guy would start to get too serious. Talking about settling down. Kids. Yards. Dogs. A house in the country. Nope. Not for her. Melissa knew what she wanted and she had come to terms with a single life. She had friends and an older brother in her life that always checked up on her. She was not alone but enjoyed her privacy. It worked for her this way.

Then there was this guy sitting at her kitchen table this morning. He was different. Older. Mature even. Oh sure she had dated older men before but it seemed they all had issues. Ex-wives. Kids. Job problems. Most of them needed a mommy not a girlfriend. Dick was the first guy she had met with confidence and certainty about who he was and what he wanted. And he was very clear that he was not interested in marriage. He liked his life the way it was and, in a way, he was just like her. When she stopped to think about it, it was scary. They were both tough, independent and sure of themselves. She liked the ground rules they had established after that first weekend together. No strings. No commitments past the next date or sleepover. A promise to communicate and always be straight with each other. That's it. So far it worked. They had been together for three months.

He noticed her in the hallway. "Hey. Morning. Hope I didn't wake you up?"

"No, it's okay. I gotta get up anyway. I have a scheduled client at the club at nine. Mrs. Jacob."

He looked up from the table with a sudden turn of his head. "Did you say her name was Jacob? She wouldn't be from Birmingham by any chance?"

"Why, yes she is. Do you know her? It's Rita Jacob. She and the husband are good friends with Charlie V. She's always talking about him. The Governor, I mean. Charlie this and Charlie that. I get the impression she and Charlie are more than friends. But that's none of my business. I've been working with her for two years now."

Motioning with his hand toward the chair next to his as he pulled it away from the table. "Sit here with me. I don't think your nine o'clock is gonna make the appointment."

As he said this, her cell phone rang on the counter next to the stove where she had plugged into the charger the night before. The called ID showed CLUB. "This is Melissa."Pause. "What? Really?"She was staring right at Dick now, her eyes wide and her mouth open. "Okay. Thanks for callin'."Placing the phone back on the charger she put her hands on her hips and looked him directly in the eyes. "Okay what's going on?"

"Sit here with me. I'll tell you."Again he motioned to the chair. "This is really a strange co-incidence. The kid who was killed in my condo complex apparently did some work for your client Mrs. Jacob. And her husband committed suicide two days ago. I am trying to put all the pieces together. What else can you tell me?"

Leaning her head back and letting her hair fall loose, she let out a sigh and stared at the ceiling for a moment. He had just confirmed what she had heard on the phone. "Jesus. I don't know what all this means, but you need to know what I know."She took another deep breath and exhaled. "Rita told me more than I said to you. When we first started out. You know when I first started helping her with her workouts, we really kinda hit it off. You know. Two girls just talking about girl stuff. I helped her stay in shape and put her on a healthy diet and stuff and we even went to lunch a few times after her sessions. She tipped me well and always picked up the tab at lunch. She told me things. You know like sometimes women tell their hairdressers their dirty little secrets. I guess she trusted me."

"What kind of things did she tell you?"Instinctively he had his pen and note pad ready.

"She and the governor were having an affair. Still are as far as I know. She mentioned it one day at lunch. We were at Panera on Rochester and Big Beaver. She likes their salads. One day she's talking about being at a thousand dollar per plate fundraiser for Friends of Charlie V. Her husband was in New York on business. She tells me that she has the governor stay at her place overnight cuz the event was in Bloomfield Hills and he was too tired to go back to Lansing. She says that after a few drinks they both knew something was going to happen and it did. I was a little embarrassed when she told me at first but she seemed so, so, happy. Excited even. It was the kind of thing she was proud of even though she was married to uh, uh Walt, I think was his name. She asked for my confidence and I never said yes or no. She just assumed. Over the past two years she has told me about some of their secret rendezvous and bragged how Charlie listened to her advice and made decisions with her help. I think it made her feel like the First Lady. I think she was hoping to be exactly that some day."

Dick put down his pen and sorted out what his girlfriend had just shared with him. He wasn't sure what it all meant just yet but there was certainly some kind of connection. He looked down at the note pad and started to write. At the top of a blank page he printed the name HODGES in caps. Then he made a line to the right and wrote KILLER. From the name HODGES he made a line down about two inches and wrote W. JACOB and below that R. JACOB. From there he made two separate lines to the right connecting to the letter V. Then he made a dotted line from the V to the name KILLER and from there, another dotted line back to the JACOB's. He knew from all of his training and experience that there was probably some names missing from this chart but this is what he had to go on for now. It was time to call Carson. He put the pen down and stood behind Melissa wrapping his hands around her just above her breasts. Bending his head down, he kissed her on top of her head and hugged her gently. "I need to call my friend Carson here in Troy. I am not going to tell him everything just yet but he needs to know where to go with his investigation. Don't worry I'll keep your name out of it."

"Yes please."She pleaded. "I don't want to get involved if I don't have to. Okay."

"Sure. Sure. Just one thing though. Will you let me know if Rita Jacob contacts you okay?"

"Yeah. Sure. Okay."

Dick kissed her again and went into the living room to call Sean Carson. He wasn't sure what he was going to say. He'd find out what the detective knew already and try to help him fill in the blanks.

Michael Ripinski

12

A deep blue Birmingham police car was stationed at the curved front driveway entrance leading to the white house. The uniformed officer approached the black Lexus as Bob rolled down the window. "I am a friend of the family. Go ahead use my cell phone to call up to the house. Tell Rita Jacob that Bob Banker is here."

The uniformed cop who had been assigned by the chief himself, retrieved a clipboard from his cruiser and looked for the name on a list provided by Misses Jacob. "Can I see your license sir?"Bob produced his wallet with his driver's license and handed it over to the cop who then held it up to the clipboard and using a small flashlight verified the name. "Okay you can go on up. Park behind the black Navigator."

Not knowing that the Navigator belonged to the Chief, Bob drove up toward the house and quickly parked as he was instructed. Another uniformed officer stood outside the front door. He did not like the looks of this and he became worried that Rita might have said too much to the police already. The cop opened the front door without asking questions and once inside he noticed several people sitting on the two large sofas in the living room. In a large striped wing back chair off to one side sat Rita Jacob, eyes moist and pink around the edges, holding a box of Kleenex. An odd sight he thought because he was quite aware of Rita's infidelity and her indifference toward Walt and this seemed like a good act.

She rose from the chair to greet him. "Bob. Thanks for coming. It's so awful. I don't know why he would do such a thing."Weeping and collapsing into his open arms he was sure it was all staged for the audience in her living room whom he now recognized as her two sisters and their husbands as well as Chief Slattery wearing casual tan slacks and a dark purple golf shirt. They nodded to each other as Rita re-introduced everyone to her husband's business partner and close family friend. She had no idea about the Big Beaver deal and she was only concerned about keeping a lid on her affair with Charlie. "There's coffee in the kitchen. Can I get you some?"

"No. No Thanks." He replied while moving to the side of the room where the Chief was seated. Leaning over he whispered. "Can we talk in the other room? I'd like to be filled in."

The chief rose and said. "I'd like some of that coffee Rita. Don't worry I'll get it myself." And then he walked toward the kitchen quickly followed by Bob the Banker. The two men were well acquainted through their relationship with Charlie V and both knew the Jacob's as well.

"Mike. Tell me what happened. Did he leave a note? How was he found?" Acting curious but not so much as to cause any suspicion.

"Well. I can tell you there was no note. At least not that we have found. Rita insists that the way she found him was the same way he was when we got here. Rope around his neck hanging from the pole in the closet in the basement. Looks like he stood on a bucket and then jumped off. Ropes marks looked pretty clean around the neck. I didn't see any other signs of a struggle." He lied about this last part because he noticed a small recent bruise on Walt Jacobs left arm when they cut him down. Not sure what it meant if anything he kept it to himself for now.

Knowing that the chief was quite aware of the affair with the governor, Bob chose his next words carefully. "Has anyone called Charlie? I'm sure he'll want to know about his good friend Walt and he'll be very upset. He and Walt go back a long way." Not mentioning anything about Rita.

"I spoke to him personally. He was at a fundraiser in East Lansing. He is very upset and said he'd help the family any way he can and I am sure he will." Just a hint of a smile appeared on the chief's mouth as he turned away from Bob and left the room.

Bob, knowing that he could count on Mike Slattery to contain the story, felt a bit relieved but he still had to talk to Rita. He had to find out if she knew anything about the project on Big Beaver and he wanted to get into Walt's office as soon as possible to examine his papers and of course his computer files to see if anything was missed.

Entering the kitchen alone, Rita dabbed her eyes with the tissue and motioned for Bob to join her in the butler's pantry between the kitchen and dining room. In the small five by eight foot space she leaned into Bob and whispered. "I'm scared Bob. I know this all looks like Walt just snapped and killed himself, but there is something really wrong here."Holding back about the note she continued. "I mean it doesn't make sense. You knew him as well as anybody. Why would he do this?"

Having been told by Paul that there was a note, he had to be careful now. He figured she held it back in order to protect her and Charlie. "Did you and Walt have any recent arguments? Did he say that anything was upsetting him at all? I mean about any of his deals or investments?"

"No. No. Not that I can remember. The last time we talked was last night and it was the usual small talk and business. Frankly, I usually tune him out when he starts talking about interest rates and construction costs and stuff like that. He did not say that anything was bothering him. At least I didn't sense that. He did say that he was supposed to meet in Farmington Hills today with an attorney regarding something routine with a deed restriction I think."

"Do you know the name of the lawyer?"

"No. I don't remember."She dabbed her eyes again. "I told all this to Mike and the other policemen already. They asked to look around in his office and I don't think they found anything."

She turned to leave and Bob gently pulled her back by the arm. "I have to ask you something Rita. And I know this is all upsetting and complicated for you and of course for our mutual friend in Lansing, but I need to know for sure if there was a note of any kind. I can understand if you have to protect him and we both want that but I may need to help you if that was the case."

Rita was a good liar and she had done a good job of playing the grieving widow so far but no one knew her as well as Bob the Banker. Her hesitation alone told him all he needed to know and she knew that he guessed her secret. She had to be careful, even with him, because right now she just did not trust anybody except for Charlie. "If there was a note, the only reason I would have destroyed it would be if it said anything about me and Charlie. Do you really think Walt would have killed himself over that? No way, Bob. He would have cut a deal. That was the way he did things even in our marriage. It was all business to him. You knew him as well as anybody. What do you think?"

He knew that she was right. But the only question now was if she actually destroyed the note or did she save it and hide it somewhere. Either way it did not appear that she had any knowledge about the deal. "Alright. Let me know if there is anything I can help you with. Have you started to plan a service yet?"

"I already called Snyder and Sons on Woodward Avenue. They will handle everything and I am planning on a memorial service on Sunday night. He'll be cremated. It would be nice if you could say a few words."

This last statement caught him off guard. His conscience creeping into his reaction to her request as he accepted and confirmed that he would speak at the service. Knowing that Walt Jacob was murdered and his part in the crime made it just a bit more difficult to be sincere. Yet in the end he was able to treat it like another business decision and poor Walt was reduced to another obstacle removed from prohibiting the success of this project. Like so many other times when he would have used his influence and power of persuasion to get it done, this was no different to Bob the Banker. He had screwed friends and adversaries alike and now it had cost the life of an old friend. Walt was just a stubborn fool and he would not listen. *Too bad,* thought Bob. "Of course. I'll keep it brief though. Can't get too emotional."

"Thanks Bob. Walt always said you were the toughest guy in the room when working on a deal but deep down he thought you were a good guy."

What a crock of shit. He thought. *She surely made that one up.* He and Walt disagreed more often than not and the only reason he brought him to these deals was Walt's ability to analyze costs and work on budgets. He was a genius at that sort of thing. Now that he thought of it, he'd miss that one thing about Walt.

13

"Carson here."The seasoned detective answered as soon as he punched the blinking green button and placed the receiver to his ear. His desk in the small office, which he shared with Mary Beth, was cluttered with files and notes and he had to fumble to find his legal pad and pen. His Detroit lions cap lay on the credenza behind his desk next to a half full Starbucks Mocha Grande. The time was eight fifteen AM and he was alone on a Saturday morning except for the receptionist and one other detective who was working on a gas station armed robbery from the night shift.

"Hey it's Dick. Your wife told me that you'd be at the office early when I called your home number. Your cell phone went directly to voice mail."

"Shit. I forgot to turn the damn thing on again."Glancing at the blank screen on his Blackberry as he retrieved it from his pocket. "Sorry man. Hey you're up early for a retired guy."

He decided to play it cautiously as he considered Melissa's request. Better to keep it close to the vest for now and see what Carson had. "I spoke to Rambo. The VIP's name is Jacob. First name Walter I think. Did you have that?"

"Well we had the name Jacobs or something from the girlfriend and we were checking with the County Morgue. We would have got it pretty soon. Anything else?"

"Well Rambo says there is some weird stuff with this guy. The Birmingham Chief has taken charge. The guy, Jacob, was a friend of his I guess. And get this. No autopsy. The body went straight to the funeral home. A little outside the norm wouldn't you say?"

Jotting few notes on his yellow pad, the Troy detective paused to digest this latest information. What he had so far was a murder in his jurisdiction and some connection to a suicide case in the neighboring town.

The difference between Troy and Birmingham was more than geographic. Although larger in area, very affluent and cluttered with modern upper end housing developments, Troy was still considered a notch below the old money, old neighborhood, and upper-class enclave of Birmingham Michigan. The only cities in all of Southeast Michigan to top it were Gross Pointe and The Village of Bloomfield Hills, its neighbor to the North. The Village, as the inhabitants called it, had one of the top five per capita incomes in the United States. Birmingham wasn't far behind. And all this wealth could buy a person some privacy and even the discreet handling of a potentially embarrassing matter like the suicide of one of its prominent citizens.

Receiving no reply to his suggestion Dick continued. "Have you been able to get through to anyone in Birmingham yet?"

"No. I left several messages last night and again this morning. I was given the name of a Detective Weingartz but he has not returned my call."

Dick decided to throw the wild card on the table for his friend and give him something else to consider. "There is another twist that I got from Rambo. Mr. and Mrs. Jacob were good friends with the one and only Charlie V."

"The governor?"

"Do you know another Charlie V? Hey you know how things work in this state. Everyone in the political power circles has some financial connections. I would bet that the Jacobs were big backers of the governor and a high profile suicide could easily be kept on the back page if you know the right people. I'd bet the Chief in Birmingham is a good friend as well."

Taking a minute to sort out this new piece of the puzzle, Carson looked at his watch and remembered that he was supposed to take his son to a soccer game at nine. He had gone in on his day off to handle some paperwork and pick up any new information that may have come in overnight. He was really appreciating the help from his old Detroit friend and considered himself fortunate to have access to Hagan's expertise as well as his connections. The Charlie V information was huge and started to explain the hush-hush attitude from Birmingham. But now he had a whole new set of questions. "Listen I have to take my son Josh to his soccer game but I want to go over some stuff later. Can I give you a call around two this afternoon?"

"Yeah I suppose. No golf today so I'll be around. Probably at my place."

"Later man."Carson had one more call to make before he left to pick up his son. He called Mary Beth to give her the scoop on the governor and the Jacobs. He wanted her to start digging on any business deals involving the late Mr. Jacob that would involve any state agency or department. It was just a hunch. In his business, hunches were part of the program and sometimes they paid off.

As he gathered his keys and cap, he thought about the new information on his way to his car, a Chevy Monte Carlo he purchased just two weeks before. He knew he'd have to interview the girlfriend again. He needed to know everything the Hodges kid said to her on his way to Troy two nights ago. He recalled the transcript that Mary Beth provided to him. She said that Hodges was worried about his client. Something about an argument. But with whom? His wife? And there was the other thing about a car. A Mercedes. He must have felt that this car did not belong to the Mister Jacob. He would have to find out what kind of cars the Jacobs drove and then there was the matter of getting the cooperation of the Birmingham P.D. He would need Hagan's help with that again.

Michael Ripinski

14

Snyder and Son's had been located in the same large red brick colonial style building along Woodward Avenue in Royal Oak for over sixty years. They were the preferred funeral directors for many of the rich and famous in the Detroit area and proudly advertised the fact that they had handled the final arrangements for a couple of U.S. Senators and at least one celebrated local TV newscaster without naming any names of course. They even handled the overflow crowd for a legendary rock star who died in a gruesome motorcycle accident after a night on the town that included a large amount of cocaine and alcohol. Their reputation was built on trust and discretion and situations like the suicide of Walt Jacob called for their expertise.

Dick decided that it was worth a visit to the memorial service, which was not a private affair. His experience had told him that sometimes, valuable information could be obtained at the funeral of a murder victim. It was easier here in the white suburbs than in Detroit. Most of the victims in the cases he handled were black and he stood out like a bright light on a rainy night. Usually the African American cops in his department were given the assignment, blending in more easily.

Rita had decided that a private service might just be too suspicious and there were many fellow supporters of Charlie that had become friends over the years. She had prepared all day for the seven o'clock service deciding to wear a black Calvin Klein suit with a subtle, deep burgundy, silk blouse. Charlie had turned down her request to attend instead sending the largest arrangement of flowers in the room with a gold satin ribbon stating *My good Friend with Deepest Sympathy* and a card that simply said *from C. Vandenberg*.

About one hundred mourners had gathered in the largest chapel inside Snyder and Son's as Dick entered, looked around and decided to take a position in the back of the room near a picture of winged angel carrying a bouquet of flowers standing on a cloud overlooking a small village church. He remembered seeing similar pictures in many other funeral homes over the years and wondered if the same company supplied these to the funeral directors everywhere. After all, burying the dead was a big business and he was sure that being a vendor to these places had to be equally lucrative. The customary organ music played from the overhead speakers. Ave Maria had just finished as a silver haired gentleman in a black suit came to the podium and the place became quiet with most of the seats being filled. He remained standing in the back with about a half dozen other men including two uniformed Birmingham police officers.

The silver haired man began to speak. "My name is Randolph Snyder and on behalf of Misses Jacob and the family I would like to thank you all for coming this evening. Tonight we are all here to remember the life of Walt Jacob our friend, business associate, family member and husband."A few ladies in the gathering dabbed their eyes with silk hankies as Dick scanned the room looking for familiar faces or just anyone that looked out of place. Randolph continued "In a few moments Walt will be remembered by his friends and family and then we will have a prayer from Reverend Cunningham of The United Methodist Church in Bloomfield Hills. Now I would like to introduce Mister Bob Banker."

Rising from a padded wing back chair near the front of the room Bob paused near the twenty by twenty portrait of Walt Jacob which was sitting on top of a golden oak pedestal. It was the only picture of Walt in the room but there were dozens of flower arrangements all of them smaller than the one from the governor. "Walt was a dear friend"he began. "We were also business partners and as many of you here know, we supported many of the same political causes. Needless to say I was shocked to hear of the news of his passing. We will never know why he made the decision that he did, but we will remember Walt as the kind, generous, civic minded man and good friend and loving husband that he was."He looked directly at Rita as he made this last statement and she looked away. Bob finished his speech with a few stories about some of their successful business ventures including the very prominent, twenty-five-floor Global Bank Building in Troy. Bob was followed by a cousin, Nick Jacob who owned a popular steak house in Southfield and Rita's sister Donna who shared a note written by Rita thanking everyone for his or her support. After the Reverend Cunningham finished, Randolph Snyder thanked everyone for coming again and invited them to stay for a while and share their fond memories of the dearly departed Mister Jacob.

Dick thought that the service was rather brief but maybe it was because of the manner of death. He was interested in Bob Banker however because of the intimate nature of their business relationships. Maybe this Banker guy would know who might have been arguing with the mister Jacob the day he died. Isn't that what Carson had said. The girlfriend stated that Hodges said he heard an argument. If it wasn't a domestic argument, and he wasn't sure that it was not, then maybe it was a business associate. He decided to speak to Bob Banker who was now standing next to Sam Ford and his young girlfriend making small talk. He stood nearby and waited for them to finish and as Bob turned toward the exit he approached. "Excuse me. Excuse me. Mister Banker is it?"He stepped in front of Bob blocking the doorway to the parking lot. "My name is Hagan, Dick Hagan. I was wondering if I could ask you a question?"

Clearly annoyed at this stranger's intrusion Bob tried to push him aside. "I'm sorry but I am in a bit of hurry and I'm upset about my friend's death."When he realized that he was not going to get through he reluctantly consented. "What can I do for you Mister Hagan?"

"I work as investigator for the Troy Police department and we have an interest in your friend's business matters. I was wondering if I could give you a call at a more convenient time to ask you some questions?"He had to make up something to give him some credibility. He figured he was, in a way, an investigator consultant to Carson who worked for Troy P.D. Not too much of a stretch.

Clearly startled by this stranger's question he replied. "Uh. Uh who did you say you worked for?"

"Troy Police. We were investigating some recent business deals involving Mr. Jacob."He had no idea that he had struck a nerve.

"Well. Uh. Uh. I haven't been. I mean I don't know about all of Walt's business ventures. He had many partners. Listen I'm upset right now. This is not a good time okay?"Reaching into his breast pocket he pulled out a business card and handed it to Walt. "Here, call my office in a few days. I'll try to help you."As he turned and walked hurriedly to the Lexus, Bob worried about this new development. *Who was this Hagan guy? And what did Troy Police want with Walt Jacob?* He didn't know but he was going to check this out first thing Monday morning.

Hagan watched as the black car sped out onto Woodward Avenue and turned north. He had interviewed enough suspects in his life to realize that this Bob Banker was nervous about something and he'd have to dig a little into what he was all about. But he had one more objective before he left the Funeral Home. Back inside he found the door marked OFFICE, which was partially open and peaking inside he could see Randolph Snyder seated at an oversized teak desk with his name embossed on a brass nameplate next to a pewter lamp with an emerald green glass shade. He appeared to be reviewing some documents in a legal size folder and did not notice as Dick stuck his head inside the doorway. "Excuse me. Mister Snyder. May I come in?"

Startled by the intrusion, Snyder quickly closed the folder and replied in his trained deep, soft, polite voice. "Yes. How may I help you sir?"Rising from behind the desk, straightening his tie and buttoning his suit coat, he approached the doorway.

"I was wondering if I might ask you a question about the deceased, Mister Jacob?"

"Are you a friend of his?"

"Well no. Not really. But I am helping with and investigation in a matter that might relate to some business that Mister Jacob was involved in."Dick had now entered the office and noticed the simple but elegant embossed wall paper and the few framed certificates on a narrow strip of wall adjacent to a large window accented by red, tied back draperies. He could make out the heading on one that read *Wayne State School of Mortuary Science*. The other read *University of Michigan*.

Wary of this man in his office, Snyder was well experienced in handling matters of discretion when it came to his clients. "Excuse me.

What did you say your name was?"

"I didn't. I'm sorry. Dick Hagan"Extending his hand to the funeral director.

Firmly, but politely, returning the gesture Snyder responded. "Well Mister Hagan, I have to tell you that I won't be of much help to you. In my line of work we treat our clients with the utmost respect and confidentially. Under the circumstances, I am sure you can understand that even if we did possess any information about the deceased, we would be reluctant to share it with strangers. Now who did you say you represented?"

Impressed with the professionalism and dignified manner of Randolph Snyder, he decided to back off a little. "I am a free lance investigator assisting the Troy Police Department. I work with a detective Carson. I can give you his number if you would like to check me out."He reached into his rear pant pocket, retrieved his wallet and extracted Carson's now wrinkled business card.

"Yes. Thank you. May I write it down? Just procedure you know Mister Hagan."After copying the phone number and returning the card he walked around Hagan and placed his hand on the door. "Now if you can excuse me I have to handle a few matters for my next client."

Dick retreated a few steps back into the hallway leading to the stately foyer. "Here's the question if I may ask and I can understand if you cannot give me an answer right now, but I was wondering if it is common practice in Birmingham to have a body delivered directly to the mortuary in the case of a suicide? You know before an autopsy?"

Snyder was clearly shaken by the question but did not immediately reply. He looked down the hall to see if anyone could hear them and then motioned for Hagan to come closer. He leaned in toward his interrogator, smiled, and in a whisper simply said, "Confidentiality, Mister Hagan. Confidentiality."

With a slight smile of his own and after repeating the gaze up and down the hallway in a mock gesture Dick replied. "Of course. I understand Mister Snyder. But based on some information we have received, there is an interest by Detective Carson in how this was handled by the Birmingham Police Department and this establishment. By the way did I mention that Detective Carson works in the Homicide department?"Without waiting for an answer he turned and walked to the foyer, placed his hand on the door handle and looked back to see the stunned Randolph Snyder with his mouth slightly open. Finally at a loss for words.

15

The meeting was to take place at four PM and as Paul Lapone glanced at his Rolex he realized that he was going to be late. *Damn traffic. Should have taken the train.* He left the downtown Chicago parking garage and walked over to State and Adams entering the plain looking office building, stopping at the elevator before deciding to take the stairs up to the third floor. There was no time to wait around because he was already late and he knew that his boss would not be happy. Hustling up the stairs he burst through the plain metal door arriving at the glass wall entrance to the office suite of Griffin and Childress, Inc. After straightening his tie and running a hand through his combed back dark hair, Paul entered through the brass framed glass door and walked directly passed the cute, blonde receptionist who recognized him with a wave and pointed to the conference room at the end of the hall. He took a breath, exhaled and entered the room joining the two familiar associates at a long mahogany table.

"Sorry. Accident on Lake Shore. No way to get around it." He took a seat with his back to the window facing the man who sat opposite to him. The Boss seated at the head of the table was turned toward a laptop computer and was obscured by the top of the large leather executive chair. He could hear the clacking of the keyboard and sat in silence waiting for the meeting to start. No one spoke for about thirty seconds before he heard the voice from the leather chair. "Now that we are all here, let's get started. Paul bring us up to date on your trip to Detroit."

And so Paul Lapone gave his report about the events of the past week and how after the meeting with Charlie V and subsequently with the bureaucrat, Greening, everything was in place until Walt Jacob decided to take the ethical high ground and threatened to blow up the whole deal. Of course this was old news to his boss who had given the go ahead to eliminate Walt if necessary. Paul was just filling in the details and providing the financial reports. It was also nothing new to the man across the table, Joey Palzonian. After about ten minutes of financial details and assurances that Bob the Banker seemed to be handling things well, as they all expected he would, he added that Bob told him something that might be a concern. "Just before I got on the plane this morning, Bob called and told me that he was approached by a guy at the memorial service on Sunday. The guy says he worked for Troy PD and that they were looking into some of Walt's business. So far he has not been able to verify who the guy is. Said his name is Dick Hagan. I ran some name checks and the only one that comes close is a homicide detective in Detroit. Joey, I may need your help on this. Let's see if he contacts Bob again."

"I ain't real interested in going back to Detroit any time soon after I had to handle the little distraction with the landscape guy. But I will if we need to cool some one else down."Joey glanced over at the boss, and then back at Paul. Everyone nodded in agreement and the meeting continued. There was much work to be done on the Big Beaver project and it was important that Paul remain the front man. The boss could not be overtly associated with any business in the State of Michigan. There was too much history there. Paul and Joey would be well compensated for their part and they knew it. They were loyal that way. As long as the money was there they would be counted on to make things happen. Paul with his expertise in getting the deals done and Joey with his own valuable skills. No one in the room felt even the slightest remorse for the murder of Walt Jacob or Tom Hodges.

After the meeting, Paul and Joey met in a side office and agreed to get together for a few drinks that evening. The two associates had known each other since they were teenagers on the South side of Chicago, frequently finding themselves in the same juvenile court room trying to talk their way out of charges for shoplifting, stealing cars or some random vandalism.

Paul was a bight kid with a B average in school and managed

to clean up his act enough to graduate from high school and attend Northern Illinois for three years before being asked to leave – actually expelled – for running a gambling and loan sharking racket in the dorms. He did manage to attend enough business classes to acquire some valuable basic knowledge, which he used to establish his own illegal operations back in Chicago. Along the way he gathered enough real estate, some of it from unpaid gambling debts, that he established a sizeable portfolio including apartments, retail space and a few small office buildings. Two years ago he was bought out by the larger firm of Griffin and Childress making him financially secure. They also retained him as a paid consultant to handle special deals like Big Beaver in Michigan. He enjoyed the freedom and the action in his new role. Still, he wondered about the reasons and rationale for taking out Walt Jacob. Why was this Big Beaver project so damn important to the Boss? The risk- reward did not add up but he would do as he was instructed. There was more money in it.

Raised by an alcoholic mother and sharing a two-bedroom apartment with three older brothers who regularly beat the shit out him, Joey made his way on the streets of South Chicago. To say he dropped out of school in the eleventh grade would assume that he actually attended classes. He was absent or expelled more than he was present since seventh grade when he was first charged with stealing a six-pack of beer from a local party store. After the usual juvenile hearing assigning probation and his mother's promise to keep an eye on him, he was back on the streets the same day. The party store mysteriously burned to the ground three weeks later. But he wasn't dumb by any means. Joey Palzonian could read quite well and was able to learn the tricks of his trade. As he grew older his crimes grew more violent and he spent time in prison for armed robbery and attempted murder during a botched jewelry store robbery where he shot the sixty-year-old owner. After he was released, a chance meeting with his old buddy Paul Lapone in a drugstore near Comiskey Park set him up in his current job. He had no official title but he was considered a security consultant for Paul's former business operations and now for Griffin and Childress who sent him to school to learn the latest surveillance systems and technology.

At eight forty five PM, Paul entered the 555 Tavern, a few blocks from the office. Dark wood panels, green painted metal ceiling, and dark, floral, stained glass lampshades hanging low over the dozen tables created the quiet secluded atmosphere perfect for the kind of meeting that was about to take place. The 555 also had a long mahogany bar with matching high back leather padded stools and Paul sat in the one near the far end of the bar. Already seated in the adjacent stool Joey was sipping a Jack and Coke.

"Chivas on the rocks"Paul announced to the bartender, a young, athletic looking, college student from Depaul named Todd.

"Got it."Todd poured the whiskey into an ice filled shallow cocktail glass and placed it on a napkin in front of Paul.

"On my tab, Todd."Joey pointed to his chest and the two men picked up their drinks retreating to a table in the darkest corner of the bar.

After getting comfortable and loosening his tie, Paul took a long sip from his glass and set it back on the table. "I need you to go back to Detroit. There may be a problem with this guy Hagan that Bob mentioned to me this morning. Bob did some research through his bank and came up with a coincidence. It turns out our guy Hagan lives in the condo sub where you offed the landscape guy. He's also been asking questions in Birmingham through a cop friend of his."

"So is this the same guy that's a cop in Detroit?"

"Yeah same guy but retired. He's doin this on his own as far as we can tell."

"I'll go back tomorrow but I need to get my car outa' the shop. I got a good deal on some new tires from a guy over in Cicero. I ordered them yesterday and his boys located some on a doctor's car in Downer's Grove. Nice rims too I hear."

"I was thinking that you should fly there and rent a Ford or something simple like that at the airport."

"I would really rather drive. I can be there in four – five hours."

"Alright. Drive then. And Joey."He took another sip swirling the ice in the glass as he set it down. "Be careful. And call me before you take any action. Okay?"

"Yeah. Okay. I'll need some cash and a new credit card when I get there. Have our friend Bob the Banker leave it in the usual place for me. "He was referring to a furnished apartment, which was leased in the name Lapone Enterprises, a shell company set up just for this deal.

"Already done. I spoke to our banker friend an hour ago right after our meeting with the boss. You're all set. I'll talk to you tomorrow night."

"Should I take Tony with me?" Tony was the goon from Chicago who helped him kill Walt Jacob He met Joey in prison and they worked a few jobs together since.

"No. I want you to go alone."

They finished the drinks and Joey placed some bills on the bar as they left.

Michael Ripinski

16

The Titliest golf ball rose off the face of his eight iron and continued in a high arc landing on the green some one hundred and forty yards ahead, stopping just a few feet from the pin. The swing, the contact, the follow through all felt just right for a change and Dick wished all his shots could turn out this well.

"Nice shot man."Said his playing partner, an older gentleman named John who he had hooked up with just that morning in the pro shop. Both were just looking for a friendly game and after a short Q & A figured they would both play at about the same level. After tapping in for birdie he added up the scores. He shot ninety-one and John came in at ninety-three. They shook hands and Dick declined an offer for a beer, choosing instead to go directly home and follow up on the investigation.

As he stopped to open the trunk and place his golf bag inside he noticed the familiar black Crown Vic approaching slowly and ease into the adjacent space. Sean Carson stepped out of the car and smiled. "I thought I could find you here. I checked at the pro shop and they told me you'd be finishing about now. How'd you hit 'em?"

"Not bad. Birdied the last hole. That'll keep me coming back."Lifting his golf bag and placing it carefully into the truck he stooped to untie his golf shoes. "You ought to play more Sean. It's a good release for some of the stress in our life."

"Maybe when I retire I'll find the time. I got about ten more years. Josh is only in sixth grade and I got to get him through college. He's a damn good soccer player so I'm hoping he can get some kind of scholarship. We'll see if he sticks with it. He hasn't discovered girls yet."

Both men laughed for a few seconds before Dick inquired about the investigation. "Anything new?"

Carson leaned against the side of the Ford and spoke in a softer voice. "I was hoping you could fill me in. I know this much. Birmingham wants this Jacob case kept in-house. Their chief called our chief and asked for some room. Says Mister Jacob might have been having marital problems and that's probably why he killed himself. As far as I can tell he didn't mention the Honorable Charlie V."

After adding his golf shoes to the gear in his trunk and slipping his Docksiders on his bare feet, Dick closed the lid and walked around the side of the car next to his friend. He still wished to keep Melissa out of this thing and he wanted to help as much as he could. "Did you tell your chief anything about where we were looking in this case?"

"No. Not yet. I want to keep digging a little further first. I think I am going to pay a visit to Mister Randolph Snyder at the funeral home. After what you told me about his reaction to your questions. Seems like he might loosen up if I pressure him a bit. What about that banker guy you talked to? Find out anything? "

Opening the passenger side door and reaching to pick up some papers from the front seat, Dick sorted through a few printed pages before pulling one from the stack. "Here it is. I Googled this guy and came up with a few things from the newspapers. This one is a pretty good bio from an award he received a few years ago – Man of the Year – from the Detroit Area Bankers and Lenders Association."Reading from the page he continued *"Mister Robert Banker, principal investor of Great Lakes Global Bank, philanthropist, civic organizer and political advisor is the recipient of the 2002 Man of The Year."*

Carson was curious. "What else did it say?"

"You'll love this part. It mentions that the award was presented by Governor Charles Vandenberg at the Ritz Carlton in Dearborn. It goes on to say that he was primarily responsible for many real estate developments in Metro Detroit and is a legend in the business community for his bulldog approach to get a project completed. In 2001 he financed the deal that secured the land for the corporate research park in Auburn Hills near Chrysler headquarters. I remember reading something about one guy holding out on a parcel of land that was part of that development. I think the guy said he was getting anonymous threats. He must have eventually gave in cuz they built that sprawling building just off I-75 that seems to go on forever as you drive by. Isn't it called Futures Park or something like that?"

"Yeah. I think they lease out the facility to the auto companies and it has wind tunnels and all kinds of high tech computer simulation stuff there."Scratching his chin and looking away toward the main clubhouse building of the golf course. "Listen man. I've been thinking and I really appreciate the help on this but I feel like we should make you official somehow. You know. Credentials and stuff. You ever think about becoming a private investigator? You know security stuff and research for law enforcement. You could be getting paid for the work you are doing."He was planting a seed that he was hoping would take root with his old friend.

Dick didn't respond at first. Instead he reached in his pocket for his car keys before turning to walk around to the driver's side, while pressing the automatic door, unlock button. Facing his friend, he spoke across the hood of his car. "Maybe. I'll have to think about it. I like being retired and something like that sounds like a full time gig. On the other hand it would be better than flashing your card while trying to explain why I'm asking questions. Anyway, I'll keep digging on this Mister Banker the banker."

They both smiled as he said this. And then Carson replied. "Kinda like a minister I know named Father Priestly."

Not to be outdone Dick came up with this one. "I know a doctor named Peter Prober. He does vasectomies."

Now they were laughing out loud. Two old friends who remembered a time when this lighthearted banter helped take the edge off while they worked on solving some of the most violent and gruesome crimes in the City of Detroit. It wasn't all that long ago that they would gather at The Old Shillelagh with some of the other cops and tell their stories and jokes. For Sean Carson it wasn't the same out in the 'burbs. Everyone went home after their shift and even though Mary Beth was a good cop and partner, she chose to just go her own way after work. Dick just didn't have the opportunity any more. He met a few new friends on the golf course but their stories were mostly about golf or their families. Pretty plain and, he had to admit, boring as hell. It felt good to be around another cop. It was good for both of them.

17

Charlie had just hung up the phone after leaving separate messages for Bob and Sam. He considered calling Lapone but decided he needed to speak to one of his old friends first. He thought about the events of the past week and now he was sure that Walt Jacob did not kill himself. Rita told him about the note and after talking with her again it was just too suspicious. And he had spoken to his friend Chief Slattery who had handled things discreetly and efficiently. Of course there was always a cost. Slattery was looking for a job at the state level and he even went so far as to suggest that Charlie appoint him to the vacant chair of the state Civil Service Commission. A job that paid considerably more than Chief of Birmingham Michigan Police. The Chief had told him that Walt sure looked like he hanged himself but it was too clean. Too perfect. And he told Charlie about the bruise but he didn't know what to make of it. But he knew that he had to handle the situation before anything could be discovered. And he said that he didn't believe Rita when she told him there was no note. Charlie had thanked him for his loyalty and assured The Chief that things would go his way in the near future.

The cell phone in his pocket began to vibrate and he quickly checked the screen. BTB – Bob the Banker – was on the line and he selected the green button on the phone. "Charlie here."

"You called. I was in a meeting."Replied Bob.

"Thanks. I need to meet with you pretty soon. Can't talk on the phone. Can you come up here to Lansing tonight? Meet me at the condo. Say eight o'clock?"

"You sound kinda upset Governor. Can you tell me anything right now?"

"No. No. I need to meet with you and Sam too if possible. Tonight. It's about Walt."

Bob knew that this was going to get complicated now. He figured that Rita must have told him something and he was worried that The Governor would become a little unglued if he figured out everything. "Okay Charlie. I'll come. But let's keep this between you and me right now. Sam is better off left in the dark. Don't you think?"

"Uh. Yeah. Yeah. Okay. About eight o'clock then."He folded the phone and placed on the desk. There was one more call to make. After telling Tonya to hold his calls he picked up the phone again and called Rita.

She answered on the first ring. "Hi, baby. I miss you. When can I come up to Lansing? I really need to see you. Oh Charlie. Please. Can I come tonight?"

He abruptly replied which caught her off guard. "No. No. Not tonight. I have an important meeting with my advisory team. We are starting to plan the re-election campaign."

Rita wished that she could be part of his 'team'. Of course if she were Misses Charlie V she would be. She still thought it was possible even after what had happened. "Oh, Charlie. When can I see you?"

He knew what he had to tell her but now was not the time. He had already figured that any relationship with Rita Jacob was now on hold until things quieted down and he was more concerned about what was known about the Big Beaver project and Walt's position. He needed some answers from Bob first. "Listen. I have to ask you something. No one is with you right?"

"No. I'm alone at home."

"Good. Now tell me what you did with the note. I told you to destroy it and you told me you did, but tell me exactly how you did it."

She was surprised by the tone in his voice. Why was he interrogating her? She had to think fast. "I burned it like you said."

"How? I mean tell me exactly. Where did you light it and did you watch it burn completely?"

"Yes. Yes. It burned completely. I lit it on fire in the patio area and it was just ashes which I scattered in the garden behind some bushes."She lied convincingly knowing that the note was neatly tucked away in the suit in her bedroom closet.

"Good. I was a little worried because people are starting to doubt. Mike Slattery thinks there might have been something fishy. Rita, I have to tell you something but I need to know that you can handle it."

"What? What?"Eagerly anticipating the question. She had been having her own doubts and needed to know what he knew.

"Walt was working on something and he may have made some people mad at him. Really mad. I am worried that his stubbornness may have cost him."

She listened intently and tried to remain calm. Charlie had just confirmed her suspicions that her poor husband was not despondent over her affair with the governor, but had been murdered. More of a concern, he was killed by someone that knew about them. Aware that their relationship was becoming less of a secret, she began sorting through a list of possibilities. She didn't get too far before he interrupted her thoughts.

"This is very serious Rita. I can't tell you everything but I have my own suspicions. I will be trying to get some answers and as soon as I do, we'll decide how to handle this. Until then I don't want you to talk to anyone. Not your sisters. Not your friends. Especially Mike Slattery. I want to see you too baby."He was lying to make sure he could keep her under control. "Give me few days and I'll have you come up to the condo. Or maybe we can get away someplace. Would you like that?"

The answer was obvious and she felt re- assured by this latest comment. After all she was in love with Charlie V and her ambitions had not changed. No matter how Walt died. It was all just part of the bigger picture for her. "Yes. I will wait for you Charlie. Please get back to me soon. And don't worry I'll keep this to myself. I love you Charlie."

"Me too."He replied as he hung up knowing that he would have to deal with her at some point. Right now it was damage control.

He noticed the red blinking message light on his desk phone and pressed the intercom button, "Tonya, what do you have for me?"

"There's a message from Senator Hall about the proposed business tax increase and Karen needs to discuss your schedule for next week."She was referring to the state senate majority leader William Hall, a close political ally, and Karen Bastow whom he trusted to coordinate his personal as well as public schedule.

"Get me Senator Hall on the phone and tell Karen to come see me in about thirty minutes. I need to arrange a few meetings."

"Yes sir. Anything else."Tonya was hoping that there was not. She was eager to finish her day and meet some friends for a drink. There was a new guy over in the Attorney General's office that caught her eye and she was hoping to meet him.

"No. Thank you Tonya."

18

Sean Carson had decided that it was time to contact Misses Walter Jacob and he persuaded his friend to accompany him. It wasn't difficult. Dick had already done some research on the Jacobs of Birmingham and was not surprised to find their names mentioned in several articles about the Governor and certain State of Michigan political causes. Between the two of them and Mary Beth who was asked to do another interview with Hodges's girlfriend Jennifer, they were putting pieces together. She was certain that Tom had mentioned the word 'fight' and that he saw a silver Mercedes. If Hodges was murdered because he heard something at the Jacob house it had to be because the murderer had already decided to take out Walt Jacob. They needed a motive and they were looking to Rita Jacob to give them some help.

They waited in the car parked a short distance from the curved driveway after their first attempt found no one at home. They didn't wait long. Rita's black BMW sped past them, slowed for a moment and turned into the driveway disappearing behind the hedges and the spruce tree. After waiting a few minutes, Carson started the engine on the Crown Vic and pulled ahead, turning into the entrance approaching the white frame house and parked next to the BMW.

"Let's see if she'll talk to us."Said Carson as he opened the door.

Dick followed without saying a word and both men walked up the few paved red brick steps to the covered porch and Carson rang the doorbell. After a short wait, he rang it again and within seconds the door opened and there stood Rita Jacob wearing tan slacks and a tight fitting black knit top with a low cut front showing just enough skin to draw some attention.

"Hello ma'am. My name's Detective Carson with the Troy Police Department. Are you Rita Jacob?"Flashing his credentials while introducing himself.

"Yes. How can I help you? Stepping backward just a little she continued to block the entrance and did not invite them in.

"Well, we are investigating a case that you might be able to help us with. By the way this is Mister Hagan. He's a consultant on this case."

"How can I help you Detective?"

"Did you hire a landscaper by the name of Tom Hodges? Drove a green truck."

"Why yes. Tommy. My husband hired him and he is doing a great job for us. I should say my late husband. I....."Without finishing the sentence just now realizing that she referred to Walt in the present tense.

"Mrs. Jacob. I am afraid to inform you that there has been a terrible tragedy. Tom Hodges is dead."

Her face turned ashen as she heard the news about Hodges. "Oh my god. When? How? He is such a nice young man."

"May we come in? I think you may want to sit down before we tell you anything else. And by the way, we are sorry to hear about your late husband. Birmingham PD informed us before we came out to see you."

Bracing herself against the doorframe with her left hand, she hesitated for a moment. "Okay. Yes. Please come in."

Holding the door open as they entered the foyer, she closed it behind them and led them into the study just off the Kitchen. The room was small, about ten by twelve but nicely furnished with a small, flower print, love seat and matching wing back chair. A golden oak rocking chair sat off to one side and an antique steamer trunk served as a coffee table in the middle of it all. One wall was a floor to ceiling bookshelf with current and classic titles mixed in. The other walls were decorated with early American prints and a Norman Rockwell copy. A brass floor lamp stood next to a small table between the rocking chair and the wingback. Rita sat in the rocking chair, Carson on the love seat and Dick settled in the wingback.

"Can I offer you some water? I don't have any coffee made at the moment."

"No Thanks."They replied in unison.

Dick decided to ask about Hodges. "Mrs. Jacob…"

She interrupted. "Call me Rita, please."

"We are aware that Tom Hodges did some work for you last Thursday and later that evening he was shot. Before he died he mentioned to someone that he was here during the day and that he had heard an argument. Do you know who your husband was with earlier in the day?"

"No. Oh my god. You didn't say he was murdered. Where?"

"He was getting ready to meet with a client and someone came up on him. We think there was some kind of confrontation."

Carson took over from there. "As he said. Mister Hodges mentioned that he was here earlier in the day and heard something."

She reached to a drawer in the table and extracted a tissue, which she used to wipe her eyes. "That was the same day that my husband died. I found him here in the basement. I thought that he was meeting with a lawyer in Farmington Hills. I don't know whom he might have been meeting with here. If he had an argument with someone, I have no idea whom it could be or what it would be about. I was out at the mall with a few friends and I found him here. Walt didn't tell me much about his business deals. Frankly most of the time I didn't understand him anyway. It was all interest rates and cash flow and stuff."

"Rita. I hate to rehash what the Birmingham police have already gone over with you, but did your husband leave a note of any kind?"Both men were watching her mannerisms and right on cue she hesitated before answering.

"Uh. Uh. No. None was found."Remembering the location of the note in her closet. "I don't know why he did that to himself. Uh. Uh. Uh. I did not have an argument with Walt if that's what you want to know."Sounding defensive she looked away from them toward the kitchen. "Maybe Walt was upset with someone or something and that's why he hanged himself."Forcing herself to cry as she made this last statement.

Carson responded sympathetically. "I'm sorry. I didn't mean to infer that you had a domestic problem. I mean we are sorry that your husband is gone."Realizing that he was not being real smooth he looked over at Dick who took over.

"Rita. Can you remember when was the last time you saw Tom Hodges?"

"Why yes. Earlier that day. I gave him a check. We discussed some additional planting in the back yard. He seemed quite happy. He was always that way. Didn't say much but always a smile. He stuttered you know."

"No. We didn't. One more thing."Dick recalled the conversation with Bob at the funeral home. "Did your husband mention anything about a big deal he was working on?"

"No I don't recall that he did. If there was anything I am sure that his friend Bob Banker would have found something on his computer or in his office downstairs. Bob was kind enough to sort through all his papers right after the funeral. He told me there were no clues. I believe the Birmingham Police also went through his things."She remembered that Chief Slattery had asked to look around and said he did not find anything of interest.

"Well we are sorry to have bothered you."Carson spoke as he handed her his business card. "Please call me if you remember anything else or if some new information comes up. Tom Hodges was an innocent young man who appears to have been in the wrong place at the wrong time."He knew it sounded cliché but he didn't care. He wanted to leave and have a conversation with Dick about what had just occurred.

"It's okay detective, I am still a little emotional. I'm sure you can understand."She rose from the rocker as the two men stood and followed her to the front door. As they left she watched them enter the Crown Vic before closing the door. *I must call Charlie right away.*

19

"You thinkin' what I'm thinking"?"Carson remarked as they drove away from the House.

"Yeah. She was lyin' like hell about the note. And she probably is covering up something else as well. Although I did believe her about her husbands business."

The Crown Vic turned left out of the driveway and came to a stop two blocks away at Maple Road. After a right turn and a short drive, they were in downtown Birmingham – a combination of designer shops, boutiques, restaurants and offices as well as a few luxury high-rise condo developments. Outside of Birmingham some called it Yuppyville but to the locals it was their own private enclave where they went to see and be seen in their latest fashions and of course, driving their Beemers, Lexes, Mercedes Benzes and sometimes a Rolls. The cars were as much an accessory as a Prada bag or a pair of Hugo Boss loafers. Drive up in a Ford or a Chevy and you might as well be riding in an ox cart. It just wasn't cool.

"Let's get some lunch. I'll buy."Carson offered.

"I know a place just down Woodward that's pretty good. It's actually in Royal Oak. called The Avenue Grill. Used to be a Big Boy or something like that but now it's a family run place. Good food. I go there for breakfast once in a while."Dick pointed to the direction as they headed south out of Birmingham.

Once inside and seated at a window booth, they ordered lunch and continued the discussion. Both agreed that it was just too much of a coincidence that Walt Jacobs's suicide and Tom Hodges murder happened a few hours apart and that Hodges heard or saw something at the house that day.

After swallowing a bite of his club sandwich and washing it down with a sip of decaf coffee, Carson removed his pen from inside his jacket and wrote something on a napkin; sliding it over to his friend across the table. *Charlie* was written in black ink at the top of the napkin.

Dick stared at the napkin for a moment and using his own pen wrote the name *Rita* in the space below and slid the napkin back across the table.

They continued this exchange a few more times, neither man speaking. Back in Detroit, they would use this same method of problem solving, usually sitting around a table at one of the bars near 1300 Beaubien, The Detroit Police Headquarters. Sometimes three or four detectives who were working on different cases would brainstorm after laying out their cases and fact-finding hoping that their comrades would make sense out of something they may have missed. Often it would result in a break that would lead to solving a case. Dick recalled a memorable situation where he was able to point out that the same name of a particular well-known doctor kept popping up in two or three different investigations. As it was later discovered, the doctor had been providing fraudulent prescriptions to married female patients in exchange for sexual favors. When two of the husbands turned up dead and a third was left in a coma, the result of drug overdoses, the clues pointed to the good doctor who was now spending a minimum of twenty years in Jackson Prison.

Turning the napkin so that they both could read the names, they stared at the list for a moment. *Charlie, Rita, Walt, Hodges, Killer.* Dick slid the napkin back toward himself and wrote one more name at the bottom. *Bob the Banker.* He then drew a line back to Walt's name and then around to Charlie.

"Yeah, but how does he fit in with the Hodges kid?" Carson asked.

"I don't know yet, but I have a feeling that Mister Banker knows something about Walt Jacob's business and that is where we need to go."

"I agree."

The waitress, a tall slender blonde girl about twenty named

Carla, stopped by the table and filled their coffee cups. "Will there be anything else gentlemen? Dessert? "When they both nodded she left the check on the table and smiled showing off her perfect white teeth. "Thank you very much. Have a great afternoon."

Dick replied. "Thank you Carla. We will."

After she left and moved on to the other tables, Dick looked at the napkin and pointed to another name. "I think that Rita Jacob leads us to both Bob the Banker and Charlie V. I want to know what the governor knows about Walt Jacob's business. He was a big supporter of Charlie's campaign. Maybe he also shared some of his business deals with the governor?"

Carson raised his cup to his mouth and slowly sipped the freshly poured coffee, his eyes peering over the lip directly at his friend. He set the cup down, folded his hands and took in a breath, exhaling before speaking again. "I want you to consider something. Okay?"

"What is it?"

"I had to tell my captain that you were helping me on this case. Mary Beth was concerned that we would cross the line somehow and with you not having any official capacity, we would contaminate the investigation. So I told Captain Banarsek and he was not real happy about it but I got him to look at it rationally. I also had to tell him a little lie. I said that you'd be interested in the vacancy we have in our department as a detective. After telling him of your qualifications and our background together in the D, he wants to meet you. Before you say anything just think about it. You can just meet him and you don't have to agree to anything."

Dick was caught off guard by Carson's announcement. He was still considering the Private Security business but this was all together new. Did he really want to get back into the game full time? It was not what he had in mind. Retirement was suiting him and he was just developing the first real relationship with a woman in a long time. But this case was pulling him in. There was something about it besides just the fact that Hodges was murdered practically in his front yard. There was something else. Melissa knew this Rita Jacob and somehow it became more of a personal thing. And what about the Governor? It sure was a fascinating case all right. He wanted in. He needed to see this thing through to a conclusion. But could he do it without becoming a full time employee of the Troy PD?

"Okay. I'll talk to him. When."

"Today. Four o'clock. Come to my office and I will arrange the meeting."Extending his hand across the table. "Thanks man."

"Sure. Just a meeting though. No obligations."

"No obligations."

20

The black Lexus parked in the driveway directly behind a blue Michigan State police car and next to a green Lincoln MKS. Michigan State Spartan-green. Charlie was a distinguished alumnus of the University and his condo was practically on the campus. It was good PR. As usual one of Charlie's bodyguards sat in the car keeping an eye on the area and he waved to Bob as he approached the front door. After one short ring of the doorbell another aide named Don Stinson opened the door and invited him inside. "The governor has been expecting you Mister Banker. He's waiting in the office."

The two-bedroom condo was sparsely furnished except for the den, which had been converted to an elaborate office complete with computers, fax, phones and wall mounted, plasma TV. A large cherry wood desk dominated the room. Like his capitol office, his desk chair was set at a level, which allowed the governor to sit slightly above his guests. Charlie stood as Bob entered and motioned for him to take seat in one of two leather armchairs situated in front of the desk "That will be all Don. Please close the door."Speaking to the aide who was also a member of his bodyguard detail.

"So what is so important that I had to drive up from Detroit tonight?"Bob said as he sat in one of the leather chairs.

"I think you might know what this is about. I don't believe Walt took his own life. This sounds very suspicious and I don't like the way things are being handled. You know damn well that Walt had some reservations about the Big Beaver project. He e-mailed me a day before he died and asked if I knew what was buried there."

"Get a grip, Charlie. Are you saying that Walt Jacob was murdered?"

"I don't know what to think right now. I know that Rita has doubts about it. And...."

Bob interrupted the governor. "Rita has doubts? Come on Charlie. Why would she even care? Hell, she's free and clear now and you two love birds can quit sneaking around."

"Cut the bullshit Bob. There was a note. She destroyed it. Based on the way it was written, Walt was trying to tell her that he was forced against his will to write it."

Bob now had to take a different approach. It was all damage control from here on and Charlie had just confirmed what he has suspected. But did she really destroy the note? "Calm down. Okay. Let's look at this rationally. Why would Walt want to kill himself? And if he didn't who would be nuts enough to want to kill him over something like the Big Beaver deal?"

"That's what I want you to tell me my old friend. Me and Rita aside, Walt was a good man. Stubborn maybe, but still a good man. I don't like the look of this thing and I want some answers. What about your buddy Paul? What do we really know about him? If he thought the project was going south would he have taken matters into his own hands? There's a lot of money at stake here isn't there?"

Bob did not immediately answer. Instead he just stared at Charlie and let him answer his own questions. He knew that he held the cards with the governor and that it was better to just let this all sink in for a moment. There was no way that Charlie V; the hot shot Governor of the Great State of Michigan would bring down his own career. His ego would not let him do that and Bob was confident that Charlie would have to play along. The game was power and these two had been playing it to mutual success for almost twenty years. Yes, he felt bad about Walt also, but in the end it was a necessary move. They just could not afford to lose.

After a minute, Bob rose and walked over to the window, opened the vertical blind and peered out into the approaching night sky; the bright orange sun dipping behind the trees in the distance. "I think we both know what the stakes are here. I believe it is better to just stop asking questions and move on. Don't you agree?"

At that moment he got it. It hit him like a blind side tackle in the ribs from his old football days at Brother Rice High School. Charlie was a pretty good halfback on a state championship team and he was known for his toughness. He would need that toughness now. He'd need to be tough or his whole life would come crashing down. He was involved up to his eyeballs having brought Bill Greening into the deal. And he was sure that his affair with Rita, if it were to be made public, would cost him. Especially with Walt now dead. He had higher goals and aspirations. He felt it was his destiny. He would ask no more questions and he would just have to live with it. But what about Rita?

"It seems to me we still might have one problem here. What do we do about Mrs. Jacob?"It sounded odd to him referring to her this way. For a moment, his survival became more important than their relationship.

Turning back from the window, Bob put his hand to his chin rubbing it softly. "Well. I think we need to make sure she doesn't ask too many questions either. She's your woman Charlie. What do you suggest? Should we buy her off like Susan? "

Charlie didn't care for the reference to his former wife. Susan never really cared for him in the first place. She took the money and ran and it always pissed him off that she could be bought so quickly. "Rita's not like that. Besides Walt left her in very good shape financially. I think it will take more than your checkbook to keep her under control. I was going to call it quits with her but now I will just have to keep things going for a while. She will want some promises so it may get a little tricky. Just let me handle it okay?"He really had no intentions of calling it off.

"You sure?"

"Yeah. If I think she's getting too suspicious I'll call you right away."In fact he wasn't sure how he was going to handle it but he needed time to think. Governor Charles B. Vandenberg had to come up with a plan to save his career. He would need some of that old high school toughness again.

Michael Ripinski

21

With nimble hands the dealer swiftly placed two cards in front of each of the five men seated around the blue felt table at **Caesars Palace** in Las Vegas. The two men to the right each folded and Bill Greening lifted the edges of his cards. King of hearts and king of spades. He raised to five hundred dollars. The next guy folded and that left the young man wearing a Yankees baseball cap in the big blind. He called the bet and the dealer turned over the next three cards in the middle – the flop. Ace of diamonds. King of diamonds. Ten of clubs. Bill had trip kings. A great poker hand. He had been playing for two days and he'd been up and down and was still about even. Now he saw the chance for the big pot. He was able to get into this table with a minimum stake of ten thousand dollars – the cash provided by his new friend from Chicago introduced to him by Charlie V himself. So what if he rubber-stamped the DEQ paperwork on that piece of land in Troy. It was probably for another parking lot anyway. Here he was in Las Vegas, playing poker for higher stakes than he had in his life. It was thrilling and he felt the rush of playing in the big game. Now he was about to make the one big hand. He wanted to play it just right. He looked down and his hand was shaking.

Hope he didn't see that, he thought as he placed his hand in his lap. Taking his time before placing the next bet. "One thousand."

"Call," said the Yankee's fan without hesitation.

Worried now. *That was quick. What's he got? Aces in the hole. No way. He would have raised before the flop.* The dealer turned over the next card. Three of clubs. No help to either player. Bill felt that he could not back off now. He wanted this hand and he was sure he had better

107

cards than the Yankee's fan. "Two thousand."Bill pushed his chips into the pot.

This time there was some hesitation from the young man. He stared at Bill and then at his stack of chips while placing the Yankees cap on his head backwards. "Call."He said again.

The dealer turned over the fifth card in the middle – the river. Ten of diamonds. Bill had three kings and two tens. A full house. He was sure he was going to take this guy down and win the big one. He wanted to enjoy the moment. Checking his stack of chips on the blue felt, he saw that he had about seven thousand left. *Let's see if I can sucker this guy into the pot.* He was sure he had him beat. "Four Thousand."Pushing the chips into the pot. A murmur could be heard around the table as a small group of interested watchers had suddenly appeared. Some of them were hoping to take a seat if one of these guys tapped out.

Yankees fan took off his cap once again and placed it on correctly – the white N and Y facing toward Bill Greening. He smiled. "How much you got there in that stack."Pointing to Bill's remaining chips.

Startled by this development, Bill nervously replied. "Three thousand."

"All in."said the Yankees fan placing seven thousand dollars worth of chips into the middle of the table.

"What the fuck."Bill whispered to himself but everyone around the table heard him. They were all waiting to see what he would do. He was so sure of himself just a minute ago. What would this guy do now? If he folded he'd still have three thousand left to play with. But no way could he fold a full house. What if the guy did have aces in the hole and was suckering him in? No he was certain he didn't have aces. The guy would have raised on the fourth card. *Maybe a diamond flush; that's it. He's got a flush and he thinks I just got two pair. Wait till he sees my full boat.*

"Call"Bill Greening stood up at the table and flipped over his two Kings as he pushed his remaining chips into the pot. "You got all diamonds don't ya Yankee boy."

"Yup."Said the young man.

Bill let out a whoop and said, "I knew it."As he started to reach for the pot, over twenty thousand dollars total.

"Wait a minute there friend."The young man lifted his cap smoothed back his hair and replaced the cap before flipping over his cards. Queen of diamonds. Jack of diamonds. A royal straight flush. The highest possible hand in poker.

Bill's face went ashen as he gazed upon the cards on the table. There was yelling and hollering all around as more people had joined the gathering.

"Did you see that? "

"Wow."

"Holy shit. What a hand."

Greening slumped back into the chair holding his head in his hands. He could not believe what just happened and he could only offer a weak handshake to the Yankees fan as he left the table stopping once to look back in disbelief.

Entering the elevator he pressed the button for the fourth floor before the door had even closed and he quickly made his way to room 401, a suite provided for him by his new friends. As he sat on the bed rubbing his temples while lamenting the unbelievable bad luck, he decided to make a call to the number provided by Paul Lapone. "If you need anything while you are in Vegas, just call this number. Ask for Dominic."He recalled Paul's exact words as he dialed the number.

"Yeah. Dominic here."The deep masculine voice answered on the second ring.

Bill thought about hanging up and just leaving. After all he had a plane ticket back to Detroit where he left his car and he could go now. Let it be. Bad luck. "Uh. This is Bill Greening. Paul told me I could call you if I needed anything here in Vegas. Paul Lapone."

"Yes. Mister Greening. He said you might call. What can I do for ya?"

No sense beating around the bush. He blurted it right out. "I need some money. Bad luck downstairs tonight. Some asshole caught a royal to my kings full. Can you believe that? Paul said I could ask you for anything. I need five grand."He was thinking of asking for another ten but decided not to get too greedy.

"I can have the money put into your hotel account. Would that be alright?"

Not expecting this to be so easy, Bill regretted for the moment that he didn't ask for ten or even twenty grand. Then the thought crossed his mind. *What do they expect in return?* So far, everything had been given to him. The plane tickets. The hotel suite. A well stocked bar. A chauffer from the airport who gave him a business card and told him he could provide the most fantastic looking hookers in all of Vegas. It was too good to be true. Maybe it was. He didn't want to think about it any more. He'd take the five grand and if things went well he'd pay it all back. That's what he really wanted to do. "Sure. That'll be great. Do I have to wait until tomorrow?"

"No. No of course not. Give me ten minutes Mister Greening and the money will be there."

"Thank you Dominic. I will be sure to tell Mister Lapone how helpful you have been."

Dominic chuckled to himself, which Bill was able to hear. "That's okay. Mister Greening. Paul and I are good friends and we help each other out often. I am sure that he knows you are being well taken care of."

"Well then. Good. Good. Thanks again. By the way I'd like to buy you a drink if you are available later on."

"No. But if I decide to stop by your hotel I'll be sure to say 'hi' in person. Good luck Mister Greening."With these words Dominic ended the call.

Bill decided to take a shower before going back down to the casino floor. He wasn't sure what he would play. Maybe blackjack for a while. Five grand would go along way at those tables. Deep down inside he knew he'd lose it all. Why didn't he just take the five grand and return to Michigan No one would know. But he couldn't do it. He was in Las Vegas and the action was too tempting. He could get on a hot streak and then he'd show 'em. Maybe get back in the game with Yankee boy. He wanted that badly. Yeah. He'd show them all.

After he returned to the casino and played blackjack and later, more poker at a smaller stakes table, he once again tapped out, losing to three fives when he had three deuces. Looking at his watch, he saw that it was seven AM. He had been playing for ten hours straight and he felt tired and now also, depressed. He couldn't ask for more money. Something didn't seem right. He'd go to the room and rest, then catch the next flight back to Michigan.

As he was opening the door to his room he didn't notice the man coming up behind him. But he did feel the hand on his shoulder. Turning abruptly he was face to face with a very tall, maybe six-three, younger man with a dark tan complexion wearing a gray suit with a white button down shirt, no tie.

"Excuse me. Mister Greening?'

"Yes. Yes. Who are you?"

"My name is Brian. Dominic sent me. He said that you might need more money."

"Well I…"Hesitating Bill wasn't sure what to say. "I thought that I might just head on back to Michigan. I've already received a nice gift from your friend."

"Oh this would not be a gift. We'd call it a loan and when you win it back you can pay us off and keep your winnings. Only a small handling charge. Dominic said he thought you'd be good for it. What do ya say?"

What was this guy saying? He'd loan him the money. He'd heard about poor suckers and getting in deep with loan sharks and then having to sell their houses or get their head bashed in. But this guy seemed so nice. Bill thought about how he might still be able to get back into that big stakes game with Yankee boy. He was sure he could finally come out ahead. And if anything happened he'd just call his friend Paul Lapone. He'd take care of things for him for sure. "How much can I get?"

"Would twenty large do for a start?"

Whoa. Twenty thousand dollars. He could sit at that table with a big pile of chips and that would make him feel real confident. He was sure he could get things going his way. "That would do just fine Brian. Just Fine. Do I need to sign anything?"

"No. We'll just stay in touch. The money will be in your hotel account tonight after five PM. Now why don't you just get some rest and have a good meal. Just call Dominic if you need anything else."

Bill meekly extended his hand and the tall young man named

Brian firmly pressed his around all Bill's fingers slightly hurting him before letting go. It was an embarrassing moment but he got over it. After entering his room he took four Advil and lay face down on the bed, quickly falling asleep.

22

Her ever-present cell phone was ringing inside her purse and Melissa noticed the name on the blue screen. Jacob. A chill went through her as she answered. "Hi. This is Melissa."

"Hi. It's Rita. Rita Jacob."

Not sure what to say or how to react she paused before answering. "Oh. Hi. I am so sorry about your loss. I read about it in the paper."

"Thank you." And then "Melissa. Can I see you? Please? I mean I need to work out to relieve some of the stress. This whole ordeal has been just too much. I need to give myself a good solid workout."

"Sure. When do you want to get together?"

"I was hoping today. This afternoon maybe. Any chance?"

In fact Melissa had an opening at three PM due to another cancellation. It was supposed to be her last session for the day. "How about three PM? You can have as long as you want. I can order you a massage when we're done. How does that sound?"

"Oh that's terrific. I'll see you at the club at three."

Melissa hung up and thought about what Dick had told her. She would have to call him but she decided to wait until after the workout.

Michael Ripinski

23

"Sean has told me some pretty good stories about you and him working violent crimes in Detroit. He says you had one of the best success rates in the department down there."Captain David Banarsek leaned back in his leather chair while placing both hands on top of his head. He was wearing a crisp white Brooks Brothers shirt with a yellow and blue striped tie.

Dick thought that he seemed like one of those guys that could run around all day long, in and out of his car, up and down in his chair and still look like he just stepped out of a GQ advertisement. Not the kind of cop who got down and dirty. A pretty boy. Dick had worked with a few like him before. It wasn't necessarily a bad thing but always made him uneasy because he was just the opposite. His clothes never fit quite perfect and by noon he looked like he slept in them.

"We worked hard in Detroit."He replied coolly.

"We're a busy shop here in Troy but not nearly as interesting as what you were used to."Dick was seated on a cloth-covered armchair in front of the desk in the office at the Troy Police Headquarters. Sean Carson was standing off to the side leaning against the wall near a small window looking out toward Big Beaver Road. Troy PD was located just a half mile from the landfill across Interstate Seventy-five and set back in the complex containing the City Municipal Offices and a library.

"Well, based on my recent experiences at my condo I am beginning to wonder."Dick replied sarcastically. "I moved out here for the peace and quiet and that's not exactly what I got. The Chamber of Commerce wouldn't want me as a spokesman."

Carson and the Captain laughed but stopped abruptly as they realized Dick was being serious. Banarsek spoke next. "Well I can understand your concern Dick. We don't get too much of this stuff out here but when we do we pretty much always get our man.....or woman. Sean, tell Dick about the Albanian girl who shot her father last year and tried to make it look like a robbery."He was referring to a case that Carson had helped solve as Sean described the details. The father had forbid the girl to go to a dance with a boy from the football team at Troy High School. The sixteen year-old walked up behind him as he was getting into his car and shot him in the back of the head. She took his wallet and watch but left a wad of fifties in his pants pocket. Her story broke down after a few hours of questioning and a discovery of gunpowder from the murder weapon on her sweater.

"Sean's a good cop."Dick said matter of factly.

"So are you my friend."Sean chimed in. "We could use your experience and skill here in Troy. Don't you agree David?"Addressing his superior by his first name.

"Yes. Yes we could. But only if he wants it. I don't want to talk somebody into something he has no passion for. Even though he has assisted on this case already."

Dick didn't know how much his friend had told Banarsek but the Captain seemed to know that he was attached to this case. He was afraid to admit it, but he was really into it. Maybe it was the location of the crime. Maybe it was the connection to some pretty powerful people in the state including one Charlie V. Maybe it was the ironic relationship of Melissa to Rita Jacob. Or maybe it was just simply his desire to see justice for poor young Tom Hodges. It was really all of it. The action. The challenge. This is what he did for over twenty years in Detroit and Dick knew that he was having a hard time letting go. Still he did not want to make a quick decision. "If you're offering me a job Captain, I'll be honest with you. I might be interested. But I want to think it over for a week or so..."

As they walked out of Banarsek's office and down the hall toward Carson's much smaller room, Dick was thinking about what had just occurred. He realized that his friend had pretty much planned this out to get him on the force. He wasn't offended. Sean knew what he was doing and he would have done the same thing if the roles were reversed. The two of them were much more experienced than the current Troy detectives. It may be a different culture out here in the suburbs, but the methods are the same. Find a motive and you find the killer. Most of the time anyway.

"I've got some work to do on another case. Can you take care of something for me?' Carson said as he placed his hand on the doorknob.

"What do you need?"

"Would you be able to pay another visit to Mister Banker? Seeing as how you already met him. There is something there with him and Walt Jacob and I just think that might be our connection to Hodges."

"I agree. Sure. Let me try to get him to see me in his office. If not I'll do a Sixty Minutes on him."Dick was referring to an ambush style interview based on the tactic made popular with the famous CBS Television show.

"Call me as soon as you have anything and one more thing."

"What?"

"Thanks man."

"No problem. We can get this one done."Dick already sounding like the Troy PD employed him.

Leaving the building and walking across the parking lot to his new car, Dick realized he had not turned on his cell phone. Reaching into his coat pocket and pressing the green button, the LED screen came to life showing two messages – both from Melissa. He pressed the instant call back feature and waited for her to answer. She was on the line after two rings.

"I've been trying to reach you."

"Sorry. I had my phone off. I was in a meeting at Troy PD with Sean Carson and his boss so I didn't want to be disturbed."

"We need to talk. I just had a session with Rita Jacob. She's real upset and it's not just about her husband."

"You met with her today? I asked you to let me know if you had any more contact with her."He sounded annoyed but quickly backed down. He didn't want to make Melissa think she did anything wrong. "Okay. Good. Are you at home?"

"Yeah. I just walked in."

"I'm on my way over. I want to hear all about it. See ya in ten minutes."

Melissa folded her phone and placed it back in the charger. She reached for the stack of mail she had brought in when she arrived home and stood by the kitchen sink, casually glancing out toward the carports next to the building. She didn't notice the silver Mercedes parked near a tree at the far end of the lot.

After following Rita Jacob to the health club and observing her chatting with this other woman in the parking lot for over fifteen minutes, Joey had decided to follow Melissa back to her condo. Just in case he needed to know more about her. He copied the license plate from her white Saab and noted which unit she entered in the attached condo building and sat there for a few minutes before driving away. As he exited the driveway he forgot to look to his right and did not see the Ford Escape turn in front of him. Both cars slammed on their breaks stopping just inches from a collision and the two drivers briefly locked in eye contact. The Ford driver mouthed the words *be careful* as he continued into the private driveway. Joey quickly sped away thankful that he had avoided an accident.

Back at his own apartment, Joey called Paul Lapone on his cell. "Hey. I just wanted to let you know I made it here okay and I followed Misses J for a while. She met with a woman at a health club and it seems like they are good friends."

"Good. Keep an eye on her. Have you found anything on this Hagan guy yet?"

"No not yet. I'm gonna call the Troy police to see what he does there. Pretty common name though. Maybe we can find out where he lives."

"Keep me posted."

"You got it."

Joey picked up the large manila envelope from the kitchen counter and using a knife from the drawer, sliced open the seal. Reaching inside, he retrieved a Visa card and a typed note with an ATM pin number. The letterhead was from Michigan Global Bank. No signature just the number. He ripped a strip from the paper with just the PIN and placed it in his wallet deciding to head out to catch a bite to eat. He would follow up on this Hagan in the morning.

As he entered the Chinese restaurant at Maple and near Coolidge, Joey noticed a middle age couple waiting to be seated. They briefly made eye contact and then continued in a whispered conversation while holding hands. The woman giggled at something the man said and then gave him a kiss on the lips. They seemed very happy and in love. He found himself wondering what it would be like to have a girlfriend and turned away before they noticed him staring. He was envious of the man. He had been with women. Many of them. Mostly whores. There was once a girl in Chicago who was sort of his girlfriend for a while. She was nice. Worked at Bloomingdale's. When she found out that he'd been in jail and suspected that he was still basically a criminal, she backed off. It bothered him for a while but he realized it was probably for the better. His lifestyle was not suited to long-term relationships. Maybe there would come a time when he that would change. He had been thinking about it more and more. Making plans even. He had made a lot of money in the past few years and he was smart enough to put most of it away.

Michael Ripinski

24

"Oh Charlie. I missed you so much. Please just hold me for a while."Rita leaned into his back, her naked breasts pressing lightly against his warm skin. They had just finished making love and as usual, Charlie was exhausted. Their routine was anything but. She liked to play full out and he was happy to oblige. He turned toward her without speaking and gently kissed her forehead as he slipped his right arm underneath her neck and wrapped his left around her body.

He had thought about ending it but he knew that was futile. Deep down he longed for her physically and he knew he could not be without her. And not just for the sex. She was his intellectual equal and he had sought her counsel on many occasions. They would sit for hours discussing political strategy or sometimes just current events – local or national. In some strange way it turned them both on and became part of the foreplay, often times in the bathtub or shower as they stroked, rubbed a touched themselves into all out passion. Charlie's favorite was discussing budget cuts while having sex.

As he laid there in his king size bed on this night he had other things on his mind. "I have to ask you something."He whispered.

"Anything baby."

"You mentioned two cops came to see you and asked some questions about your lawn guy."

"Yeah."She tilted her head so that her eyes met his.

"Then you said they asked if you knew anything about Walt's business. Correct?"

"Yeah. And I told them the truth. I didn't know about anything. But these cops seemed to think I did. I could tell. And they seemed to think that Walt and this kid Tom Hodges were connected."

He pulled away from her and sat straight up in the bed, his back leaning against the walnut headboard. "Baby. We got a problem."

Joining him in the same position, she let the bed sheet fall around her lap and sat there exposed from the waist up, turning her head toward him. "What do you mean?"

"I mean that Walt was into some kind of business deal and I think he had help hanging himself. I don't know how the lawn kid is connected, but I have a feeling he is."

"Are you saying you are certain that Walt was murdered? And you might know who was responsible?"

"I didn't say that. But I'm worried that's all. You did burn the note didn't you?"

Rita climbed from the bed and grabbed a velvet robe from his closet wrapping herself tightly before sitting on the edge of the bed. "I told you I did. Didn't I?"

"Yeah but did you?"Leaning over he placed his hand on her shoulder. "I got to know Rita. There is more to this than I can tell you right now."

Turning quickly toward him, she could see the worried look in his eyes. It was real and she thought about the note, safely tucked away in her suit pocket hanging in her closet. She had come to grips with the fact that Walt's death was suspicious to say the least, but now that she had what she had always longed for, always hoped for, she was thinking that maybe she should have destroyed that note in the first place. Why let anything get in the way of her and Charlie. She thought in that moment about being Mrs. Charles B. Vandenberg, First Lady of the State of Michigan. She wanted that more than anything else and she would have her way.

"It's gone. I burned it in the backyard like you told me to."She lied.

"Good girl."He reached across the bed and wrapping his arms around her, he kissed her on the neck. "Now we need to have a plan on how to deal with this."

Tilting her head to the side she allowed him to continue as his lips moved slowly along her neck and back. The robe slowly parting and falling away. "A plan for what?"She whispered heavily.

Interrupting his kissing, he spoke with his mouth close to her neck. She could feel his warm breadth. "A plan for keeping you safe and for keeping me out of all of it."

"Why do I need to be safe? I didn't do anything. And I sure as hell don't know anything about Walt's business. What do you mean baby?"She turned around and unexpectedly kissed him full on the mouth, her tongue exploring his as her hand reached into his lap.

Pulling away and breathing hard he looked into her eyes and replied. "We are in this together. You should know that this is a dangerous game we are playing and you know some of the other players."He then reached inside the robe and placed a hand on her breast before returning the full kiss, which lasted for a minute.

"I love danger as long as I get to be with you."She slipped the robe away and wrapped herself around him falling into the bed. For the next half-hour there were only breathing sounds as they moved and twisted and probed each other. Eventually resulting in exhaustion - for both of them this time.

Opening his eyes Charlie realized that he had been asleep for a few hours and he noticed that the other side of the bed was empty. "Hey baby."He yelled toward the open door leading to the bathroom. The door was closed and the light was on. Inside, Rita dressed in the robe once again, sat on the floor thinking. She remembered that Charlie said he was concerned for her safety and that she would know the people that might be responsible for Walt's Death. He was right. *This is a dangerous game.* And she loved every minute of it as long as she had Charlie.

Michael Ripinski

25

"All in, "said Bill Greening to the Oriental looking man seated at the opposite end of the table while pushing his remaining chips in to the center. He was down to his last five hundred dollars after playing all night once again. At one point he was ahead by twenty five thousand, which would have been all his to keep, but he kept on playing. Always looking to make it grow. Looking for that big pot that would have the other gamblers talking about him with respect. Like a winner. He would walk away with a smile and never play again. He would prove that he was indeed a winner, Not, Oh God how he hated that word – a loser. He would show them. He would pay back the twenty grand and take the winnings back to Michigan and call it quits. Maybe he could talk the wife into taking him back. He would give some of the money to charity he promised himself. That would be the right thing to do and it would make him feel good. That was his plan. But in the end he was still William Greening, inspector with the Michigan Department of Environmental Quality and a gambling addict destined to lose as long as he could not just walk away.

The cards in the middle were ten, five, ace, three, jack.

"Call."The Oriental man counted out enough chips to match the bet and turned over a pair of jacks giving him a set – three of a kind.

Bill just stared as he flipped over his pair of tens giving him a set but still not good enough. Watching as the dealer pushed the pile of chips over to the Oriental man he finally mumbled "Good hand."He paused for a moment before turning away from the table and as he began walking away it hit him that he had just lost twenty thousand dollars of someone else's money. He froze in his tracks and he felt weak and disoriented. What would he do now? He was pretty sure this was a loan and they would want to be paid back. He couldn't just walk away and fly back to Lansing. There would be some kind of arrangement to be made. He counted out how he would have to pay it back month by month. If he paid five hundred dollars a month it would still take almost four years. But there would be interest too he suddenly realized. How much would that be? He had heard of guys being charged twenty percent or more. Then that would take longer to pay back.

"Shit. What did I do?"he asked himself out loud. Then remembering that his good friend Paul said he could ask for anything, he returned to the room and quickly dialed the number.

"Yeah. Paul here."Answering the call with a deep raspy voice.

"Uh. Uh. This is Bill. In Vegas. Bill Greening."

"I know who you are. What do you want now?"abruptly he asked.

Detecting the difference in the attitude he wondered if his new friend already knew about his losses and about the loan. Of course he would. They would have called him and told him by now. He hesitated before speaking. "Uh I. Uh. I hate to ask you again but. I. Uh. I need your help with something."

"This wouldn't have anything to do with the twenty grand you borrowed from those guys in Vegas?"

"Well yeah. Sort of. I mean yes. Can you help me out one last time?"He was trembling now as he sat on the edge of the bed holding the phone tightly. "Your friend Dominic loaned me another twenty and of course I want to pay him back but…"

"Shut up and listen to me dumb ass. Dominic had nothing to do with lending you that money. Those guys that approached you are loan sharks that work the casinos out there and they don't like to be messed with. I can't get you out of this and neither can he."

"But. But. The guy, Brian was his name, he said that Dominic sent him."

"Did you call Dominic to check it out? No you didn't. You just assumed that this guy Brian was cool and you took the money. Well let me tell you something Bill. You got to pay that back."

He was sweating now and realized he was in serious trouble here. "Can you help me? You got to help me. I won't come back here again. I'll quit. Please Paul. Make it right with these guys and I'll come back to Michigan and you'll never hear from me again."

Thinking that he would need to explain this to the Boss he decided to let Bill simmer a while out in Vegas. Maybe it would teach him a lesson. He knew that he could send the money but he was worried that this guy might just head right back to the tables and lose it all again. "Listen. I don't know if I can do anything but I'll get back to you. Just sit tight and wait for my call."

"When? When will you call?"Nervously switching the phone from one hand to the other.

"Just sit tight I said."

"Yeah. Okay. Thanks man."

"As I said, just sit tight."

Bill heard the phone click off and placed his in the holder on the nightstand. Not knowing what to do next he decided to try and sleep for a while but it was no use. He kept staring at the phone waiting for Paul to call back. After a few hours Bill Greening made the biggest mistake of his life, deciding to take a walk alone out on the strip. He had about twenty dollars left in his pocket and headed out into the night. As he walked down the street away from the hotel he turned the corner and bumped into a very attractive young lady wearing a short black cocktail dress. She had shimmering auburn hair, bright green eyes and a gold chain draped around her neck cascading onto her ample breasts, which he noticed right away. "Excuse me. "He mumbled.

"No. I won't excuse you."She replied.

"Huh? What did you say?"

Smiling back at him the young lady said. "I was just joking. Sorry. Just trying to be friendly."

"Oh. Oh I'm sorry too."Smiling back at her. "Got a lot on my mind."

Extending her hand. "My name's Mandy. What's yours?"

"William. I mean Bill."Hesitating as he thought about his problems for a second and then let them go. "Hey are you with anyone

Mandy?"

"No not really. I just got off work here at the casino. In the cages."She lied. "I'm sorry if I interrupted your thoughts Bill. I wasn't paying attention myself. It has been a rough time for me."

Taking a step back and noticing how good-looking she was, he was totally attracted to her beauty and her friendliness. And right now he needed a friend. "Well I guess we have something in common. It's been a rough few days for me too. But I'll be okay. Just got to take care of a few details and a friend of mine is coming through for me."Trying to sound confident. "What about you?"

She offered that friendly smile again and said. "I think I just need some time to get it together. But yeah, I'll be okay."

"Well then Mandy, can I buy you a cup of coffee?"He was surprised by his own assertiveness.

"I guess so Bill. That actually sounds good to me."Taking his arm they continued walking in the direction he was headed. After a few blocks they entered a Starbucks and spent the next hour talking about dreams and bad luck. He was feeling pretty good about being with such an attractive woman as he was telling her stories about his job with the State, making himself sound more important even mentioning his good friend Charlie V. the Governor.

While he was rambling on about soil testing, she slid her hand over to his and began stroking his palm. He almost spilled the coffee and it wasn't long before she invited him to her apartment. Before the night was over Bill Greening would realize that a very high priced hooker had picked him up. Of course he had no money to immediately pay and that did not make Mandy or her pimp very happy. He stubbornly refused to admit that he had access to the funds and he did not want to call Dominic or Lapone or any body else. They would all think he was just a big loser. His body was found two days later in ditch two miles outside the city limits. The autopsy showed that although he was beaten pretty badly about the face and had his right arm broken, William Greening had died of a massive heart attack while trying to walk back to his hotel. Once he arrived, he would have received the message that Paul had taken care of the loan and he was free to return to Michigan without worry.

26

"So what did Rita Jacob have to say?"Dick was standing in the kitchen at Melissa's Royal Oak condo, while twisting the cap from a bottle of Bud Light, which he had taken from the fridge.

"It was really weird. She just started talking and I listened. For like twenty minutes. All I said was 'Uh Huh' and 'is that so?' It was like she needed to confess her sins or something. Of course she asked me to keep it all to myself. But how could I? I need to tell you everything. You need to know this."

After taking another sip from his beer, he slid a chair away from the table, turned it around and straddled it so that he was facing her. "I'm listening."

Melissa began by telling him how Rita asked to meet with her on short notice and they had a good work out first. As they began the cool down Rita shared some of the details of her relationship with Charlie. "She has been seeing the governor for a few years now which I already knew but she told me that he asks for her advice on many issues and she really wants to marry him as soon as the time is right. Heck her husband's body isn't even cold yet and she wants to become Misses Charlie V. Then she tells me that her husband's death was suspicious and that she thinks that he may not have acted alone. She thinks that some body made it look like suicide."She paused for a moment while staring out of the window and then resumed. "Then she tells me that Charlie thinks the same thing. He thinks that Walt was getting some pressure from some business associates and they wanted him out of the way for some reason. Then she tells me the real bombshell. Everyone believes there was no suicide note but there was. Charlie told her to destroy it but she didn't."

"Why would the Governor want it destroyed?"he inquired.

"Apparently the note says her husband killed himself because he found out about her and the governor. But she says she thinks that he was forced to type the note and sign it against his will. If anyone finds the note it could mean big trouble for Charlie V and of course that would end their relationship."

"Where is it? The note."

"She wouldn't tell me. She said that she was thinking about destroying it now but wasn't sure. She's afraid. She thinks that someone could be putting pressure on Charlie and she thinks he knows more than he's telling her."

"Hmmm. So she said there was a note and she may still have it?"

"Yeah. I think she feels that it gives her some security. She says that she loves Charlie and she says that he loves her back but I don't think she trusts him totally."

Lifting the bottle to his lips, he took a long slow sip and placed it back on the table. After a few minutes he asked Melissa if she was worried about Rita's safety. "Do you think she is in any danger? I mean based on the way she acted, do you think she is afraid that the people who allegedly killed her husband may come after her too?"

"Well she won't go to the police because it would mean trouble for Charlie. She can't trust anyone else and she says that I'm the only one she can confide in. It was like she wanted me to know in case anything happened to her. You know what I mean?"

"Does she know about me? Does she know who your boyfriend is?"

"She only knows that I have a regular guy. She doesn't know your name or what you do."

"Let's keep it that way."

Dick began sorting out this latest information and realized that this was getting to be more than a random murder case. It was, in fact, a potential major scandal that would bring down a Governor and possibly several prominent business leaders in the state. Obstruction of justice. Conspiracy to commit murder. Fraud. It was all there. He just had to keep connecting the dots. He needed that suicide note if it even existed.

27

"Tonya. If anyone calls, take a message and tell them I'm in a private meeting and I'll call back soon." Charlie instructed his assistant while walking passed her desk into his office and closed the door. After removing his suit coat and carefully hanging it on the back of his chair, he sat behind the big golden oak desk. A blank yellow legal pad lay off to one side and a stack of manila folders sat in a tray awaiting his review. But Charlie was in no mood to conduct official state business today. He had other matters on his mind. Loosening his tie, he swiveled the large black leather chair so that he was facing the window looking out at the gathering gray clouds. Using his cell phone instead of the office phone on the desk, he pressed the speed dial for the familiar number.

"I was expecting you." Bob the Banker recognized the call immediately while driving to his office. "Where do we stand with Rita? Did you tell her that it's over?"

Hesitating, Charlie knew that Bob was going to be upset that he didn't do as they had agreed but he really felt that he could control her. "No. But don't worry, everything is cool. She won't do anything to hurt me, or our relationship. Hell. I think she's glad that Walt is out of the way." He was sure of this last statement.

"You know something Charlie. I believe you. And I hope for your sake that she is worth it. But just to eliminate any doubts we are having her followed for a few days and we're keeping an eye on who she talks to."

"Who's following her? I don't like it." Sounding indignant and objecting to the tactic.

"Calm down Governor. We need to make sure there is no possibility that she can expose the Big Beaver Project. And."He paused for emphasis. "We are looking out for your interest as well."

Charlie took a minute to digest the possibility that this whole thing would come crashing down and he would be caught up in the debris. Even though he cared for Rita and he valued his friendship with Bob, the one thing he cared about most was keeping the power and growing in the Party. He had been approached by an advisor to the President about a possible Cabinet post in the next term. There was going to be some turnover, which is customary when a sitting President is re-elected and the current President was a lock with an eighty percent approval rating. The one he wanted was Transportation Secretary. An awful lot of funding came through that department and he liked the idea of wielding that kind of influence. Nothing. Not even Rita would stand in his way. "Alright. But keep me posted if anything turns up. I want to be able to handle things on my end."

"We will Governor. We will."Bob reassured him. "Paul has arranged it and we talk every day."He was about to end the call and then remembered the other reason for the call. "By the way, there is going to be a ground breaking for the project in Troy next week. We want you there. Great photo op."

Charlie thought about the risk involved with the ceremony. Did he want to be associated with this project in the unlikely event that somebody would find out about Greening and the way he influenced things. But, on the other hand, he loved to be associated with any project that brought jobs and economic growth to his state. Oakland County, where the Big Beaver project would be built, was his long time base of support – financially and politically. It was important to be perceived as a source of growth and prosperity in this part of Michigan. "What angle are we presenting?"

Bob had already figured out how to include the Governor. "You'll say that this is the kind of project that gets built because people believe in this area and we need to be more diversified in the state economy. Here's the good news."He was saving this for the big surprise. "We have signed a lease agreement with Consoft Systems for thirty thousand square feet of office space. They have promised fifty new high tech jobs. Their CEO, John Miller, will make the announcement the day before the ground breaking. He's going to say that he likes the potential for doing business with the recovering global auto markets from this location and he going to thank you personally for your support of this project."

Charlie could hardly contain his enthusiasm. "Are you kidding me? That is great news. I think Miller is an old fishing buddy of the President. It could be a good kiss up opportunity." Then thinking for a moment he had to ask. "Uh. Exactly how did I support this project? "

"Tax credits. Don't you remember? You signed that bill last year."

"Oh yeah. We had to push that thing through the house and that guy from Ann Arbor, what's his name from the 29th District, made a big deal about selling out to big business. What a jerk. Garza is his name I think." He remembered how they had to cut some back room deals in order to get the bill passed. In the end they promised some state money to the Ann Arbor district for educational research projects that would never happen.

"Next Thursday. At ten AM in Troy. Have your staff make sure you are there by nine forty- five. We'll keep it short and sweet. Throw a few shovels of dirt and you get to say a few words thanking Consoft for believing in Michigan and its people." Bob was used to orchestrating these events for the Governor. It was all about the power machine and he was the one at the controls, pushing the buttons and creating the grand illusion that made the constituents believe that the system worked for them. That they were the ones benefiting from all the new development and investment. In fact a few of them might actually be able to pick crumbs from the pie in the way of maintenance contracts and a few jobs in retail. But the real big pieces were divided among a few, already fat and happy men, like Bob the Banker whose appetite seemed to never diminish.

28

Joey Pal or Pal Joey. He went by those names back on the streets of Chicago and in the joint. He had heard of a Sinatra movie where the famous star was called by the latter name and he kinda liked that association. He fancied himself a rather heroic sort of character in spite of all the crimes he had committed and he had profited handsomely from his work with Paul Lapone. Wearing designer clothes, driving luxury cars and traveling around the country made him feel important. Back in Chicago he liked to show off to his old buddies on the South Side but behind his back he was still known as a tough guy and a loser who would eventually get what he deserved. Right now he didn't care about anything except the job at hand.

As the black BMW came bouncing out from the driveway of the house on Blissfield Drive, he recalled the last time he was there – inside the big white frame house – the day he took care of Walt Jacob. It was just another job. He was hired to take care of things and he did his job well. Waiting until the BMW reached the corner stop sign before starting his engine and slowly rolling forward, he eventually picked up speed in order to follow his objective.

Rita Jacob didn't notice the silver Mercedes in her rear view mirror because she was too busy checking her lipstick making sure it was just right. A slight rub with the little finger on her right hand removed a slight smear and she smiled showing her perfectly straight cosmetically whitened teeth. It had only been a few weeks since Walt's death but she was enjoying her freedom more and more each day. She had a full schedule this day starting with a workout at the Health Club and ending with a complete makeover at the Salon Edgar in Bloomfield Hills. In between she was planning on shopping at Somerset for a few hours and lunch at J Alexander's. Perhaps Melissa would have time to join her. This budding friendship was something she looked forward to and she hoped they would be able to have another talk.

For Joey, this was very boring and he hoped that some thing exciting would happen. Like maybe she'd sneak away to meet the Governor for a quick screw. Not that he'd get to watch or anything but just the idea made him laugh. He had never met the famous Charlie V but from seeing him on TV, he didn't much care for the fake smile and salesman-like attitude. He'd just have to wait and see. After watching the BMW pull into the parking lot at the health club on Long Lake Road, he parked in the adjacent lot of a strip center featuring a dry cleaner, a video rental store and the necessary Starbucks. He was barely fifty yards from where she parked and had a clear view as Rita grabbed a large canvas bag from the back seat and headed toward the entrance. Then something strange happened. A dark haired man, wearing a dark sport jacket and tan slacks, suddenly walked up to her and began speaking. It appeared to him that they were acquainted but he couldn't hear the conversation, all he could do was watch. Based on her body language it appeared that she was eager to enter the health club and end the conversation. He decided to watch and wait.

29

"Excuse me. Mrs. Jacob? Rita?"Dick emerged from the space between the covered entryway of the health club. "Do you remember me? Hagan is my name. We met a few days back. I was with detective Carson from Troy Police."

Startled, Rita took a step back before recognizing the gentleman from the visit to her home. "Oh yes. Hello detective Hagan."

"You can call me Dick. I'm actually not a detective. At least not any more. I'm sort of a consultant to Troy Police."He realized that his explanation sounded kind of dumb. "Do you mind if I ask you another question?"

"I'm in a hurry. I have an appointment with my trainer. Could we do this later?"

"Maybe we could meet after you are finished. I don't mind waiting."

"Alright Mister Hagan. Here is my cell phone number."Handing him a card from her purse. "Call me and we can set something up. I'm very busy today though."It finally dawned on her that he must have followed her or somehow got her schedule from inside the club. "How did you know I'd be here? Are you following me or something? "

"No. I belong to this club also. I saw you the other day when you were with your trainer."He lied. "I was just leaving when I saw you drive up and park over there."

"Oh. Well then I have to get going. Call me and I'll be happy to answer your questions."She nervously reached for the door handle but Dick had already gotten his hand there first, opening the metal frame glass door in a gentlemanly gesture. Slightly bowing his head as she entered.

"Thank you."She said as she hurriedly entered the building, a slight smile on her face. After a few steps she turned around and smiled and he was still there, watching her and returning her smile without speaking. It was the first time she really noticed how handsome he was and she quickly turned away thinking that she would actually look forward to his call.

Entering the club, she signed in at the front desk and took one more glance back at the entrance before proceeding to the locker room. She would have to tell Melissa about this for sure.

Dick returned to the Ford and sat taking notes for a minute. Rita's business card lay on the seat next to his cell phone and a magazine. Thinking that he still had the touch with suspects and witnesses. His buddies on the force called it The Old Hagan Bullshit. He didn't know what it was but he sure did have a way with females when interviewing them. Maybe they were distracted by his handsomeness and polite manner, which he found to be a useful in all situations especially in his line of work. People were just more cooperative if you treated them with kindness and courtesy. It always surprised him that they didn't teach that at the Police academy.

Glancing at his watch he saw that he had enough time to grab a quick cup of coffee before his next meeting. Carson had called and asked to meet him at his office. As he exited the parking lot out onto the side street, he glanced to his left and noticed the man sitting in the silver Mercedes. A familiar feeling emerged in his gut sensing that he had seen this car and the driver before. Continuing on his way to the coffee, Dick tried to remember where he might have seen the man in the Mercedes but couldn't quite recall.

30

"Hey man. Something strange just happened. I was sitting in my car watching Misses Jacob go into her Health Club and this guy comes up and starts talking to her. They talk for a few minutes and then she goes in and he starts to drive away. When he's leavin the parking lot, he stops and I get a good look at him and guess what? It's the same guy I almost ran into when I was leavin the trainer chic's place. I'm telling you this guy has cop written all over him."Joey had driven away and immediately called Paul in Chicago.

"You said that you almost ran into him? Where was that again?"Do you think he recognized you? "A little nervous about this latest development.

"Yeah a few days ago. I followed the trainer back to her condo in Royal Oak and this guy was drivin' in as I was drivin' out. I almost hit him. Same car. Black Ford Escape. Guy has wavy hair and a square jaw. Looks like he came right out of one of those cop TV shows. The only thing I can't figure is how he's connected to the trainer and the Jacob lady? I followed him back to his condo and it's the same complex where I offed the kid."

Paul tried to think this through for a moment and came up with an answer. "Let me ask you something. Did you ever track down this Hagan guy? I have a hunch you may have stumbled on to him. I think you should watch his place and see if you notice anything. I don't have to tell you that you can't let yourself be seen cuz we may have to take this guy out. You know what I mean?"

"Yeah. Yeah. I think I can stake out his place from a wooded area behind his house. It faces the garage and it should be easy to see when he drives in."

Paul didn't like this latest development and he sure didn't like the fact that Joey may have been ID'd by a cop who had been snooping around. He couldn't figure out how this guy was connected to everyone. Was it just a coincidence? Joey shoots the landscape kid in his front yard. He knows both the trainer and Rita Jacob. Who is he working for anyway? He wanted to get some answers before he reported back to the boss. "Be careful and report in as soon as you confirm."

"Yeah. Okay. ."Joey placed the cell phone back in his jacket pocket and decided to head back over to the condos where he shot Tom Hodges. It didn't bother him at all, returning to the scene of the crime. He parked the Mercedes in a crowded office building parking lot and walked a few hundred yards back to the wooded area that faced the backside of Dick Hagan's condo. A weathered green and gold sign announced that the property was FOR SALE and gave a phone number to call. Noticing the name Baxter Realty and he decided that he would say he was interested in buying the land if anyone challenged him. A well-worn path led into the brush and then the wooded area and eventually to the tree line facing Hagan's garage. He chose a spot between two large maple trees with some overgrown ferns as his vantage point where he was certain he could not be seen from the buildings some sixty to seventy yards away. Deciding to make his way back to the car and return in the evening he hoped to catch the cop as he drove in.

When he returned at six PM he didn't have to wait long. The black Escape slowly rounded the corner of the entry driveway and proceeded to the second to last garage door making a wide arc in order to enter straight into the space. He got a good look at the driver and there was no doubt that it was the same guy he had seen on the previous two occasions. He observed for a few moments, ducking down below the bushes as Hagan pressed the auto garage door opener and pulled right in closing the door behind him. Joey thought for a moment that this would be the perfect spot for an ambush if he needed to eliminate this guy. Two or three quick shots from the Glock into the driver side window and he would sneak back into the wooded area. No Problem.

"What do you got?" said Paul as he answered his phone, recognizing the caller ID from Joey.

"He's our guy alright. Same one that I saw both times. Must be some kind of coincidence that he lived here when I did that lawn kid. But yeah, he's the same guy."

"Well I just confirmed with Bob the Banker that he does not work for anybody. He's not a member of any of the local departments. Must be some kind of freelancer or just pissed off that the kid was killed in his yard there. What I don't get is him and the trainer chic."

"Maybe she's his girlfriend." Joey took a stab in the dark and didn't realize he made the correct guess.

"You know. You may be right. Let's keep an eye on them both. See if he shows up at her place again."

After finishing talking to Paul, he started the engine of the Mercedes and headed back to the apartment to plan his next moves. He liked the excitement of this job and he was hoping that he would get a chance to confront this ex-cop or whatever the hell he was. There was something about this guy that made him feel uneasy. If it was indeed just a coincidence that Hagan lived in the condos where he shot the Hodges kid, then he didn't like him getting involved. He should just stay retired and keep his nose out of this. It was bad luck for him that Hagan lived there and it was going to be bad luck for the ex-cop if he got in the way. Joey had no reservations about what he might have to do.

Michael Ripinski

31

After meeting with Carson on Monday, they decided that it was time to contact Charlie V directly. In all his years in Detroit, Dick had developed a skill at interviewing suspects that usually made people cooperate. He was eager to take on the Governor if for no other reason than to see if he could rattle him. Charlie was known as a smooth communicator and expert politician. In Dick's eyes that meant he was very good at embellishment and deception. He didn't much care for most politicians and it didn't matter if it was a city councilman, mayor, senator or Governor. If they were elected, they owed something to someone. And then there were the appointed officials who owed their jobs to the politicians whom they helped get elected. To Dick, the whole system was flawed. He was sure that the founding fathers in this country didn't envision the current two party set up with all the big money controlling who had the power while giving the illusion that the people really had representation in government. It was a cynical point of view and he didn't see much hope for change. Every attempt at election reform seemed to be a hollow gesture because it was like asking a thief to rewrite the laws on stealing.

Carson thought it would be best to contact Charlie in an unofficial capacity, which meant that Dick would be the one to make the attempt. Through some record checks and investigating they determined that Walt Jacob was very close to the governor and they already knew about Rita. He wanted to see how the Governor would react.

As he drove into the garage at his condo, Dick had no idea he was being observed from the trees just beyond the paved driveway at the rear of the complex. All he had on his mind was the phone call he was about to make and how he would persuade Charlie V to meet with him. His background and experience in Detroit was beneficial to accessing any phone numbers he needed to reach his desired person and it usually only took a few calls to someone he knew at the State Police crime lab or even the FBI's Detroit office. He still had lots of contacts.

Inside his home, Dick opened a bottle of spring water and started making his inquiries. After obtaining the correct number, he made the call eventually reaching Tonya at the Governor's office. "It's a great day in Michigan, Governor Vandenberg's office."The greeting was Charlie's idea.

"Hello. My name is Hagan and I am a private citizen. I was hoping to speak with Governor Vandenberg."

"I'm sorry Mister Hagan, the governor is in a meeting at the moment and I would be happy to give him a message."She usually lied about the meeting but in this case it was true. Charlie was meeting with the head of The State Health Department and a few key aids regarding a health care reform package currently stalled in the House. It was another one of his campaign promises that he wanted to push forward

"I understand. Perhaps you could give him a message and he could return my call. Tell the governor I would like to speak to him about Walt Jacob. I have some information that he might find very interesting."So he left his phone number and asked that she give the Governor the message as soon as he finished his meeting. Dick expected to hear back from one of the governor's staff who would then ask more questions in order to see if this was something worthy of his time. He knew that Charlie would have to take notice of the message – assuming that he actually received it. His hunch paid off about an hour later when he received a response.

"Hello. Hagan here."Answering on the second ring.

"Mister Hagan, this is Karen Bastow with Governor Vandenberg's office. He asked me to return your call. How can our office help you?"Karen was one of those who knew about Charlie and Rita and realized that follow up was required on this message if only to determine whom this guy was and whether he really had information about Walt Jacob. Charlie trusted her more than his chief of staff or his communication director. Karen and Tonya were a team in a very special game created just for the purpose of protecting the public image of Charlie V, Governor of The Great State of Michigan. They seldom failed to win, closely guarding information about his personal life and often placing misinformation into the media in order to direct curious reporters in a different direction. Their most successful effort involved a gossip columnist from one of the Detroit papers who thought she saw Charlie and Rita in the back seat of his limo in a rather close encounter. They were able to convince the reporter that the governor had loaned his limo to Rita and Walt and that is whom she saw in the car. Charlie convinced Walt to cover for him making him think that he was with a woman he met at a fundraiser. Poor Walt had no idea he was covering for his own wife.

Dick decided to play it cautious. "Thank you for calling back Miss Bastow, but I really need to speak to the Governor. Privately. It is a matter that I think he'll want to discuss with me. It is important."

"Well I can assure you that the governor can decide what is important. He asked me to get more information from you first. I'm sure you can understand that he is a very busy man and can't possibly speak to every citizen who calls. Of course he'd like to, but it is just not possible."She was used to the approach, having screened Charlie's calls since he was a State Senator.

Dick knew what she was doing and had expected the delay. "Of course. I understand. I suppose the governor has no time to discuss the way the Birmingham Police Department handled the potential crime scene at the Jacob's house on the day he died? I'll just have to speak to Mrs. Jacob again. She seemed so eager to cooperate."

Karen was rattled for a moment. "I don't know who you are Mister Hagan, but I can assure you the Governor has no information on the Birmingham Police investigation of Walter Jacob's most untimely and tragic death."

"Maybe you should ask him yourself Miss Bastow. He can still call me if he changes his mind."Not waiting for a reply he ended the call knowing he had hit a nerve. Now he would wait again.

Michael Ripinski

32

Joey entered the health club at five PM on Tuesday. He hoped to catch Melissa as she was finished for the day or just hanging around. A short, stocky young man with a crew cut wearing a blue Tone House sweat suit approached him. "Welcome to Tone House. I'm Derek. What can we do for you today?"

"I'm interested in having a personal trainer. I like to work out but I think I need somebody to push me. Know what I mean?"

Derek noticed that his guest seemed to be in pretty good shape already. Not like most of the other clients that walked in the door who were overweight and flabby. This guy looked like he was serious about his body. "Well we have four trainers on staff right now and a few who freelance here. I am the assistant manager and I also do some training. Are there any special goals that you have?"

Joey was looking around and didn't make much eye contact. He was looking for something. Names. "Uh. Uh. No. Nothing specific. Just. You know. Tighten up."

Realizing he didn't ask his name, Derek decided to go into all out sales mode. "I'm sorry I didn't get you name."

"Joe. I just moved here from Chicago"

"Well Joe. I'd like to show you around. We have a great facility and I'm sure we can set you up with a fitness coach who'll help you meet your goals. We have a variety of memberships that we can tailor to your needs and right now we a have a special introductory offer of…."

Interrupting the young man, Joey spotted what he was looking for. "Let me ask you something. Do your trainers keep a set schedule?"Realizing he was getting a funny look from Derek he continued. "I mean are they able to work at different times or do I have to fit myself into their schedule? I work odd hours and I may need to change times often."

"Well the club is open five AM to midnight and I'm sure we can meet your needs Joe."Pointing to a table near the front desk. "If you'll join me over here. I'd like to get some information before I give you the tour."

As they moved toward the sitting area, Joey noticed the sign behind the front desk with the heading Trainers. Below were the list of names and a box next to each name with a green or red marker showing if they were IN or OUT. The third name from the top was Melissa and the green marker showed that she was IN. As they were about to sit at the table an attractive woman wearing the same style sweat suit at Derek came through a side door and moved around to the front desk. He immediately recognized her as the woman he saw with Rita Jacob and he watched as she replaced the green marker with a red one.

Having collected a folder with brochures and a clipboard with a guest card attached, Derek proceeded to take a seat at the small round table. "Would you like to join me here Joe. I just need to get some info before we take the tour."

Melissa walked toward them and said. "See you tomorrow. I'm here all day. Till six."Then she waved as she confidently headed out the door and into the parking lot.

"See ya."Replied Derek

Turning to Derek who was still seated at the table Joey looked at his watch and said. "Ya know. I just remembered I have to be someplace. I'll come back tomorrow and we can do this. Okay?"Before Derek could reply Joey was headed out the door as well.

"Yeah I guess. Tomorrow is fine."Disappointed as he watched his client walk away, not making the connection that Joey was following Melissa.

Before he could get to the Mercedes, she was already heading out the driveway on to the main street so he jogged to his car and exited the lot just in time to see her turn at the stoplight.

33

Carson had arrived at his office after dropping his son at soccer practice and was planning on going over a few details before contacting Bob the Banker. Dick had informed him of his plans to call to the governor's office but Sean still did not know the extent of the relationship between Melissa and Rita Jacob. Remembering that Hagan sometimes worked outside the box while investigating murders in Detroit, he didn't want to know right now where he was getting his information. What was important to him was that they were fairly certain of the existence of a suicide note and for some reason Rita was hiding it. He was sorting through his messy desk looking for a legal pad when Banarsek poked his head into the cramped office. "Sean. I need to see you and Mary Beth right away. Where is she?"

"She just went to the john. Why what's up?"

"We got a new one. Just came in. Meet me in my office as soon as she gets back."

Two minutes later Mary Beth returned to the office and before she could sit down he informed her of the urgent meeting. With legal pads in hand they marched quickly to the captain's corner office and noticed the stranger seated in front of Banarsek's desk.

"Sean, Mary Beth. This is Detective Mike Paulous from Sterling Heights. They have a case that they think involves us as well."Waving for them to sit in the two vacant chairs facing the side of the captain's desk. After handshakes all around Banarsek continued. "They found the body of a woman in a vacant lot over on Mound Road. Looks like she may have been killed here in Troy. Mike, go ahead and fill them in."

"Well here's what we got so far. Victim is Katie Mathews. White female. Twenty-nine years old. Worked at Arnold's Market here in Troy. She was produce manager or something. Her car is still parked at the store in a back lot. We found signs of a struggle in the car. Some blood. An anonymous call came in saying she was having an affair with the owner, Arnold Dubanna. Looks like crime scene is here in Troy so you guys may have to take over."

After a discussion about coordination of resources and sharing information Detective Paulous left and promised to meet with them at the crime scene within fifteen minutes. Troy uniformed personnel had taken over and the forensic team had already been called.

Banarsek closed the door and looked at the two detectives. "You know that Arnold Dubanna is a prominent citizen here, Chamber of Commerce and all that stuff. I want you guys on this pronto. I'm taking you off your other cases for now. You haven't gotten anywhere with the Hodges case anyway have you?"

Mary Beth turned to Carson and waited for him to speak up. She had been kept in the loop on the leads from Dick and the interview with Rita Jacob but they were playing it cautious because of the possible Charlie V connection. The last thing they wanted to do was blow the thing open before they had all the facts. Careers went down in flames for mistakes made in these kinds of cases.

Sean spoke for both of them. "Not really. No witnesses and few leads. We were checking on some of the Hodges kid's customers but nothing panned out just yet."He had already decided to let Dick work on the investigation on his own. Sometimes the best way to solve a case was using slightly unorthodox tactics. Sean believed it was simply a matter of leveling the playing field and he wanted to let Dick do the digging so he could step in when the time was right. Besides this new case could become a front-page story and he knew that they were the best detectives to handle it.

"Okay then. Keep me posted. If any media get wind of this one, refer them to me. It's best that we speak with one voice. I'll keep the chief informed. He will want to know what's going on. He knows Dubanna personally. It could get delicate."

They left the building and entered the black Crown Vic in the parking lot. Sean reached Hagan on his cell as Mary Beth drove them toward the crime scene at Arnold's Market. "Hey me. Listen we just got pulled to another big case here in Troy. We need you to stay on the Hodges case. Let's keep talking by phone but I may be tied up for a while."

Dick was caught off guard but understood the way things worked. It was the same way in Detroit. Sometimes the high profile cases took up all the resources and other ones fell into the unsolved file a little too quickly. But he knew that they were onto something with the Jacob and Hodges murders. "Yeah. Okay. I'm working on something right now. I'll let you know if it pans out. Talked to somebody in the Governor's office."

"What did they say?"

"Oh they were trying to screen me out at first but I think I have his attention."

As they approached the market they observed the police cruisers of both Troy and Sterling Heights parked at the entrance to the back parking area. Two or three uniformed officers were milling about and one of them waved to the detective vehicle as it approached. "Okay. I guess maybe I don't want to know what you're doing there but Dick, be careful."

"Yeah. Don't worry. I'll handle it the right way. Our friend the governor will be eager to cooperate if he acts the way I think he will. Good luck on your other case Sean. I'll call you soon."

Carson folded his phone back into his pocket and looked at Mary Beth as she parked the vehicle. "Let's go to work partner. I'll fill you in on what Hagan told me later."

It was a sunny morning and both detectives donned sunglasses as they emerged from the car and approached the scene. They immediately recognized Detective Paulous and he waved them over to where he was standing next to a white Chevy Malibu.

"All yours Sean."Taking a step back after handing him a preliminary report.

Michael Ripinski

34

"Hagan here." Answering the phone in his customary cop way. Short and direct. He was waiting for this call and when he observed the 517 area code he was eager to pick up.

"Mister Hagan." The female voice said. "Please hold for Governor Vandenberg."

After a few seconds the distinctive voice came on the phone. Dick had heard the Governor many times in TV sound bites and campaign ads and was quite certain that he was speaking to Charlie V. "Mister Hagan. This is Governor Vandenberg. A member of my staff has informed me that you have something important to discuss with me in regards to my late friend Walt Jacob. Is that correct?"

"Yes sir. Thank you for returning my call. I would like to talk to you about Mr. Jacob." He waited for another few seconds and then added. "And also Mrs. Jacob."

Charlie refused to be intimidated but was eager to play along for the moment, wanting to discover just whom this guy was and whom he was working for if anybody. His first thought was somebody from the opposition party trying to shake him up and uncover any hint of scandal that could damage his approval rating in the polls. In the back of his mind he was concerned that somehow this man had found out details about he and Rita. "You'll pardon me for asking Mister Hagan, but who did you say that you represented. Are you a lawyer or a police officer?"

Finding the question to be precisely what he expected, Dick was prepared. "Well sir. I sort of work with a local police department but to be quite honest I am a private citizen right now and I have an interest in a related case that just seems coincidental. I am retired from the Detroit Police Homicide Department."

Charlie found this last bit of information intriguing. "Detroit Huh? Homicide. You must have had some real adventures there. I know the chief in Detroit very well. Eddie Harris. Long time friend of mine. And of course Mayor Gilliam and I go way back."

"Yes. I am quite aware of your support in the city. You have helped them get back on track and I know the police department appreciates it."Obviously playing up to Charlie's ego and creating a softer tone. "What I was wondering sir is if I could just have a minute of your time in person? I just hate to discuss this on the phone and I would be sure to keep it brief, as I know you are a very busy man. I would be happy to drive to Lansing if necessary. Do you think it can be arranged?"

"I think so Mister Hagan. As a matter of fact I will be in your area in a few days for a ceremony regarding a new development going up on Big Beaver Road. Maybe we could spend a few minutes that day. I assume that you are aware of my long time friendship with the Jacobs and how deeply saddened I am about Walt. I am also very concerned for Mrs. Jacob. She is taking this very hard. I hope that you do not wish to create any more anguish for her."He was keeping his cool but intentionally fishing for anything he could get from this caller. *Just how much does this guy know about Rita and me?*

"I was hoping we could meet sooner actually. I could be in Lansing tomorrow if you could spare a few minutes. I will try to be as sensitive as possible but I really think that you and I need to talk sir. Privately if possible. It's just something I think you should be aware of for your own protection. I do not wish anyone any harm and I am not looking for anything for myself."He relayed the sense of urgency and created a context for Charlie to respond without thinking there was another agenda.

Listening to this request, Charlie became concerned about where this was headed. What did this guy know and what did he want. Against his better judgment, he agreed to meet. "We'll see. I will have one of my people call you back with a time and place. I'll try to fit you in before lunch tomorrow. I look forward to meeting you and I hope I can help you with your problem."

Dick smiled to himself knowing that he had succeeded in his plan to get in front of the governor. "I look forward to it sir. Thank you."

As soon as he hung up the phone Charlie pressed the intercom button for Tonya. "Get me Police Chief Harris in Detroit on the phone please."He needed to find out about this Hagan fellow right away. What kind of cop was he? Any skeletons? Was he ever suspected of being on the take? That would explain his desire to meet with him. A proposition. Buy his silence. All sorts of thought ran through his mind but after speaking with Chief Harris, he was even more puzzled. "Good cop. Honest and dedicated. Decorated for bravery. Left due to burnout according to other cops. A real loss for the department."These were the comments from the Chief. *So what does he want then*? Charlie V would find out soon enough. But first he would call Bob the Banker.

He left a message on Bob's phone, decided to call Rita next and was surprised to hear that she was familiar with the man with whom he just spoke. "Are you kidding me? This is one of the guys that came to your house. I thought you said they were both cops?"

Rita was concerned that Charlie had talked to this gentleman thinking that he was a cop and that they would find out about her and Charlie. She didn't think about Walt right away but then it started to add up. There was something rotten here and she was beginning to panic. "I thought he was a cop. Maybe he is. What if he's with the FBI or something? Oh Charlie what if they find out about us and then they'll start asking about Walt and all."

"Hold on there baby. We don't know anything yet. If he were FBI he would have said so. I don't think he is working for anybody but himself right now. Lets just stay cool and we'll see what he knows. I can handle this."Reassuring her that he could keep it under control. The old Charlie V confidence. "I don't get the feeling he wants to make anything public. If he did he would have already gone to the media. He wants something else but I'm not sure."

Rita was not so confident. She remembered that they kept asking about the note and about Walt's business dealings. What if this Hagan guy found something and the landscape kid knew saw something he shouldn't have? She was nervous and upset but she was not stupid. There was something about Walt's recent business deals that got him killed and she had an idea that Bob the Banker knew something too. "Charlie. I want to know if you were involved with anything Walt was working on before he died? There is some connection with another murder in Troy that may involve the same guys that got to Walt. That's why this Hagan guy is snooping around. He was with a detective from Troy when he was here and they think our landscape guy saw or heard something when he was hear that same day. It makes sense."

Listening to her he already knew the answers but didn't want to let on. She could become a loose cannon if these cops got to her and shook her up. He need to think it through and he needed to keep her away from this ex-cop. "Listen up. I want you to go away for awhile."

"What?"

"Trust me. I think it would be a good idea if you went on a trip or something. People would understand. You need time to get away from the site of the tragic loss of your husband. I can arrange a trip to Mexico or The Bahamas. What do you think? Just till things settle down around here."

Rita thought this was not a good idea but she didn't want to tell Charlie right now that she disagreed with him. Besides maybe she would be able to sort things out from a distance and make some plans. "I'll think about it. If I go somewhere, will you promise to stay in touch? Call me every day?"

"Of course baby. I really think this would be good for you. Hell I wish I could come too." At this time he really did wish he could get away for a vacation. He was a little envious.

She realized that he did not answer her question about Walt's business. Instead of pursuing the matter she decided to wait and consider her options. After all she still had the note. She decided to do as he asked. "Okay. I remember one time we went to Cozumel on a vacation and I really liked the laid back atmosphere on the island. I think we stayed at a place called the Cozumel Palace. Can you get something arranged for me there?"

Charlie knew he could count on Bob to arrange something and he would get her on the quickest flight. "I'll have Karen call you with the details. We can trust her and she will understand your need to get away for a while. Be ready to go tomorrow or the next day. I'll call you as soon as you get there."

"Alright. But only for a few days okay. I'll miss you too much."

He knew it would be longer but he wanted her to feel at ease with his plan. "Yeah Okay. I promise to get you back here as soon as possible."

Michael Ripinski

35

When Bob the Banker found out that Charlie was planning to talk to Dick alone and that this was the same guy that approached him at Walt's funeral, he became furious. No way was he going to allow the meeting to take place but Charlie stood firm and told his old friend that he was running the show as far as his relationship with Rita and any business that this ex-cop wanted to discuss. He knew how to handle things if necessary. The one thing they did agree on was sending Rita away for a while. She was less of a risk while this Hagan guy was asking questions. The project on Big Beaver was under way and all the obstacles were taken care of. He had talked to Paul and everything was still on track. The report from Greening was complete and there was no problem with DEQ on the site clearance. The first shovel of dirt was to be turned in a week and then he could start counting the money. It would take a few years to complete but he knew that this would be the biggest achievement of his business life. He was even sorry that he agreed to name the project after Edna Biddle Norris. He thought Banker Center sounded better. But he would get over it. His only regret remained the way they handled Walt Jacob.

Sitting in the governor's office, Bob and Charlie were discussing the speech for the groundbreaking ceremony when the call came through. "Sir. I have Mister Lapone on the line. He said it's urgent." Tonya announced through the intercom.

"I'll take it." Pressing the blinking green button and speaker at the same time he answered. "Paul what is it? I have Bob with me here."

"I am sorry to bother both of you but I just got off the phone with my people out in Las Vegas and we have a little problem. Our friend

Bill Greening is dead."

"What? How? What the hell happened?"Bob shouted into the speaker as Charlie sat there with his mouth open.

"It seems our friend Bill got mixed up with one of the local working girls and when she found out he was broke, her pimp beat him up pretty good. Funny thing was, the guy died of a heart attack not from the beating."Paul continued with the story. "One of my boys out there got the word from the street that this hooker was talking about him to her girlfriends before they found his body. Vegas police are checking him out. They want to know how he got all the money he lost in the casino. We might have a problem if they trace it back to Michigan."

"Oh shit."said Charlie. "That's all I need. We got to figure a way to smooth this out."Looking directly at Bob. "What do we do?"

"How much did he lose?"Bob asked.

"Well he was into us for over fifteen large and I was covering him with a local guy for another twenty."

Bob was thinking of a way to create a bank account for Greening that would look like he had some money stashed away and a line of credit. It would take some doing but as long as Vegas police didn't dig too deeply he might be able to pull it off. "I have an idea."He said. "We need to find out which bank he did business with and I can make a few calls. We'll open a back dated line of credit with my bank and make it look like he was borrowing the money legit."

Paul said. "Are you sure they won't figure it out?"

Charlie spoke up as well. "Can you really do that without getting caught?"

"Guys. Guys. I own the bank. Let me worry about it. If they see the possibility that he had access to the money, I doubt they will fly out here to dig any deeper. The important thing here for us is."turning to Charlie "We need to check his records at DEQ to make sure he didn't leave a diary or something about our little meeting. You need to handle that Charlie."

"Okay. Okay. Damn it all. I don't like getting into this any deeper than I already am."

Listening in, Paul could sense some reservation in Charlie's voice.

"You already are Governor. So just deal with it. I am sure someone on your staff can find a way to check his computer and office files."

He knew that Paul was right He could call Karen Bastow and she would make a few calls and gain access to Greening's files. They would make up a cover story about campaign information that might be in his possession since he worked on the last election. He didn't really want to bring her into this mess any further but he had no choice and he knew he could count on her loyalty. "Alright. I'll handle it. But make sure we cover that money trail. The poor shmuck can't help us any more and I don't want any accusations floating around."

Bob spoke up again. "Paul. When are you coming here? We need to have a meeting in person with Sam and some of the contractors. I'd also like you to be at the ceremony with Consoft on Thursday. You won't have to say anything. I'll handle the PR and Charlie gets some good face time. It will be important to the project."

He didn't want to come to Michigan any more than he had to and he already had Joey keeping an eye on things. He still needed to discuss the matter of the ex-cop Hagan as well. After talking with the boss earlier in the day he was instructed to keep a closer tab on the situation so maybe a trip was going to be necessary. He had no idea of what was to come. "Yeah. Okay. I'll be there but we need to discuss few other matters. Some can't wait till Thursday."

"I have something else to bring up as well. This ex-cop who approached me at Walt's funeral has contacted Charlie. The guy says he has information about Walt's death and something about Rita as well. He has already spoken with her according to Charlie and this Hagan seems to think there's a connection to another case."Bob added. "The Governor agreed to meet with him. I'll keep tabs on the meeting. You should also know that we are sending her away to Mexico for a while."

Charlie chimed in. "That's my idea. It'll be good for her."

Paul couldn't believe what he was hearing. If this was the same guy that Joey was on to, then they had a bigger problem than they thought. "Are you talking about that ex-cop named Hagan?"

"Yeah."They answered together.

"Do not. I repeat. Do not meet with this guy. He has definitely been asking questions with Rita and we think he has a connection with her personal trainer. She may be his girlfriend. My guy there is checking it out right now. We can't risk a meeting with him."

They were both stunned. Not sure what to do, they would have to come up with an excuse to cancel or postpone the meeting.

Then Charlie had an idea. "Wait a minute. We don't know what this guy already knows. If we cancel he might think we have something to hide."

"You." said Paul.

"What do you mean, you?" Asked Charlie.

"You might have something to hide, not we. He's after you Governor. We are assuming that he concentrates on you. We can't be part of it."

Bob had heard enough. Sensing that Paul and Charlie were about to get into an argument he decided to take charge. "Wait a minute. Charlie's right. We can't cancel the meeting. We have to go through with it or he'll smell something. The guy was a top-notch detective in Detroit. He is good at this stuff. I still don't know what his angle is?"

Waiting for someone to speak, Charlie thought of how to handle this Hagan. And now there was the possibility that Rita had said something to her personal trainer who just might be this guy's girlfriend. He wondered if she even knew. "Okay guys. I meet with this ex-cop and see what he has to say. I won't give him any direct answers and I'll manage to put him off he presses me on anything. Let's just see what he wants. And I'll find out about Rita and her trainer."

Paul was not thrilled about this development but he was not in a position to call the shots. Plus he didn't want to give out too much information bout what Joey was doing. It was looking like he'd have to spend more time in Michigan. "Okay but be careful. Bob. I'm counting on you to make sure this thing doesn't get out of hand."

Now Charlie was getting annoyed. He had had just about enough of this guy from Chicago treating him like he was somebody's fool. He was wary of him from the start but he always depended on Bob to do background checks. It just so happened that Bob relied on his friend Sam who told him that Paul was solid. He made the mistake of trusting Sam's judgment. Bob realized this but Charlie had no idea.

"Hey. I can handle this. I don't need Bob to hold my hand and I sure don't take orders form some Chicago boy who…"

Bob cut him off. "Hold on Governor. I know you'll handle this. Paul, I've known Governor Vandenberg"using his title for emphasis. "For over thirty years and he is one of the smoothest guys in a room that you will ever meet. He can talk the feathers off a duck. I trust him."

Paul was still nervous but decided not to continue any confrontation with Charlie at this time. One day though, he would let him know just who was in charge. "Okay. Please keep me posted as soon as you're done. Thanks."The phone call ended.

Now that it was just the two of them again, Charlie let Bob know how he felt. "Look. I never liked this guy from the start. You brought him into your little deal and I trusted your judgment. I did what you asked of me and we got Greening to handle things. Look where that got him. I don't want to know everything about how Walt died, but I can guarantee you that I'm not going to admit anything. Let's just hope Greening doesn't leave a trail."

"He's the least of our worries."Bob responded. "I'm more worried about Rita.'

"I'll handle her."

"You'd better."

Forgetting about the speech, they talked about the meeting with Hagan and how they would bug the office. Bob had experience with a security company he had hired to record conversations with competitors. He knew whom to call.

Michael Ripinski

36

Exhausted from a long day at the Club, Melissa decided to take a long warm bath. After plugging the phone into the charger, sorting through her mail, starting the water in the tub she entered the bedroom and threw herself onto the bed. It wasn't often that she was this beat. Maybe it was the mental fatigue as well. She couldn't stop thinking about her conversations with Rita Jacob and she was worried about how Dick was handling the situation. He told her in advance about approaching Rita as she entered the club and she wasn't happy about it, but he insisted. Now there was this business with the governor. As she lay there thinking, she was not aware of the man sitting in the silver Mercedes in the parking lot staring at the second floor balcony just off her living room. Pulling herself up from the bed, she quickly disrobed and walked to the bathroom slowly slipping into the tub and enjoying the soothing, relaxing warmth of the water.

Joey observed that the balcony was close enough to a mature maple tree so that it would afford him enough of a platform to ascend the side of the building and pull himself up to the wooden deck. Once there, it would be no problem to enter the condo and surprise his subject. He was rather looking forward to the encounter but not tonight. He had other business. Putting the car in gear and slowly rolling away from the building, he gave it just enough gas to drive away quickly while making sure there were no other cars turning in this time. Paul had called and wanted him to spend more time tracking Rita before she headed to Mexico. He was also told to plant a listening device in her house so they could find out if she and Charlie were up to anything. They were beginning to trust The Governor less and less.

As he approached Blissfield Drive, Joey parked on the street a few houses down from the curved driveway. There were other cars parked on the street so he did not stand out and at this time of day no one noticed his presence as he walked toward the house carrying a small duffel bag and hurried up the driveway to the brick porch. He recalled the last time he was here. The day he strangled Walt Jacob. Remembering that there was a sunroom on the West side of the house, he used a small knife to pick the lock and entered the screened in room. Once inside he was able to easily open the other doors necessary to gain access to the entire building. He already knew that Rita was on her way to the mall to pick up a few items for her trip. Charlie had mentioned it to Bob who relayed the information back to Paul. He had about an hour and finished in thirty minutes after planting devices in the kitchen, bedroom and dining room. A small recorder with a receiver and transmitter was placed on a shelf in the garage in order to provide a clear signal back to another receiver in his car where he could pick up any conversation from a quarter mile away.

While shopping at The Somerset Mall, Rita decided to take a break and grab a coffee at the food court area. She sipped her café mocha while thinking about the pending trip. She wasn't in favor of it at first but now she was looking forward to getting away to the laid back tropical island. The cell phone ring awakened her form the daydream. It was Charlie.

"Hi baby."

He was whispering which caught her by surprise. "Hi. Listen. I'm coming in to town tonight and I want to see you before you leave."

She was excited by this news. "I'm so happy to hear that. I need to be with you so bad. Oh Charlie when will you be here?"

"Late. I'm coming in around nine and I'm staying at the Townsend. I want to come to your place."

More of a surprise. "Are you sure that it's a good idea? I mean what if someone sees you coming here."

"No problem. I'm just checking up on the wife of my late friend who is still grieving her loss. I covered it with Karen and she is going to arrange everything. We are going to wait until my regular detail is off for the night around eleven and I'll have one of the assigned state troopers from the Detroit office on guard at the hotel. We'll just tell him to wait for us while we run out for a few minutes. She'll drop me off and pick me up when I call her."

This news couldn't have made her any happier and she was looking forward to being with him. She was hoping they'd have enough time for sex. "I'll be waiting for you in the bedroom."

He hadn't been thinking about that at the moment but now that she mentioned it maybe he could. But after they had a talk. "We have to talk first. That's why I'm coming over. I don't want to use the phone okay."

"Is everything all right?"Now she was worried.

"I think it will be. But we need to make some plans. We'll talk later. I miss you."

"Me too."She answered but he already hung up. She gathered her few bags and quickly headed to the parking garage where she practically ran to the BMW. The drive home was a blur as she was filled with anticipation of the evening. It was only eight PM and she was looking forward to seeing him later.

Joey was sitting in his car when he saw her drive past and head into the curved driveway. He immediately drove to the small shopping center on Maple Road where he parked in front of a busy wine shop and deli; confident he would not be noticed as he sat in the car. He was able to pick up her sounds clearly as she entered the house and he thought he heard her singing as she prepared for her visitor. He had no idea that Charlie would show up later so he headed inside the deli to pick up a snack and a coke. Upon his return he was able to distinguish the shower running and decided to head back to his own apartment. The recorder in the garage would pick up anything else.

Michael Ripinski

37

Karen Bastow had known Charlie V for over fifteen of her forty years and she was perhaps the most loyal person on his staff. Her devotion to the job had already cost her a marriage and she sacrificed any kind of social life. Her time was spent in service to the people of the Great State of Michigan by being the Governor's top aide and a key strategist for his campaigns and the legislative initiatives for which they shared a passion. Tall, five-ten and thin with dark brown hair and pale skin, she was considered attractive but not beautiful. When they were both in the final stages of their respective divorces, she and Charlie had a one-night stand, prompted by sharing a few bottles of red wine. Neither one could remember much and they agreed that it was nothing to pursue and nothing to get excited over. Their working relationship was most important and nothing would get in the way. Considering herself to be a crusader for the cause, she was willing to do whatever was necessary to protect him and the image of the great Charlie V and that included assisting in the cover up of the Rita Jacob affair with the potentially career-damaging news should the story be made public. With Walt's death still fresh in their memory, the press would have a feeding frenzy and she was in charge of keeping the lid on. She actually liked Rita and thought the relationship was good for The Governor because she understood his needs as a man. He seemed to be more focused and driven after seeing her and often mentioned some new insight or strategy after their little trysts.

As requested, she picked him up at the Townsend Hotel at ten forty five PM greeting him as he let her into his suite."Hello Governor."Karen always used his formal title when conducting official business or on a night like this when the line was a little vague. If they were discussing the weather, sports or some non-official subject she often called him Charlie - or Charles if she wanted to tease him. She could sense the tension as soon as she entered.

Charlie pointed to a couch near a fireplace and he sat in an antique armchair facing her.

"Karen, there is something we have to discuss before you take me over to Rita's. I have not shared some things with you regarding a matter that I am involved in with Bob, Sam and a few others. I can't tell you the details but should this situation unravel, I am in big trouble. What I am about to tell you cannot be repeated unless I authorize you to speak. I need your word on this."

She looked at him puzzled and worried. "You know you can trust me." And "Does this have something to do with that Mister Hagan who called?"

"Perhaps." After a short pause he continued. "But more importantly, I don't think Walt Jacob took his own life. Rita doesn't think so either. There is a situation he was working on that became very complicated and he was stubborn and the next thing I knew he was dead. Do you remember the time I asked you to get me somebody in DEQ that we could contact?"

"Yes. Wasn't it William Greening? I just heard that he died of a heart attack or something." she said.

"Yes. That was him. He handled a problem for this group who includes some people from out of state."

She knew right away. "Paul Lapone?"

"Yep. He represents some people that apparently don't like to take no for an answer .I didn't even get a chance to talk to Walt about it. Next thing I know he's dead and it makes my relationship with Rita a little more suspicious. I am sending her away for awhile till things cool off but I want you to know about this in case anything happens to her…" pausing to look around the room even though he knew they were alone. ."Or to me."

Karen was shaken. She could tell that he was worried about this and it was the first time she saw him afraid of anything or anyone. "Oh God. What are you going to do?"

"Once Rita is safely away from here, I am going to confront these guys. This shit has got to be stopped and I am the only one who can stop it."

Now it became another strategy session for Karen. "What if they blackmail you? Can't they do that?"

"I've thought this thing through. It would be a stand off. If they try to bring me down, they go down too." He sat there wringing his hands and then finally added. "You are the only one that knows besides me and in a little while Rita will too. When all this settles down I fully expect to be offered a position in Washington. I want you there with me. Rita too, eventually."

Just sitting with him alone in this room, she realized how fragile their hold on the power had become. Not wanting it to end either, she willingly became his accomplice. "Let me know what you need me to do for you. I am still here and I will be there in DC as well."

"Right now I want you to drive me over to Rita's. I have arranged to exit out a back entrance near the kitchen. Just honk your horn twice and I'll come out."

Doing as instructed, she pulled up in a black Jeep Grand Cherokee and pressed the horn twice in quick short bursts. Charlie came bounding out the door and jumped in the passenger seat closing the door as she drove away. They were only a few minutes from Blissfiled drive and as she drove he outlined another plan. Something he might need her to lie about if asked. She readily agreed. Turning into the curved driveway past the spruce tree, slowing to a stop, she turned to Charlie. "I'll stay right here if you want me to wait."

"No. I'll call you on your cell when I am ready. If I don't call before midnight I want you to call me."

"Got it."She replied.

Before opening the door he turned to her and did something she did not expect. He kissed her on the cheek. "Thanks. This means a lot to me."

She watched in silence as he hopped up the porch steps to Rita's front door, which quickly opened and he was safely inside. Driving away, she worried about his ability to stay in control. She had known Bob the Banker as long as she knew Charlie and never really liked the man. He once made a pass at her and when she rebuked his advances he tried to have her fired. She had also met Paul Lapone and he was just a little too slick. She didn't trust either of them and she felt Charlie shouldn't either.

38

Throwing herself into his arms as soon as he entered the house she kissed him passionately on the mouth but there was no reciprocal gesture on his part. "What's wrong?"

Leading her into the kitchen where he unknowingly would be recorded, Charlie lifted her onto a bar stool adjacent to the coffee bar and looked her in the eye."Remember when I told you we could be in danger because of the situation that Walt was working on?"

"Yes. You said it was a dangerous game."

"Well I need to know something. What have you told that girl at the health club?"

Surprised that he knew about Melissa she put her hand on his shoulder. "I didn't tell her anything. Anything important anyway. She is a friend. We talk about girl stuff. She knew I was having an affair but that's all."

He suspected she was being less than honest and it bothered him. What else might she be lying about? "Did you know that her boyfriend is an ex-cop named Hagan?"

The color drained from her face and she felt her stomach tighten up. Could this be the same guy that approached her at the club and was here at the house with the detective from Troy? What had she done? "How do you know that?' She begged.

"Christ, Rita. What did you tell her?"

Pushing him away, she stood up and walked over to the window by the sink. Staring out into the darkness she confessed. "I told her about us. After Walt died I was upset and I also told her that I wasn't sure he killed himself. She just listened. I had no idea about her boyfriend. She rarely mentioned him. We had lunch a few times and she was someone I could confide in. I was going crazy here. You were not available for a few weeks and I needed to talk to somebody."

Walking over to her, he gently put his hand on her shoulder and put his lips in her hair. He could not get angry with her. At this moment he realized that he really did love her and he had to protect her. "Listen. You need to get in touch with her and tell her that she might be in danger as well. I don't know what will happen after you leave for Mexico but I am about to do something that will risk everything."

She turned around to face him. "Oh Charlie. I am so sorry if I messed this up."

"It's not your fault. You need to know everything."Returning to the chair where she sat just a moment before he continued. "Walt was killed because he knew something that could undermine a very big deal. A deal that was put together by our good friend Bob and some outsiders. Walt was being stubborn and it cost him. And there's more."

She came to his side and put her arms around him. She needed to hold him as much as he needed to be held. "Tell me."

"I am involved. I arranged for a guy in DEQ to shuffle a few papers and make a problem go away. Walt discovered that this problem was serious enough to cancel the project. It would have cost millions to everyone involved. Especially Bob. There is another guy named Lapone from Chicago. He's the one that I believe had Walt murdered. Bob knows everything and he has no remorse. He more or less threatened me over it and this Lapone fellow is bad news. He's the one we have to worry about. And one more thing. The DEQ guy has turned up dead in Vegas. They say he had a heart attack but I'm not so sure. He was out there with money provided by Lapone and now the Vegas cops are wondering how a bureaucrat from Michigan could blow over thirty grand in the Casino. Bob is supposed to fix it like he had the loan before he went out there."He continued telling her about the original meeting they had in his office and how Sam, Bob, and Paul had taken Greening to lunch. He did not know at the time how serious the hazardous waste problem was at the Big Beaver site.

Explaining that he wanted to put a stop to the project without having the thing blow up in his face he asked her for her help. "I need you to give some information to your friend. I'd like to throw this Hagan guy off track if we can."

Relieved that he wasn't angry with her, she happily agreed to cooperate. "Sure. What do you want me to say?"

"Before you leave for Mexico, tell her that you discovered some information about what Walt was working on before he died. You'll tell her that he was talking with a guy from Chicago about an investment there. A big project near the lakefront. We'll divert him from any snooping here in Michigan."Charlie held her close and added. "Tomorrow I am attending a ceremony in Troy that will be on the local news. It is a big investment with a new company coming into town. Consoft. They have deep pockets and I am told they have connections in Washington. Their CEO goes bass fishing with the President. I need to get a few words with him alone. After that I am going to tell Bob and his partners that they need to stop the project or someone in DC gets the information."

Figuring it out on her own she realized that this was the deal that had gotten Walt killed, she was fearful for Charlie. "Are you sure you know what you're doing?"

"Yeah. I'm still the Governor. I can expose this thing and make it look like they were doing this without my knowledge. I don't think we can prove that they killed Walt, but it will screw up this project and the DEQ guy is dead so he can't say anything. Walt was trying to do the right thing. I am not going to let Bob or anyone else run this show any longer. I will need you and Karen to help me pull this off. If they try to say that you and I have been carrying on for the past few years, Karen is ready to say that she and I were seeing each other on any days you and I were together."

There wasn't much else to say. Rita placed her hand around his neck and pulled him closer while reaching his mouth with her lips. Placing her hand around his, she tugged him gently toward the stairs leading to the bedroom. Charlie took a quick peek at his watch and saw that it was eleven thirty. After calling Karen and telling her to pick him up at one AM he followed Rita up the staircase to the master bedroom. He hadn't planned this part but he knew he could not resist.

A small recording device in the garage had captured the entire conversation.

39

The meeting in Lansing was postponed at the Governor's request. Deciding to wait until he had more information on the retired cop, Charlie also wanted to get the Big Beaver ceremony out of the way. It would also be a good thing that Rita was on her way to Mexico.

For Dick, it actually worked out better. He wouldn't have to drive all the way to Lansing and he would catch the Governor in a moment of high visibility. The local paper had announced the ceremony for the Big Beaver project and when the names were listed for the speakers he began to put some pieces together. Bob Banker, Sam Ford, John Miller and of course Charlie V. He wondered if Walt Jacob was originally part of the deal. He made it a point to attend the ceremony.

On her way to Detroit Metro Airport, Rita speed dialed the number for Melissa. When the voice mail came up she waited for the tone and began her message. "Hi Melissa. It's me Rita. I am sorry to have to cancel my next two sessions, but I am on my way to Cozumel, Mexico on a quick get- away trip. I need to sort a few things out. I also need to tell you that I know that your boyfriend is Dick Hagan and he's an ex-cop who has been asking a lot of questions. It's okay. I need to tell you that you may be being followed. Tell your boyfriend that I'll talk to him off the record when I return. One more thing. There is an envelope in my locker at the club. Leave it there and do not open it unless I don't return safely from my trip. Have someone open the locker and tell them that I left you some money that I owe you. Do not try to contact me. I'll contact you in a week or so. Take care."

She hoped that Melissa would understand. Although she was annoyed that she had never mentioned who her boyfriend was exactly, it didn't matter now. Inside the envelope for Melissa, she left the suicide note and a letter explaining her suspicion about Walt's death. It was insurance and she hoped she didn't have to cash it in. There was also a note for Dick telling him that he should dig into the cover up surrounding the Big Beaver deal.

Meanwhile the ceremony at the development site was just finishing. There was the usual assortment of local elected officials and dignitaries as well as a contingent made up of members of the local business press. Charlie had delivered a short but eloquent speech acknowledging the people who had the vision and foresight to invest in Michigan especially Metro Detroit. The crowd loved it and he made it a point to thank John Miller and Consoft for their commitment. Before they left the stage Charlie had a chance to schmooze Miller about his relationship with the President and how Charlie was looking forward to the next term and oh by the way, he hoped that he'd get to spend more time in Washington. For his part, Miller being captivated by the Charlie V charm, agreed to pass along his best wishes to the Big Guy.

Among the group of reporters and members of the local Chamber of Commerce, Dick blended in well. As Charlie mingled, shaking hands and accepting congratulations from well-wishers, he did not notice the man in the black blazer and tan slacks waiting his turn. Bob would have recognized him but he was in a hurry to attend another meeting and quickly rushed off right after the ceremony leaving Sam to answer questions from the media. As the crowd started to thin out, Dick approached the governor while he was talking with a pretty young reporter from the Free Press who was thoroughly enjoying his attention. Karen and a few other members of his staff were standing about fifteen feet away and could not hear the conversation. "Excuse me Governor."

Charlie barely noticed him but he interrupted again. "Excuse me. My name is Hagan. We spoke on the phone."

The startled look on the Governors face was not noticed and he quickly finished with the Free Press girl. Turning to Dick, he replied. "Did you say your name was Hagan? The same one who wants to meet with me? I thought I told you I would set something up in my office." Annoyed by the interruption he continued. "I don't have time right now Mister Hagan. I'm afraid you'll have to speak with my staff."Motioning to Karen to join them.

Dick knew he only had few moments. "Look governor. I know about you and Misses Jacob and I think you should hear me out."

Karen hurried to his side. "Yes sir. Is there something wrong here?"

Holding his hand up toward her he said. "No wait. It's okay. I need to talk to this gentleman for a moment."Then, turning to Dick and placing his arm around his shoulder like they were long lost buddies, they walked a few steps away from the group. "Okay Mister Hagan. If it has to be right now, I only have a few minutes."

"Thank you Governor. I won't keep you long."Looking around to make sure no one could hear them. "I want you to know that I have no political agenda hear. My interest lies with an incident that happened in front of my home but is connected to your friend the late Mister Jacob. I don't yet have all the pieces but you should be aware that if this turns out like I think it will, you could be implicated in a serious crime. I am asking you to cooperate with the Troy police on their investigation or I'll take what I know and make it public."

Charlie wasn't prepared for this confrontation right now but he had thought about how he would handle this ex-cop. "I see. So you want me to assist the police with something I know nothing about and for that you'll not go to the press about an affair I am not having."He chuckled out loud. "Mister Hagan. I am going to be frank with you. I don't know where you got your information, but someone is feeding you a sack of fertilizer. If you know what I mean."

The Governor did not intimidate Dick. "I assure you that it is not cow manure sir. I won't go away. This may be your only chance to control the damage. Unless you are more involved than I think."

Charlie decided to end the conversation as his aids came up to him sensing that he was not happy. "Well, Mister Hagan. Let me think about your request and I'll get back to you. I believe my assistant has your number. I'll call you in a few days."

They shook hands and Charlie was whisked away by his staff to an awaiting limo.

Michael Ripinski

40

Once again Joey entered the house on Blissfield but he had no worries this time knowing that Rita was on her way to Mexico. Retrieving the disc from the machine in the garage, he left the rest of the equipment in case they would need it later. As he listened back at his apartment, he couldn't dial the number fast enough.

Noticing the caller, Paul answered. "Yeah. What have you got?"

"You are not going to believe this. Our friend the Governor is getting ready to throw you and Bob under the bus. Listen."He played the recording into the phone.

Paul was furious but kept his composure. "So the son-of-a-bitch thinks he can play us for fools on this. We have to act fast. I'll take care of Misses Jacob in Mexico. One of Dominic's boys can handle that one. I need you to take out the ex-cop and his girlfriend. Let's hope he hasn't given too much to the other cops. Do it quick. Tonight."

"What about the Governor?"Joey asked.

"When I get through with him he'll wish the hell he was never born."

Having already thought about a plan to deal with the ex-cop and his girlfriend, Joey was prepared to follow his instructions. "I am going to wait inside her condo and when she gets home I'll have her call the boyfriend to come over. When he gets there I'll do both of them."

"Okay. Call me when you're in the clear."Paul hung up and immediately called Bob Banker getting his voice mail. He decided to leave a short message telling him to call back as soon as possible. It was an emergency. It didn't take long.

"What's the emergency?' Bob inquired.

"Your buddy Charlie is out of control. We bugged Rita's place and we have him telling her how he's going to blow the whistle on the project and put the blame on us. He also has an alibi for his little affair. We need to meet with him right away and set him straight. Call him and set it up."

"Are you shitting me? I can't believe Charlie would do that? He doesn't have the balls."Bob was in disbelief. After all these years he thought he knew his friend and could not accept that Charlie could do such a thing. He was smart enough. That wasn't the issue. Bob just felt that Charlie didn't have the courage to risk his entire career.

"We got it recorded. He has it planned with Rita to make themselves come out of this thing without a scratch. Get that son-of-a-bitch òn the phone and tell him we know what he's up to. Tell him to keep his mouth shut or he'll end up like his friend Walt."

Bob was taken back. Things were getting a little crazy and he realized that he was playing a game that was out of his own league. Paul couldn't be serious. They wouldn't murder the Governor would they? There had to be another way. After all, he and Charlie went way back and he always listened to him. "I want to hear it. I need to know exactly what he is planning. I know him better than anybody and I can figure him out. Maybe he's cracking up."

"I'll be in Detroit by seven tonight. I'll have the disc by then. Meet me at the apartment where Joey is staying. You should call Charlie and tell him that if he's even thinking about doing anything he should wait until he hears from us later. Tell him we can work something out."Paul was already on his way to the airport to catch a flight to Detroit and he was not looking forward to telling the boss about this latest development. That was his next call.

"I'll call him right away."Bob hung up and attempted to call Charlie on his private cell number. The message said that it was no longer in service so he called the Governor's office. Tonya told him that Charlie was still in Detroit and she would give him the message. Charlie had taken steps with his staff to shield himself from Bob and Paul if they tried to contact him. Karen and Tonya followed their instruction to a tee and they refused to give out his new cell phone number. He gave it to Rita before she left.

"Where's he staying?"Bob demanded.

"Well he is still at the Townsend as far as I know Mister Banker."She usually called him by his first name but she was instructed to maintain formalities.

"Cut the Mister Banker shit, Tonya. You tell him to call me right away or I'll...."He didn't finish, realizing that she was following instructions. "Okay then. Just tell him to call me. It is an emergency."

"I'll tell him as soon as I hear from him."

Michael Ripinski

41

As previously planned, Joey was able to access the balcony to Melissa's condo by climbing the adjacent tree and once there, he was able to pry open the balcony sliding door with ease. He was aided by the fact that a security light, which normally illuminated the back of the building had been burned out for weeks, leaving the area in the shadows of the fading light of early evening. Once inside he sat in a reclining chair near the window where he could observe the parking lot through the open blinds.

Melissa had stopped at Walgreen's on her way home from the club to pick up a few personal items and the latest issue of Newsweek. It had a story on the latest trends in national politics and the next election. Not knowledgeable on the subject, she rarely voted but she had become more interested since the friendship with Rita. As she drove into her carport, she did not notice the silver Mercedes parked among the other cars at the end of her building in the spaces designated for guests and visitors. Retrieving her bags from the back seat she shut the door as she turned and headed to the building entrance. Noticing that the security light was still burned out she made a mental note to call and complain as soon as she got inside.

Joey saw the familiar Saab enter the carport, heard the door slam, immediately rose from the chair and stood in the kitchen next to the doorway so that when she entered he would be behind the open door. He could soon hear the rattle of keys as she unlocked the deadbolt before entering the apartment and reached for the light switch on the wall. Swiftly, he reached around her and placed his gloved hand over her mouth, put his gun next to her temple and said. "Don't make a sound. I am not here to rape you or anything. I am after your boyfriend."

Dropping her bags and keys, her first thought was to ram her elbow into his ribs like she had been taught in a self- defense class that she had taken at the club, but the presence of the gun barrel against her head changed her mind. Wisely, she did not struggle as he pushed her toward the center of the room, directing her first to turn off the light.

He could tell that she was strong and would put up a fight if he let his guard down for even a moment so he calmly positioned her in front of the recliner. "I'm going to pull my hand away and if you scream or make a sound your brains will be splattered all over this lovely apartment. Understand?"

She mustered a muffled. "Uh huh."as he lowered his hand and stepped in front of her, still pointing the gun at her face. "Who are you? And why are you doing this?"she said calmly even though her heart was beating out of her chest.

"Do you really think I'm going to tell you that?"he replied. "Just do as I say and you won't get hurt."

"Does this have anything to do with Mrs. Jacob?"remembering the voice mail she had heard just a few moments before while in her car. She hadn't had time to call Dick to tell him about the message from Rita.

"That is not important right now. I want to speak with your boyfriend. I want him to come here. You should call him and tell him to get here right away but you can't say why. Where is your phone?"

Pointing to her purse on the floor. "In there."

Motioning with his free hand "Get it and call him."

In her mind she was trying to figure out a way to call Dick and tip him off while leading him to her apartment. She was stalling for a moment when she finally rose from the chair to get the phone. "My battery is low. I'll have to plug it in first."Displaying the phone to him as she retrieved it from the purse. It was the first time she got a really good look at him and it was like she had seen him before. *Was it at the Club?* She thought maybe she did.

"Call him now."Joey demanded impatiently. "And just tell him that you have to see him right away. Tell him you have a message from someone important. When he asks who it is just tell him to get here and then hang up. No funny business."

Worried that this guy was going to kill them both, she tried hard to think of something but she was too rattled. Then she remembered seeing him at the club the day before as she was leaving. "I saw you at the Tone House Health Club."

"Just make the call."

"Okay. Okay."She nervously selected his name from the speed dial list and made the call. When Dick answered she spoke exactly as she was directed and then hung up. She knew that Dick would suspect that something was wrong but she could not stop him from coming to her apartment and into the trap.

Joey contemplated killing her first and then waiting for the ex-cop but decided against it thinking that he might need her to persuade Dick to enter the apartment. For the first time he noticed how attractive she was and could understand why the ex-cop was interested. His mind drifted again for a few seconds. They were the lucky ones. To have each other. He wanted that too. Again pointing at the recliner, he told her to take a seat. "Sit down and shut up until he gets here."

Melissa was terrified but did her best to maintain her calmness as she remembered her self defense class. The instructors told her it was best to be passive until an opportunity arose to strike back. She wasn't sure she would get the opportunity.

Joey took a chair from the dining table and sat just a few feet from her; still pointing the gun at her head and there they sat in silence waiting for Dick.

Michael Ripinski

42

One problem with being Governor was that it became difficult to move around without being recognized. After checking out of the Townsend, he had Karen rent a furnished apartment in her name in Farmington Hills on a one-month lease. Charlie was running out of options and he worried that people on his staff would eventually become suspicious of his behavior. Even Karen was having some doubts. She was asking more and more questions about what was going on with Bob and his friends and he also did not want to tell her that Walt Jacob was murdered because of what he knew. He was trying to find a way out without being implicated in the Big Beaver development and especially Walt's death. He had the affair with Rita handled with the help of Karen and Tonya. Of course he would have to take care of them later by bringing them to Washington with him. With Bill Greening dead he made sure that there was no record of their meeting at his office and they were able to check his files for any information regarding the inspection at the landfill. It was clear that Greening had rubber-stamped the paperwork without an actual site inspection, but to Charlie's benefit there was no mention as to why. The only thing left was to distance himself from Bob, Sam and Paul Lapone. He knew it would be a challenge because of his long association with Bob.

Karen drove him to the apartment and handed him the keys. Before driving off she inquired about his safety. "Are you sure you are going to be alright here? We canceled your appointments for the next few days and I told the State Police that you were dealing with a very private matter and asked for their cooperation. You regular guards will be waiting at the official residence but we can't keep them in the dark very long. I'll be staying at the Sheraton in Novi and I've programmed your phone with my name and number as well as the hotel in Cozumel to reach Rita. I'll be back at eight-thirty tomorrow morning."

Taking the key he touched her hand before getting out of the car. "I owe you a lot Karen. When this is over I'll try to explain everything but I expect we will be on the defensive as soon as the news stories start coming out. I'll see you tomorrow."

Waiting until he was safely inside she drove off wondering what was going on. Charlie had only shared that Bob and his associates were responsible for the Big Beaver development and he had no knowledge of the serious hazardous waste problems. He only introduced them to Greening because he wanted to make sure they knew whom to call if they discovered any issues. He said that he never directed anyone to cover it up. Karen was skeptical, but she was loyal first and foremost, having hooked her wagon to his rising star and there was no turning back now. Whatever he may have done, it was now her job to help him.

Inside the apartment, Charlie sat on the couch and placed his head in his hands while forcing himself to get hold of his emotions. He had planned his next move but it made him nervous nonetheless. He dialed Bob's number on the new phone and hoped get an answer.

Looking at the strange phone number on his cell phone screen, Bob was reluctant to answer but he had a hunch. "Banker here."

"It's me."Charlie announced.

"Where the fuck are you?"Bob demanded.

"I am somewhere safe. Did you know that the ex-cop Hagan is snooping around asking questions about Walt Jacob? He thinks he knows about Rita and me too."

Bob was furious. "Listen my old friend. He may be the least of your worries. Lapone has a recording of you telling Rita about your plan to screw us over. They had her house bugged when you were there."

Charlie was dumbstruck. It never entered his mind that they were bugging him. After he thought about it though he knew he was stupid to be so careless. He could not deny anything. They knew what he said and now he would have to figure a way out of this. But how? "I don't have anything to say. Everything is all fucked up and you got me into this."

Hearing Charlie put the blame on him, Bob immediately countered. "You got a lot of fucking nerve. I got you into this?" He repeated himself more loudly. "I got you into this? Let me remind you who has bankrolled all of your little escapades over the last fifteen years and who arranged the buyout for your ex-wife and who cut you in on enough of my investments to make sure you are a wealthy man. And don't forget who the hell covered your ass with the lovely Misses Jacob. I got you into this? Fuck you, Governor. I never twisted your arm. You went along with everything every step of the way. You made your own choice. I tried to help you and what do I get?" Hearing no reply from Charlie he continued. "I'll tell you what I get. Fucked. Because now I have to try and save your ass again. And I don't know why I'm doing it but I'm going to help you Charlie. Do you hear me?"

Sitting on the couch with the phone sitting limply in his right hand, Charlie felt like he had the wind knocked out him. He felt claustrophobic. He was breathing heavily. What had he done? He had the ex-cop squeezing in from one side and Bob and company spying on him from the other. He finally responded. "Yeah. I hear you. What did Lapone say?"

"He's mad as hell and he's flying here tonight. In fact he should be here any minute. He'll want to meet with you Charlie. He's probably going to give you an ultimatum. Either stop your little plan or you'll go down in flames looking like the bad guy in all of this."

"What should I do?"

"If I was you. I'd do whatever he says. Remember he's the one who had Walt eliminated. I don't think he's afraid of you being the governor. He can get to you. I have no doubt."

This last statement stunned him. *Was that a threat? Would they dare try to kill a sitting governor?* "What about Rita?"

Bob knew that the subject would come up but he didn't want Charlie to know that she was in danger. "She is in Mexico. I think she should plan on staying there a while longer don't you?"

"What should I tell her?"

"Just tell her that it is not safe to come home yet and that you'll call for her when it is time. She will have to understand. You make her understand. Got it."

"Yeah"

Bob decided he needed to get off the phone with Charlie and contact Paul who by now had landed in Detroit. "I have this number you just called from. Stay put after you call Rita and I'll call you as soon as I talk to Paul. Don't do anything stupid either."

Charlie had no choice. They would have to help him deal with the ex-cop and he would have to go along with their demands. "Okay. I'll wait then."

As soon as he got off the phone with Bob he dialed Rita in Cozumel. There was no answer so he left a message for her to call him as soon as possible.

43

The call from Melissa worried him so Dick was already suspicious when he entered the parking lot at her condo. Pulling into the only vacant space, he turned off the ignition and immediately stared at the vehicle parked to his left. He had seen this silver Mercedes before. Or at least one just like it. As he walked around the vehicle and peered inside, there was nothing obvious yet something about it was familiar. Then, after taking a step back he noticed the Illinois license plate. This was the same car he had seen as he exited the health club and he remembered that the plate was on the front bumper. Michigan only had rear bumper license plates. He quickly dialed Carson's number on his cell phone and fortunately received a quick answer.

"Hey I was wondering when I would hear from you. What's up?"

Dick replied immediately. "I've got a lot to tell you but I need some back up right away. I'm in Royal Oak at my girlfriend's condo and I think she may be in trouble. No time to give you all the details right now but I think someone is in her apartment with her and he may be our suspect."Giving Carson the address, he told him to hurry and get some help there right away. "I'm going in. This can't wait but get here and tell them to hold back. Can you get here too?"

"I'm on my way. Maybe you should wait till I get there. "

"No. I can't wait. She may be in danger. Just get here. I'll try to keep you posted on my cell phone."After placing the phone back in his pocket he quickly opened the building entrance door with the key Melissa had given him and climbed the stairs to the second floor hallway stopping a few doors down from her apartment.

Inside Joey was waiting for him after noticing Hagan walking toward the building. But he was concerned that it was taking him so long. Melissa's cell phone began ringing. "Answer it."He ordered.

"Hi. Where are you?"She answered nervously.

Whispering into the phone, Dick asked. "Just answer yes or no. Is somebody with you?"

"Yes."

Grabbing the phone from her hand, Joey talked directly to him. "Listen. I've got your girlfriend in here and if you don't want her to get hurt you'll do as I say. I'm going to have her open the door and let you inside. Remember I've got a gun pointed at her head. You slide your gun on the floor before you come in. You try anything and I'll put her brains on the wall. Understand?"

Dick was thinking fast as he had many times in Detroit but it was never this personal. "What do you want?"

"Shut up and do as I say"came the reply.

He wanted to get inside her apartment because he felt that he had a better chance of dealing with this guy than from outside. He thought if he were planning to hurt her it would already have happened. Arriving at the door he knocked and announced. "Okay. It's me. Don't hurt her."

Joey motioned for Melissa to go to the door as he instructed and held the gun a few inches from her head as she unlocked and opened the door. Pulling her backwards with him toward the middle of the room he waited to see the Hagan's Smith and Wesson 357 magnum slide along the floor. He kicked it to the other side of the room. "Good. Now come in with your hands on top of your head."

Waiting in the hall with his back against the wall Dick responded. "Not until we talk. Are you okay Babe?"Directed toward Melissa.

She looked at Joey and he signaled her to say she was. "Yes! So far."

Using all of his training and experience he knew that he had to buy some time. "Look. I don't know who you are but I saw your car at the health club and I recognized it outside the building here. You won't get away. I already phoned in for a back up from the Royal Oak cops and another detective. You can't escape. You may as well give it up. "He decided to throw out one more hunch. "We know everything about your friends Bob Banker and Charlie V."

Surprised at this development, Joey had to react quickly. If the ex-cop was right then he'd have to get out of there. But what should he do? Still holding his gun to Melissa's head, he decided to take her as a hostage and he'd need to handle this Hagan guy as well. But killing them now seemed out of the question. Something didn't feel right about it. He realized that he would be captured for sure but that wasn't it. Maybe it was time to just get out. He'd done enough killing and he wanted to just get away. He had plans. "Listen cop. Or is it ex-cop? Your name is Hagan. Right? I haven't shot anyone yet but if you want to keep it that way, you do as I say. I'm takin' your girlfriend here with me as I walk outta here but first you'd better get your ass in here where I can see you with your hands on top of your head."

Taking a chance, Dick slowly emerged from the hallway and stood in the doorway with both hands laying flat on top of his head. His gaze quickly met Melissa's and he could see the fear in her eyes. He then stared directly at Joey Palzonian – face to face for the first time. It was the same face he saw twice before. "Take me with you. Let her go."

"No way. You'll both do as I say."Still holding the gun on her he reached around from behind and placed his hand around her neck, pulling her along with him. He had previously noticed a closet door just off the entry to the kitchen with a key lock from the outside. "What's in that closet?"

"Just some cleaning supplies and some old boxes of personal stuff."She replied.

He motioned for Dick to move toward them and to follow them toward the room.

"Give me your phone. Put it on the table there."He demanded that Dick hand over his cell phone and after Dick complied, he pointed to the closet. "After she opens it you get in there."

"You can't get away."Dick reminded him again. "I believe you know about the Jacob murder and maybe the Hodges kid. Maybe I can get you a deal if you give up now. We don't want you."He lied. "We're after these other guys. Charlie V's friends."

"Shut the fuck up. I don't need your deal."He was worried now. This ex-cop knew more than he thought. Maybe it was time to shoot them both and take his chances. He decided to stick to his plan and make a break instead. "Get in there and face the wall."As Dick entered the closet with his hands still on top of his head, Joey used his free hand and shoved his back causing him to tumble into a pile of boxes that originally held reams of copy paper but were used by everybody for storage of personal items and files. Slamming the door shut he asked Melissa for the key. "Get your key and lock that door."

"It's in my purse."

Still holding her by the neck he walked her to the purse and as he grabbed it he emptied the contents onto the table. Her leather strapped key ring with the distinctive Saab emblem tumbled out. "Which one?"

"The brass one with the green dot."Melissa had the habit of color-coding her keys and right now she was glad that she did. He still held her neck as he handed her the key and motioned her to lock the door. Afterward she handed the keys back to him.

As he heard the door lock, Dick decided to give it one more try. "We don't want you. We want your boss and Charlie. Let her go and you can still get away. Take my car. They have a description of the Mercedes and you won't get far."Hearing no answer, he sat there in the darkness and began feeling around the room for anything that might be helpful. His hands moved over the boxes and various items on the shelves until he came to a familiar shape. A toolbox. But as he tried to open it he realized that it too was locked. It would have to be forced open. He could hear movement in the apartment and he decided to wait until he heard them leave. Then he wondered where the Royal Oak cops were and what was taking them so long.

Joey let go of her neck and grabbed Dick's cell phone. Pushing her toward the bathroom, he stopped by the open door, moved quickly to flip up the toilet seat and tossed the phone into the water. "Let's go."he whispered forcefully and shoved her toward the open apartment door. After sticking his head out into the hallway and making sure no one saw them, he held the gun close to her head. "After we walk outta here I will have this gun in my pocket but if you try anything I'll shoot you right here. Understand?"

"Yes. Please can't you just let me go? You can take my car."She pleaded to no avail as they walked to the stairwell and descended the six steps to the door where he again surveyed the area before exiting the building. Realizing that he had to take the Mercedes because the cops would trace it back to Paul, he handed her his keys after clicking the doors open.

"You drive."He commanded, opening the driver's side door and shoving her in, while quickly moving around the front and into the passenger seat, holding the gun on her the whole time. She started the engine and backed out of the space turning toward the driveway and out onto the street. "Turn here."He pointed to an alley about a half block from her condo and she continued past a couple of dumpsters and trashcans and finally, out onto Thirteen Mile Road. They were a half-mile away when the Royal Oak Police arrived.

Michael Ripinski

44

Sean Carson kept trying to call his old friend on his cell phone and kept getting a message saying the customer was not available. As he and the Royal Oak police arrived at Melissa's condo and he immediately noticed Dick's Ford, he eased his car into the space vacated by the Mercedes.

A Royal Oak detective named Rolston was right behind him and approached his car as he was getting out.

"We would have been here fifteen minutes ago if you gave us the right location."Sean had mistakenly given Melissa's address as Roseland Avenue when she actually lived on Roselawn. In his haste he copied the wrong street name when he was on the phone with Dick. The Royal Oak police approached a small bungalow at the former address and scared the living hell out of an old widow as they loudly pounded on the front door. When Carson arrived they realized the mistake and immediately headed to the correct address but they were too late to catch up with Joey and his captive.

After carefully surrounding her condo and realizing there was no activity inside, Sean had a fearful sensation that maybe he was too late and that something terrible had happed to Dick. He made the decision to break down the door even though it was the Royal Oak jurisdiction. It always surprised him how flimsy these interior doors were and after throwing his two hundred and twenty pound frame into the door a few times it started to give way.

"Wait a minute."Said Rolston. "You can't just break down the door. We don't have a warrant."

"Fuck your warrant."Said Sean. "My friend may be in trouble

here and this is his girlfriend's place anyway."He gave the door one more shove and it finally broke open. "Dick you in here?"he shouted, entering with his gun pointed straight out moving toward the interior of the condo.

He heard a voice from the closet. "In here. Shoot the goddamn door lock. Get me out."

Doing as requested, Carson fired his weapon at the lock and the door came free. . Out sprang Dick wiping some dust from his eyes and running to the kitchen sink to throw water on his face.

"He took Melissa. They left about fifteen minutes ago. What the fuck took you so long?"

"Sorry man. A mix up on the address."Carson replied.

Looking around the condo floor, Dick noticed his gun right where Joey had kicked it by the TV. He placed the weapon back into his pocket and headed to the door as Carson and the Royal Oak detective followed.

"Where we going?"Carson asked.

"I don't know for sure but I know we are looking for a silver Mercedes with Illinois plates."He announced after noticing that Melissa's Saab was still parked in her carport.

Sean caught up to Dick and grabbed him by the arm. "We'll put an all department on this. He can't get far. We'll catch this mother."

Dick wheeled and came within a few inches of his face. "This prick has Melissa. I'm gonna get his slick Chicago ass and when I'm done he'll wish the fuck he never heard of me."

Carson knew that look. He had seen Dick when he was focused on a case back in the D and nothing was going to stand his way. Not Royal Oak PD. Not Troy PD. Not any jurisdiction. The best he could hope for was to keep Dick from getting himself shot as they tried to save Melissa and apprehend this guy. "I'll help you. We got to coordinate. We can't just go off. We don't even know where they are headed."

Dick knew that he was right. He had no idea where they were going and where to start looking. His main concern was Melissa's well being and he was feeling guilty about using her. Thinking that he should have told her to stay away from Rita Jacob when he first found out about her and Charlie. Now she was in real danger and he didn't know how to help her. "Goddamn it Sean. We got to find them. Did you trace the Mercedes yet?"

Sean had phoned in the plate after getting the number when Dick first called him and he just received a message on his cell phone with the information. "The car is registered to a company in Chicago. They don't know why it would be in Michigan. They say it had been parked in a storage lot for the past month and were not aware it was missing. We're checking out their story."

"Sounds like bullshit to me. Can your guys check out this company? What's their name? What kind of business? Who is the CEO? And who normally drives this car?"

"Already on it man. I should know something soon."Carson put his hand on his friend's shoulder. "We'll find her and we'll get this prick."

Without responding, Dick began walking toward his car. Sean went after him. "Where you going?"

"I don't know but I can't stand here and hope he brings her back. They have to be somewhere nearby. Melissa's is probably driving and he's got his weapon on her. She's cool. Has a good head on her shoulders. She'll try to talk him into letting her go and it'll be someplace she is familiar with."He pulled out his keys and unlocked the car door.

"Wait."Said Carson. "Let's take my car. I have the radio and we can use my flashers if we have to."

Agreeing to Sean's request, Dick locked his car and climbed in the passenger side of the Crown Vic. After arranging back-up from Royal Oak and informing Troy what they were doing, they drove out onto Woodward Avenue heading north because that's the way Dick thought Melissa would go – toward Birmingham – not Detroit.

Michael Ripinski

45

Paul had taken a taxi from Detroit Metro and arrived at Bob's office. Throwing his leather garment bag on a chair by the door, he walked over to the desk where Bob was sitting and didn't waste any time giving orders. "I want to see Charlie right now. Where the fuck is he?"

Standing to show that he was not going to be intimidated, Bob replied. "I just talked to him. He's in seclusion. Don't worry he'll cooperate."

"Seclusion."Paul screamed. "What the fuck does that mean? "Realizing that Bob didn't know exactly where Charlie was staying, he was even more furious. "You don't know where he is, do you?"

"I told you that I just spoke to him. He's scared. He'll do what we want but you got to understand what the deal is. He's the goddam governor Paul. You can't just put the squeeze on him and expect no one to notice. We have to talk about this."Bob walked around the desk and stood a few feet from his business partner - acting confident and in control as he had in so many situations over the years. Under the surface he was fearful, for Charlie and for himself. He knew that this was not just about money any more.

Turning away from Bob and walking toward the window, Paul stopped and began speaking without looking at him. "I know who he is. Let me remind you that your friend the governor was about to throw us all under the bus to save his own ass. How do you know he won't do anything stupid like cut a deal with the Feds? Maybe he has already and he is getting protection or something. How do you know he can be trusted?"

Bob hadn't thought about that. He was certain that he still had Charlie in his pocket and that they would be able to keep things from getting any further out of control. "Our biggest worry right now is not Charlie. The way I see it, this ex-cop Hagan is the one we need to worry about. If he gets any closer he'll be in our shit for sure. We need to come up with a story that will keep him off the track."

Checking his cell phone, expecting a call from Joey at any minute, Paul replied. "Let me worry about Hagan. I'm taking care of his situation as we speak. I expect that we won't have to worry too much about him after tonight." Then turning back to face Bob he continued. "After Charlie the only other one to take care of is Rita and we are handling that as well."

Bob was stunned. He had a sickening feeling in his gut that told him what was happening. This was way out of control. Out of *his* control. He had come to grips with Walt Jacob's murder but if he understood correctly, the body count was about to escalate. Clearly underestimating the ruthlessness of this man standing in his office, he stepped backward and slowly sank into one of the Victorian wingback chairs next to his desk.

Flipping open his cell phone, Paul couldn't wait any longer and punched in Joey's ID number. After four rings it went directly to voice mail and Paul left a quick message. "Call me. Tell me how it went." He closed the phone and placed it in his suit jacket pocket. Glancing at his watch, he began to feel some concern. It was already past eight PM and he expected to hear from Joey by now.

46

Feeling the vibration of the cell phone in his pocket, Joey decided not to answer it just now. He needed to concentrate. "Go left at the next light."he ordered.

Melissa carefully guided the Mercedes to the left turn lane and waited for traffic to clear before completing the turn onto northbound Crooks Road toward Fourteen Mile road. "Where are we going?"she asked nervously, her eyes focused straight ahead wondering what her captor was planning to do next. Somehow she felt relieved that he had not yet harmed her and for the first time felt more confident in her predicament.

"Just keep going this way and don't do anything stupid. I ain't interested in having to hurt you."Keeping the gun on her at waist level, he took a quick glance out the rear window to make sure they weren't being followed. His strategy had changed. The ex-cop clearly knew more about him than he originally thought. For a moment he regretted not killing them both when he had the chance back at her condo.

After passing Maple Road – Fifteen mile – the Mercedes was approaching the major intersection of Crooks and Big Beaver. Going west would take them to the Somerset Mall and that's what Joey decided to do, remembering this area from his recent travels. "Head on over to the mall and go into the parking garage over by Saks."

She obeyed his instructions and headed west past several office buildings and a few restaurants. Ironically the Big Beaver Project site was just a quarter mile to the east on this same street. A large sign proclaimed the future development - RETAIL and OFFICE SPACE COMING SOON.

The Somerset Mall was one of the largest upscale retail developments in the Midwest. Originally developed on the south side of Big Beaver road with Saks and Neimen Marcus as anchor stores, a major expansion was added on the north side of the street with Nordstrom and Hudson's, which is now Macy's. A long umbilical in the form of a covered moving walkway joins the two sections with hundreds of designer shops and boutiques representing the most affluent retail shopping experience in America. From Abercrombie to Tiffany and Brooks Brothers, they had it all. On a weeknight in July, the mall was not very busy and after turning on to Coolidge Road, Melissa entered the parking area adjacent to Saks Fifth Avenue. Joey glanced back once again and was satisfied they were alone.

"Go all the way to the top deck."He ordered her to drive up to the top of the four level parking garage.

Slowly she proceeded up the ramps careful not to bottom out on any of the speed bumps placed every fifty feet or so to discourage those in a hurry and avoid collisions. Reaching the top level which was open to the air she paused to survey the mostly empty parking deck. Seeing only a dozen or so cars she surmised that these vehicles belonged to mostly store employees who were instructed to leave the bottom three levels for the customers convenience.

Not seeing anyone around, Joey pointed his weapon toward a red Taurus parked against the retaining wall at the south end of the deck. "Pull up next to the red car over there. Keep your hands on the wheel after we stop."

Melissa eased into the space, placed the shifter into the P position and waited for his next command. If he was going to shoot her, she thought, this would be the perfect place. No one would find her for hours. Her heart began racing and she felt like throwing up. "What are you going to do with me?"She asked.

Joey knew that he was running out of options. They probably traced the Mercedes by now and he knew that Paul would deny knowing him. He'd say the car was stolen. He told him as much when they discussed the various jobs he had performed over the years. That's why he was well paid. His salary included taking the fall if things ever got dicey. It was definitely that way right now. He would be on his own.

Fortunately Joey had prepared for this very day having stashed away a hundred grand in a Bahamian Bank under an assumed name. A safe deposit box in Miami contained his new passport and enough cash to get him to Nassau. He'd be okay for a few weeks until things settled down. An old friend from prison was working in one of the casinos down there and promised to help him out when the time came. Now was that time. This was his plan and he needed to move fast. "Give me the keys and put your hands on top of your head." As she did so he quickly exited the Mercedes pointing the gun at her face as he came around to the driver's side and opened the door. "Now get out."

Standing at the side of the car Melissa looked around hoping to spot someone coming but there was no one. Realizing her legs were shaking, she thought that this was it. He was going to kill her. Then she heard the click of the trunk latch opening and turned her head to see Joey extracting a small leather duffle bag. She pleaded once more. "Please. Just let me go. I don't want to die. I won't say anything to anybody. I'll forget what you even look like. I promise. Please." Then she saw him smile.

"I told you I wasn't going to hurt you. If I were going to kill you I would have done it back at your place along with your boyfriend. Now be a good girl and climb into the trunk."

"What?"

"I said get in the trunk. Lie down and close your eyes. And keep your hands by your side and keep your mouth shut. After I close the lid you can count to one thousand before you start to yell. You know. Like the kids do. One-one thousand. Two-one thousand. Not that anybody will hear you right away. But if I hear one sound before I leave the area. I'll open the trunk and blow your head off. Understand?" He motioned with the gun toward the open trunk and Melissa climbed in, curling up into a fetal position as he closed the lid. She could hear him moving around outside and she began to count in her head as he had ordered.

Joey placed his gun in the bag and exchanged it for a small metal tool that resembled a screwdriver with a funny looking pronged end and a pair of wire snips. After surveying the deserted roof area again he walked over to a black Pontiac G-6 parked a few spaces to the left and placed the tool into the door lock, which opened, sounding the horn alarm. He pulled the hood latch and quickly lifted the hood and cut the battery cable quieting the alarm. In a matter of seconds he located the horn, cut those wires and re-attached the battery cable using a small connecting clamp from his bag. The whole episode lasted less than a minute. Tossing his bag in the back seat Joey climbed behind the wheel, jamming his specialty tool into the ignition key slot and started the engine.

Inside the cramped trunk, Melissa could hear the brief car horn and then the engine start nearby. She stopped counting and felt a sigh of relief thinking that he was on his way. Feeling around inside the darkened space her right hand came upon a piece of material against the side- wall of the trunk. It felt like a belt strap and had a looped end. She tugged on the strap and realized that it opened a compartment containing an emergency kit. She felt what seemed to be a flare and some tools and a first aid kit. A small canvas bag contained some papers and a small cylindrical object with a flat end on one side and a round end on the other enclosed in plastic. Feeling a sliding button along the flat bottom she moved the switch and the truck became aglow in yellow light. She had found an emergency flashlight beacon. Now she could survey her enclosure and maybe find a way out. Her good luck continued as she grabbed a screwdriver from the bag and started prying against the trunk latch from the inside. To her surprise it opened on the third try. Poking her head out, she saw the rear end of the black Pontiac as it disappeared down the ramp. She stopped for a moment, feeling weak and dizzy as she realized what had just occurred. Leaning against the hood of the Taurus with her right hand, she bent over and threw up while holding her head with her other hand. "Oh God. Oh God."She cried over and over.

The voice of a young woman caught her by surprise. "Hey. You there. What are you doing? Where's my car?"

Brushing the hair away from her face and stumbling slightly Melissa reached out to the woman who immediately backed away. "I need your help. Please."She begged. Then realizing that she had frightened the woman who seemed to be in her early twenties with long dark hair and glasses. "Your car was stolen by a man who kidnapped me. Do you have a cell phone? My boyfriend is a cop. He can help."

The woman was still unsure whether believe Melissa or call 911 herself. Concluding that this disheveled woman standing in front of her was in distress, she agreed to help. Reaching into her purse she offered the compact flip phone to Melissa. "Here. Are you all right? Do you need medical help?"

"No thanks. I'm okay." Taking the phone she had to think for a moment to recall Dick's number then dialed quickly. Before he answered she turned to the young woman and extended her other hand. "My name's Melissa."

"Brenda." Returning the gesture the young woman moved closer as they waited for Dick to answer.

Michael Ripinski

47

He didn't recognize the number of the incoming call on his cell phone display, but Dick answered in his familiar way. "Hagan here."

"Baby. It's me. I'm all right. I'm not hurt, but he stole a black car and took off."

Relieved that she was not harmed and seemed calm considering what she had gone through, he looked at Carson and mouthed her name as he continued. "Where are you? Are you alone?"

"I'm at Somerset. Parking garage, top deck behind Sak's. There is a woman named Brenda with me. It was her car. This is her phone."Smiling as she said this to show her appreciation.

"What kind of car and do you have the plate number?"

Handing the phone to Brenda, she repeated his request.

"Hi this is Brenda. It's a black Oh Five Pontiac G six. My plate number is PTE one oh one."

Scribbling the make and plate number on his note pad he showed it to Carson who immediately was on his radio announcing the information to his communication center back in Troy. In a matter of minutes it was broadcast to all area law enforcement agencies. "Thanks Brenda. We'll send a police car there to take a report right away."

Before handing the phone back to Melissa, Brenda offered further assistance. "I work in the mall at J Jill. We can go back in there until the police come."

"Okay. Thanks."Melissa replied before speaking to Dick again. "We'll be inside the mall at the J Jill store. It's right near Saks on the second floor. Are you coming?"

"Yeah sure. I'll be right there."It was not what he originally planned. His instincts pulled him toward continuing the search.

He wanted to get this guy. The pieces were falling into place. The Mercedes driver was suspect number one in both the Hodges murder and Walt Jacob's death. Dick was sure of that. He was also sure that Bob the Banker and Charlie V were covering up the whole mess and he suspected that the development on Big Beaver was connected.

"Am I taking you to Melissa?" Carson asked.

As he contemplated the answer, Dick thought about his conversation with Charlie at the ceremony. "Yeah take me to the mall. I need to make sure she's okay. Then we have to find this asshole, if he's still driving the black Pontiac. My guess is he'll be out of town soon. We also need to start looking into that new project on Big Beaver where they had the groundbreaking a few days ago. I think the late Mister Jacob was originally involved with that group and something he knew got him killed."

Carson turned toward Dick for a moment and then looked ahead as he continued driving. He wondered how Dick had put all this together. He was sure he'd find out soon enough. "We are running the plate on that Mercedes. We'll know more on our suspect soon. But I'd like to get him in a room in order to ask some more questions. Do you think this guy would cut a deal in order to give up the others?"

"Nope. Don't think so. Whoever is pulling his strings has him under control. We'll need to lean on him before he's arrested. That means you find him first. If another department picks him up, you got to get to him right away. I want a piece of him and I want him to give up the governor and Mister Banker. These pricks are going down. All of em."

The voice on Carson's radio interrupted their conversation. "We have some details on the Mercedes." The voice crackled on the speaker in the dashboard. "The car is registered to a company in Chicago. We tried to look them up but nothing so far. We're checking the stolen vehicle reports.

"Thanks. Keep checking on the Chicago Company." Carson spoke to the two-way radio device and then switched to an all department frequency just in case anyone spotted the Pontiac.

Right on cue a minute later. "This is Birmingham unit four eight. We have the black G six going south on Woodward near Fourteen

Mile. White male driving. No passengers. Just pulled out of a gas station."

"Four eight, do you have a plate number?"asked another voice as Dick and Sean looked at each other.

"Yup. PTE one zero one. Do you want us to stop him?"

Pressing the button on his radio, Carson chimed in. "Birmingham four eight, this is Troy. Detectives. He's our guy. Homicide suspect. Take him. I repeat, take him but approach with caution. He is armed."

Another voice came on as soon as Sean stopped talking. "All Birmingham and Royal Oak units in the area. You are requested to back-up Birmingham four eight."

Flipping a switch on his console, Carson activated his flashers, made a U-turn and sped southbound toward Thirteen Mile Road. "I'm going all the way to Twelve Mile, maybe we can cut him off if they don't stop him further up on Woodward."

"Good idea. Cut over on Vinsetta. It'll save time."Said Dick referring to a residential street that angled toward the main road and would cut a few minutes off the trip.

As he drove on Woodward at normal speed so as not to bring attention to himself, Joey Palzonian was thinking ahead to his getaway from Detroit. First he'd have to ditch this car. Remembering a small shopping center a short distance ahead at Thirteen Mile, he figured he'd be able to grab a different car and then he'd be on his way. His glance at the rear view mirror showed the flashing light of the Birmingham Police vehicle that was rapidly approaching about ten car lengths behind. His reaction was immediate and aggressive. Flooring the gas pedal, the Pontiac lurched forward almost hitting a mini van and a small SUV as he swerved around the traffic.

"Shit."he said aloud observing a jam of traffic at a stoplight ahead. He had no choice. Gripping the wheel and pressing the pedal to the floor, he jumped the curb up onto the median, narrowly avoiding a small crabapple tree and a metal road sign. Approaching the intersection, he drove back onto the paved surface in front of the stopped vehicles and sped through as cars screeched and swerved to avoid a collision. Joey again glanced in his mirror and saw that the cop car had slowed to avoid the cars in the intersection and the distance was widening between them.

In the newly built, brick fire station located on the corner of Woodward and Thirteen Mile, Firefighter Mike Walters was monitoring the chase on the radio and realizing that the suspect was approaching this corner, he quickly jumped into the cab of the new five-ton pumper. Having just returned from a false alarm twenty minutes before, the station doors were still open. The diesel engine quickly fired and with sirens and flashers blaring, Mike drove out onto Woodward as all the traffic stopped expecting the fire truck to pull away. Instead the large vehicle came to a stop blocking all the southbound lanes and part of the northbound ones. A Royal Oak police cruiser approached from the east on thirteen mile and he could hear other sirens rapidly getting louder from all directions.

Joey was thinking that he needed to get off this main road but knew that he'd be at a disadvantage if he drove into one of the neighborhoods on either side of Woodward. The local cops clearly had the upper hand on those streets. Approaching the intersection, he could see the flashing lights on the fire truck and all the cars pulled to either side of the street. He had little time to react. With horn blaring he steered the Pontiac around a pickup and scraped the front end of a white Honda causing it to slide into a signpost near the entrance to a Mobil station. Half on the grass and two wheels on the driveway entrance to the gas station, he jumped the curb and plowed into an A-frame sign listing the price of cigarettes, speeding through the station and out onto Thirteen Mile road on the other side. He narrowly missed a woman with two children in a mini van turning into the station.

The other drivers were staring in disbelief while the attendant in the Mobil station came running out yelling in a foreign language. Meanwhile, sitting in the cab of the fire truck, Fireman Walters radioed the details as the scene played out in front of him. "I see the black G-6. He just plowed through the Mobil Station and he's on Thirteen Mile. Now he's heading back toward Woodward. He just turned southbound again."

Dick looked over at Sean as they approached the intersection of Woodward and Twelve Mile. "He's coming our way."

As he swerved again to avoid another row of cars, Joey reached over into his leather bag on the passenger seat extracting a Glock 9 millimeter, his heavy-duty weapon. With one hand on the gun and the other on the wheel he sped through a red light at Coolidge Highway causing several cars to slam on their breaks while the drivers cursed and flipped him the bird. A Royal Oak police car approached too fast from Thirteen Mile and skidded into the rear end of a large UPS truck. Fortunately no one was injured but the cruiser was disabled. Southbound on Woodward he passed the McDonald's and a camera store among a row of other small businesses. *No time to change cars now.* He thought. *Got to keep going.* A quick glance in the rear view mirror showed no flashing lights but he could hear the sirens. Passing cars and zig- zagging through the traffic he noticed the cemetery on his right. It was not an option of escape. He knew there was a freeway, I – 696, just a few miles ahead and he thought that he might have a better chance in the faster traffic.

Hearing the sirens, Dick motioned for Sean to drive up onto the median- a ten yard wide stretch of grass and dirt separating the southbound and northbound lanes of Woodward Avenue - the City of Berkley on the west side and Royal Oak on the East. The famous Shrine of The Little Flower church dominated the northeast corner, with its one hundred foot, gray stone bell tower protruding upward like the tall stump of a petrified tree in the middle of a grassy field. The surrounding neighborhood was a mixture of upper middleclass homes built between the twenties and the seventies. As they slowed, moving carefully over the median, the remaining traffic had moved off to either side of Woodward or turned onto Twelve Mile road to avoid the approaching police vehicles with their whirring sirens and alternating red – blue flashers.

Looking ahead, it appeared to Joey that the intersection was clear and he felt fortunate to be able to blow through unimpeded, but then he saw something moving in the median strip a few hundred yards ahead on the left. Flashing lights. *Damn. Another cop.* He had to think quickly. An abrupt shift to his left brought him into the turning lane just as Sean Carson eased his vehicle onto the pavement blocking the approaching Pontiac.

"There's our boy."Shouted Dick as he reached into his pocket placing his hand around the grip of his 357 magnum.

The G-six hit the curb with sparks flying and clipped a metal sign post before crossing over the median onto the northbound lanes of Woodward. All traffic had now stopped on both sides of the avenue and Joey saw a chance to head onto a side street near the big church tower. Carson skidded on the grass and fishtailed as they spun around to follow the Pontiac. Both cars swerved as they bounced over the curbs and Dick noticed where they were headed. "He's trying to get to the side street there next to the church. Cut him off."he said while pointing to the oncoming lanes and another narrower median strip for this street. Carson floored the Crown Vic and cut the angle between them as the fleeing suspect jumped another curb, both men briefly hitting their heads on the padded inside roof.

Seeing that he was about to be cut off by the larger cop car, Joey reflexively jerked the steering wheel to the right, bounding up onto a sidewalk and the lawn adjacent to the side entrance to the church. There was no time to avoid the large maple tree which was now directly in his field of vision. "Oh Fuck."He yelled as the Pontiac collided with the tree on the front passenger side. Not quite head on, but enough to deploy the air bag and knock the wind out of him for a moment.

Following up onto the sidewalk but avoiding the trees, Carson skidded to a stop about fifty feet from the suspect, both he and Dick came bursting out of the car with their weapons drawn and knelt behind the front and rear fenders.

Joey regained his breath and quickly ducked down on the front seat, his hand still on the Glock. Scrambling over the console, he reached for the passenger door handle and rolled out onto the grass next to the maple tree. He continued his roll for a few yards before jumping to his feet and headed toward the steps to the church.

"Police."Shouted Carson. "Give it up."

Turning toward the Crown Vic, Joey fired a round that shattered the windshield and another hit the sidewalk next to Sean's leg sending a chip of concrete up into his face."Fuck you."He yelled as he continued running toward the large wooden doors to the church.

Sean yelled "Goddam it Dick. I'm hit."while dropping his

weapon and placing both hands to his face. "My eye. Shit. It's just the concrete. Not a round. But I can't see."Carson turned and pointed toward the church and said, "You go. Get the prick."

Dick didn't need to be told. Instinctively he had already begun moving around the side of the car and crawled on his stomach toward a tall spruce tree and observed the suspect reach the church doors. Moving ahead to the crashed G six he stopped while ducking behind the trunk. "You won't get away. Throw down the gun and give up."

Realizing that the church doors were locked, Joey moved to his right out onto the raised stone patio area before ducking behind a three-foot wall and fired another round in the direction of the voice. As he looked around he saw that the wall extended around the front of the tower in a semi circle and there was another set of steps on the opposite side near Twelve-mile road. If he could get there, he might carjack a vehicle and make a run for it before the other cops approached. He could hear the sirens getting closer. He fired another round toward the G-six shattering the driver's side window and he began a stooped run toward the other side of the patio.

Dick had made his way around to the front of the patio below the stone wall about twenty feet to the right of where the shots came from. He guessed right that Joey would try to make his way out the other side and as he took a quick peek over the wall, he saw him about half way to the exit along Twelve Mile road. "Hold it."He shouted.

Joey dropped and rolled to his right firing toward the wall. Dick ducked amid splintering fragments of stone as the round hit just inches from where his head was a moment before. Sliding on his stomach, Joey tried to make it to the exit and out to the steps that lead to the street. Dick rolled a few feet to his right and rose above the wall aiming his weapon toward the man crawling on patio floor. He fired two quick rounds in succession at the figure that was now just five feet from the exit. Cloth, blood and bone exploded from the shoulder of the man as he suddenly stopped and rolled against the section of stone- wall next to the steps.

The sting of the bullet registered immediately in Joey's brain. As he slid over to the wall he felt another sensation in his abdomen as he realized that the second round had entered near his left kidney and swiftly exited out through his chest. Looking down he could see the crimson liquid flooding his shirt and felt the warm sensation running down his legs. For an instant he thought about his plan. Florida. The Bahamas. His new life. It was not to be. Shock had settled in but he shook the blurriness long enough to focus on the face of the man standing above him with the barrel of his gun still pointed in his direction. "You."he whispered. "It was you."His eyes rolled back into his head and he slumped to the floor of the patio. The last thing Joey Palzonian saw before he died was the face of Dick Hagan.

The Royal Oak police arrived on the scene seconds after the final exchange of gunfire and with their assistance, Carson joined them on the patio in front of the church holding a gauze patch next to his damaged eye. Dick was standing over the lifeless body of Joey Palzonian, his weapon held loosely in his right hand. A uniformed cop stooped over the body to confirm that Joey was dead and somewhere in Miami, a safe deposit box containing a new identity and ten thousand dollars in cash would remain unopened. More cop cars and an EMS vehicle arrived in the adjoining parking lot.

Dick turned to Sean. "Are you alright?"

"Yeah. I think so."Looking down at the body of Joey Palzonian. "Too bad. We could have tried to get him to talk."

Dick turned away and noticed that his hand was shaking. A nervous reaction he remembered from other times he was forced to fire his weapon in the line of duty. He realized that this would be different. Even though Sean Carson was a cop, he was not. He was a civilian and this was in Royal Oak, outside Sean's jurisdiction. There would be many questions and an investigation with the required paperwork. All he wanted to do right now was go sit down somewhere and figure out how to get the guys who were behind this thing. Bob the Banker and anyone else who knew anything including Charlie V. His next thought was about Melissa. Reaching for his cell phone he called to explain what happened and to tell her that he would catch up later at her place.

On Woodward Avenue the traffic began moving again as a small crowd of curious onlookers gathered; pointing and whispering as the police arranged yellow crime scene tape around the entire area.

48

"Buenos Noches. May I help you Madam."Said the Mexican bartender wearing a white cotton shirt with a colorful emblem in the shape of a dolphin on the breast pocket

Rita noticed that he was a little taller than the other Mexicans working in the resort and his English was very fluent. The others were mostly of Mayan descent with their round faces and short stubby arms and legs and they spoke with heavy accents. The bartender was obviously not one of them. Probably from the north, maybe from Mexico City like some of the workers who found their way to the resort areas of Cancun and the Mayan Riveria - lucky enough to find work in the tourism industry. Plus she thought he was handsome, for a Mexican anyway. Wearing a yellow sundress and a white cotton wrap around her waist she eased onto the bar stool and replied. "Margarita por favor."

"One Margarita for the lady."Flashing a smile showcasing his perfect white teeth against his light brown skin. "My name in Herman."Pronouncing it ' err – mon' with the emphasis on the second syllable.

She just smiled in return and watched as he swiftly mixed the ingredients into a stainless steel shaker. Ice, tequila, grenadine and limejuice. After shaking the mixture a few times he poured concoction into a large salt lined Margarita glass, squeezed a sliver of fresh lime on the rim and added small green straw before carefully placing the drink on a napkin in front of her. "Anything else for you this evening?"

"No. Not right now. Muchas Gracias."

"De nada."

Lifting the drink to her lips, Rita noticed only three other people sitting around the outdoor bar under a large palm palapa. A young couple sat on the end stools to her right and couldn't keep their hands off each other as they sipped their drinks from tall colored tumblers – tiny red umbrellas sticking out the top. Five stools to her left sat a man wearing baggy tan linen slacks, leather sandals and a powder blue cotton short-sleeved shirt. His large forearms extended from muscled bi-ceps and he held a Dos Equis beer bottle in one hand. Leaning with his back against the bar, facing the ocean, he seemed to be enjoying the view. On the opposite side she could hear the laughter of some tourists at the swim up portion of the bar, which was attached to the fifty-foot long outdoor pool. The sun was sliding into the horizon amidst a few stray clouds, appearing to drop right into the deep blue, water between Cozumel and Playa Del Carmen on the eastern mainland shore and she noticed the lights from one of the cruise ships as it steamed away from port on its way to the next destination on the popular Western Caribbean route. She wondered if they were headed back to Miami or to one of the other ports where the tourists enhanced the local economy by purchasing overpriced souvenirs and taking sightseeing side trips to the beaches, ruins and other landmarks. Glancing back to her left, she noticed the man in the powder blue shirt had turned back around and was speaking to Herman but she could not make out their conversation.

Finishing the Margarita, slurping the last few drops of flavor through the straw, Rita was enjoying the moment. Just taking it all in with the cool evening breeze washing over her, she had almost forgotten about the problems back home in Michigan. She thought how wonderful it would be if Charlie could join her here for a few days. Just the two of them. No guards. No aides. No cops. No Bob The Banker.

The bartender interrupted her little daydream as he placed another margarita on the bar. "Compliments of the gentleman."Nodding in the direction of the man on her left.

Immediately glancing that way, she got a good look at his face for the first time. Blue eyes, slightly large nose with light brown hair and eyebrows almost blond from the bleaching of the sun. He smiled without showing his teeth and lifted his beer bottle in her direction. Rita reached for the margarita and returned the gesture with a smile of her own. Not expecting this act of generosity, she sipped the drink tasting a little more tequila than the first one. She was wary of socializing with anyone she didn't know right now but the guy in the blue shirt seemed friendly enough and she convinced herself that she could handle it. Even if he was trying to pick her up, she was flattered that she could still draw the attention of most men. With Charlie tied up handling the situation back in Michigan she had no one else to talk to. A little flirty conversation wouldn't hurt anyone. She was enjoying the attention. As she took another sip, she noticed him walking toward her.

"May I join you?"Pointing to the stool next to hers.

"If you wish."Playing it coy. "Thank you for the drink."

"My pleasure."Extending his hand palm up. "My name's Jake. Jake Anton. Does the pretty lady have a name?"

Smiling, she didn't answer right away. He was direct but something about him made her feel comfortable. She reminded herself that this would only be conversation. "Rita."She decided not to give her last name.

"Well Rita. It is nice to meet you. First time in Cozumel? "

"No. I actually came her a few times with my late husband."She almost regretted saying this. She really didn't want him to know she was alone. She thought about making up a story that she was traveling with a friend who was not feeling well at the moment but decided against it.

"I'm sorry."He said, turning back toward the ocean. "I don't mean to intrude. Was it recently?"

"Yes. Yes. I am actually here to unwind a bit. I needed to get away from home back in Michigan. It is a good place for that isn't it?"Sweeping her hand in the direction of the now almost absent sunset. All that remained was an orange glow against the gray-blue sky illuminating the horizon absent of any clouds. It was a romantic moment and she wished that Charlie were here with her to enjoy it. Forgetting about Walt altogether. Another taste of the Margarita and she could feel the alcohol taking effect. Maybe it was the tropical heat. She always seemed to get drunk a little easier down here. She kept thinking she had to stay in control.

"I would have to agree."said Jake. "I have been coming here for many years with a group of divers from Ohio. I am their dive master and I organize the trips."

She looked at him and responded. Recalling that it had been a few years since she last went scuba diving. "Really. I used to dive myself."

"Why don't you do it any more?"

"No time. And I have other interests now."She thought about her life back in Michigan for a moment. Her interest was Charlie V and how she still hoped things would work out.

"Listen Rita. If you are going to be here for a few days I would be happy to take you along on one of our dives. We are going over to Palancar reef tomorrow. I can get you all the equipment you need and you can keep it simple Twenty feet or less. Just enough for you to get reacquainted."

The thought of being able to enjoy the splendor of the colorful underwater world along the reefs appealed to her. She remembered how much she enjoyed the solitude amidst the creatures in their natural habitat and the bright red, blue and yellow coral rising from bottom. What could it hurt? Charlie said she might have to be here a few days anyway. "You know. I might just take you up on that. How can I reach you Jake? "

He smiled at the response. "I'm staying at the Vista Del Mar, right in town near The Plaza. Are you here at the Coral Princess? "

"Yes. I…"She almost gave him her room number but wisely held off. "I am here but I'm not sure for how long. I planned this trip kind of open ended and I may need to go back at any time."

Lifting the Dos Equis to his lips he took a long swallow and set the green bottle back on the bar. "Some members of my group are staying here. I just dropped them off. If you would like to join us just be in the lobby at eight AM tomorrow."

"Okay. I'll think about it. If I'm not too tired and can get myself up maybe I'll join you."

The first rays of the morning sun reflected off the marble floor and stainless steel frame of the patio door as Rita awakened from a hard sleep. Looking at the clock it was only seven and she had plenty of time to make it if she wanted to go on the dive. *What the Heck* she thought. Slipping from the sheets on the queen size bed, Rita rose and made herself a cup of instant coffee in the microwave. After taking a long shower and putting on a new red one-piece swimsuit and white cotton cover up, she placed a few personal items in a large canvas handbag. She though about trying to call Charlie before going out but she knew he would talk her out of this. She wanted to go. She would tell him all about it later. Maybe even make him a little jealous so he'd want to come down and join her.

"Good Morning, Rita."said the handsome man that she met the night before at the bar. He was wearing red and blue, baggy, surfer-style shorts that extended slightly below his knees. He seemed taller than she remembered from the night before. After the second margarita she didn't remember that much. Looking around she noticed a family of four checking out at the front desk but no one else was in the lobby except for the concierge sitting at the desk near the door.

"Am I early?"she replied still looking around.

"No. No. Don't worry. My group decided to go into to town for an early breakfast. We are going to meet them at the pier near Dzul Ha. Is that all right?"he sounded reassuring.

With just a little apprehension Rita decided to go along. "Okay I guess. How many are going with us?"

"Four others plus you and I. There were supposed to be more but there are a few hangovers this morning and they decided to go out this afternoon. Come. I have a Jeep outside."

She followed him out the front doors and down the marble steps to a green Jeep Wrangler, the kind common to the island. He opened the passenger door for her and offered his hand as she boosted herself into the seat. Without saying a word he climbed into the driver's seat and with a quick turn of the key they were off heading south toward the town of San Miguel. The morning salt air washed over her and she enjoyed the view along the malecon – the promenade and main road along the western coastline. The man she knew as Jake drove toward their destination, shifting gears and slowing down for the occasional speed bump. Passing the ferry pier in front of the plaza, a crowd of locals, workers and tourists disembarked and descended upon the awakening central district with its shops, restaurants and bars. The always-present time-share kiosks were already open for business shouting out to the obvious tourists with their cameras, over sized bags ready to cram with souvenirs and pinkish red, sunburned complexions. "Hello Senor. Free Jeep. Free snorkel tour."They barked from the podiums and huts around the plaza. Proceeding further southward, they passed the small soccer field in front of the municipal building and the Mexican Navy barracks. Jake turned toward her and smiled giving her reassurance that they would soon be at the dive boat. Pointing to the newly remodeled hotel on the right she said, "I stayed there when it was called Plaza Las Glorias. I understand that it's an all inclusive now."

"Yes, yes. I remember it."He replied as he picked up speed heading away from town. But as they passed the cruise ship pier at the far end of the strip, where the road split into a four-lane highway, the Jeep pulled off to the side of the road letting a few taxis pass by. Then with a lurch Jake maneuvered a U-turn heading back north and then took a quick right turn onto a dirt road extending into the interior of the island.

"Where are we going?"She asked worriedly.

"I have to stop for a moment at a friend's house. He owes me some money and I need it to pay the boat driver."Kicking up dust on the dirt road the Jeep bounced on the rutted dirt road.

A nervous feeling entered her stomach as she observed his demeanor change. The smile was gone, replaced with furrowed eyebrows and gritted teeth. Further away from the main road and the ocean, the Jeep slowed again and made a sharp right turn down a narrow one lane road with the jungle now extending its reach, leafy branches from banyan trees and other native foliage slapped against the metal frame and window. She had to keep her arms inside to avoid being scratched. Suddenly there was opening and the Jeep pulled into a small clearing and skidded to a stop at the front of a small cinder block shack with a corrugated metal roof and yellow cloth covered windows.

Reaching under the seat, Jake pulled something up with his right hand and pointed it in her direction. The barrel of a small handgun was staring her in the face. "Get out."

"Oh my God!"She exclaimed. "What? What is this?"

"Just get out."He motioned for her to exit the Jeep and pointed with the gun toward the shack.

Grabbing her bag and quickly sliding out of the Jeep, her feet barely touched the ground before he jammed the vehicle into reverse kicking up stones and dust and with equal urgency, lurched back forward sending dust into her eyes as he sped back into the jungle. She never saw the person whose hand reached around her face and covered her mouth and nose with a cloth soaked in an ether-like substance. Rita Jacob barely resisted as her body went limp and was guided to the ground by the man with the rag.

Without uttering a word she was dragged into the dark shack and fitted with a scuba suit and tank. The man – a Mexican, now joined by an accomplice who looked like him only taller, arranged her equipment with expert care and as she began to come around from the slumber, applied the rag one last time before carrying her to an awaiting small white truck at the rear of the shack, placing a blanket over her -out of site in the back cargo area before speeding away toward the oceanfront road. Passing the Chakanob Park and turning down the old road that ran parallel to the new highway, they reached a secluded turnout that led directly to the ocean a few yards from the rocky shore. A small eighteen-foot skiff with a seventy-five horse Honda outboard was waiting for them. After making sure they could not be seen, the two Mexicans wrapped their victim in the blanket and carried her into the boat; laying her in the bottom before shoving off and heading out away from shore. The motor roared and the water churned as they sped out to the reef area. Making sure the oxygen tank was fully expended they placed the mask over Rita's face and tied a heavy sand bag to her feet with a loose knot that would come undone in the currents, but only after the life was gone from her body. Checking the horizon to observe that they were not within eyesight of any of the other dive and snorkel boats, they lifted her over the side watching her sink below the waves with only a few air bubbles rising to the surface.

The next day, the local newspaper Por Esto, reported that the body of a female American tourist had washed ashore, apparently the victim of a diving mishap. It would take another few days before the authorities suspected foul play and by then Jake Anton – not his real name – was back in Las Vegas working for his brother Dominic. The two Mexicans collected a sizeable fee and were soon long gone from Cozumel. The case was ruled a drowning under investigation.

49

Pacing around the living room of the apartment Charlie again dialed the number to the hotel only this time instead of reaching the room the call was intercepted by the front desk. A polite female voice with a slight Mexican accent answered. "May I ask whom you are trying to reach?"

"Miz Jacob. Room four oh one."He replied.

"Excuse me. Can you hold por favor? The hotel manager would like to speak to you."

"Yes. Of Course."Charlie stopped pacing and sat on the couch facing the TV set, which was tuned to CNN. He as worried. Something was wrong. Rita had not retuned his calls for two days. Two days that he had spent in virtual seclusion; his only contact being through Karen Bastow and phone calls to Bob the Banker. He was trying to negotiate a deal that would keep him out of the loop with the Big Beaver project. They would pin the whole thing on Bill Greening who could no longer defend himself or implicate any of them. Karen meanwhile, was diverting all inquiries to other staffers who were told that the Governor was taking a few days to relax from the heavy- workload of the past few months. No one questioned his excuse, as they all knew Charlie V as a high-energy guy who often put in twelve to fifteen hour workdays. Most assumed he had retreated to the Governor's summer residence on Makinac Island, which was in fact exactly what he had planned for his next move.

"Hello. My name is Ernesto Hernandez. I am the hotel manager. Whom are you trying to contact?"

Taking a moment to digest the sequence of events and the

unusual handling of his call, something told him all was not well. Why did they not just connect him to the room? The hotel manager was talking to him not just a desk clerk. "Misses Jacob. Rita Jacob."

"What is your name Senor?"The manager asked.

"My name is …"Hesitating. Not sure if he should give his real name. "Charles. Charles Vandenberg. She might have left my name as an emergency contact. Is everything alright?"

After a pause while Ernesto Hernandez checked over the form that indeed listed the emergency contact name as C. Vandenberg, he delivered the news. "Mister Vandenberg. I am afraid there has been a terrible accident. Mrs. Jacob went diving yesterday and she did not return. Her body was found this morning near one of beaches on the south end of Cozumel. I will give you the number for the local authorities. Perhaps they can provide more information. I am terribly sorry Senor."

Stunned, Charlie dropped to one knee still holding the phone to his ear but unable to speak. This could not be happening. Rita was dead and although the manager said it was an accident, he had his doubts. After taking the name and number for the Cozumel Policia, he thanked the hotel manager for his help and said that he would be in touch regarding Rita's personal effects. Moving to a chair near a window, his eyes were the stage for his grief as the first tear emerged, slowly sliding down his cheek, quickly followed by a steady flow. Realizing, perhaps for the first time, that his love for Rita was deep and profound, not just the physical, playful, relationship they had cultivated over the past few years. His world was coming apart and the one person he knew he could count on was no longer a part of it. Alone. Sad. Confused. Charlie Vandenberg, Governor of The Great State of Michigan was left with a broken heart, soon replaced by anger, as he suspected that Rita's death was no accident. At this moment he gave up any hope of saving his reputation. "Lapone."He said out loud. "Goddam him."

50

Melissa could not stay at her condo. The events from earlier in the day were too upsetting so she collected some clothes and a few personal items and agreed to accompany Dick back to his place in Troy. They barely spoke before finally arriving at one AM. The past few hours had been spent giving statements and answering questions regarding her abduction and the very public shooting death of Joey Palzonian in Royal Oak. The story was now prominently featured on the eleven PM newscasts. All of the local Detroit TV stations had parked distinctively painted vans around the Shrine Church with their station ID numbers boldly featured on all sides and the antennae extended to the sky. Each carefully located so as not to allow the other station's van to be seen. Of course they all had "exclusive" stories. Their number one street reporters, standing with microphones in hand, were taping the reports and preparing for the inevitable live shots during the newscasts. Based on the information that was released they all reported that the still unidentified suspect was wanted for a kidnapping and auto theft. The rest of the background and details were being closely guarded by the Police agencies. No one yet suspected the potential of this story could reach all the way to Lansing.

Shortly after arriving and tossing her bags on a chair, Melissa walked over to the couch and let herself fall back onto the plush leather cushions. As Dick emerged from the kitchen carrying two glasses of brandy, he reached over to turn on a lamp on a side table and handed one of the glasses to her. "Here this will help take the edge off."

"What happens now?" Melissa asked after taking a full sip of the Brandy, welcoming the warm burn as the liquid entered her body.

After a second sip, she already felt light headed and remembered that she had not eaten since lunch which consisted of only a small salad with bread at Panera.

Joining her on the couch he resisted the urge to turn on the TV located on the opposite wall and instead put his arm around her, gently pulling her closer. "There are a number of questions regarding the connection to Mister Jacob and the Hodges kid that we may never get answered now but I do need to speak to Rita Jacob as soon as possible."Not knowing of her murder he continued. "She might be the one that can identify how this guy is connected to a certain development here on Big Beaver near I-75."

"What do you mean?"slightly pulling away and looking at his face. "Do you think Charlie V is behind this?"

Swallowing the last of the brandy with one gulp and throwing his head back momentarily. "I don't think he's behind it but he's involved. So is Bob Banker the principal owner of Great Lakes Bank. I just can't prove it all yet. That's why I need to talk to Rita."

Melissa remembered that she saw a missed call on her phone from Rita's number. There were also unanswered voice mails. "I need to check my voice mail. I think Rita tried to call me a couple of days ago and she might have left me a message. I haven't checked my mail in a few days."

Retrieving the phone from her purse she pressed the buttons to retrieve her voice mail and waited through a few messages from other clients and one from her mother who was always checking in just to be nosy. Finally reaching message number five she listened to the computerized female voice "Thursday, ten fifteen AM."Then the familiar voice of Rita Jacob, telling about her trip and about the envelope in her locker. After hearing the complete message Melissa hit repeat and put her cell phone on speaker. "You should hear this."

After they both listened to the message twice, Dick stood and said. "We need to see the contents of that envelope."Looking at his watch, "Can we get into the club tonight?"

"No. They have an alarm system and I don't have the pass code. Besides it's one AM. I'll take you there tomorrow."She thought about the locker. "We can't just break into her locker you know. I believe there are laws against that."

He stared at her and briefly recalled the many times that he sidestepped the laws in order to further an investigation back in Detroit. As long as you covered your tracks and the prosecutor's office cooperated it was not a problem. But he knew this would be more difficult. He decided to call Carson first and bring him up to date. But all that would wait until morning. The brandy was doing its job and he slumped back into the cushioned couch letting his arms fall by his side and his head lean back. "You're right. We'll deal with all of this tomorrow."

She sat next to him once again and laid her head on his shoulder and neither one spoke as soon they were nodding off. After a short time Melissa, awoke, tugged at his arm and they both shuffled into the bedroom not bothering to turn out the lamp. Exhausted, they fell into the bed without removing their clothes and quickly fell asleep.

Michael Ripinski

51

Paul had been in a few close calls before but through his connections in the Chicago Police Department and city hall, he was always able to avoid being directly linked to any illegal activity. The closest he came to being prosecuted was a bribery scandal involving an Illinois State Senator who was sent to prison for exchanging money for votes on a highway construction bill. The route of a new highway connector ramp was conveniently moved to force the demolition of two vacant building owned on paper by his mother Maria Lapone a silent shareholder in Lapone Enterprises. An Alzheimer's patient in a nursing home, she had no idea what her son was doing. Paul received much more than the buildings were worth. The construction company, which built the project and overcharged the state for materials and labor, was owned by the senator's nephew. By the time the prosecutor got done with the senator and his nephew there was no desire to go any further.

It had been six hours since he last heard from Joey and he sensed something was not right. Almost absentmindedly he picked up the TV remote control from the coffee table and pressed the red button as the eleven PM news had just began. A very cute, thirty something, blonde holding a microphone standing in front of what appeared to be a gray, stone church began her report by saying that the Royal Oak police still were not releasing the name of the man who was killed in the spectacular chase and shoot-out earlier in the evening. The camera panned the scene showing the crashed G-six and several bystanders lined up next to the yellow crime scene tape stretched around the area. A couple of teenage boys jumped up and down behind the blonde, their goofy faces alternately popping in and out of the frame. Among the minimal information released to the media was the allegation that the deceased suspect was involved in the kidnapping of a health club employee and the theft of a vehicle at Somerset Mall. Paul sank into the couch as the last bit of information came from the blonde on his TV screen. "One more thing Steve."Speaking to the news anchor back in the studio. "One of my sources tells me the suspect was from Chicago and may be connected to other crimes in Metro Detroit. I'll keep working on this story."

Having checked into this hotel after leaving Bob the Banker's office he knew right away that things had gotten messed up. His next phone call would not be pleasant. The boss was going to flip out when he delivered this news. It was going to be very difficult to stop the bleeding on this whole situation and he knew that it would take drastic action. He hoped that Joey was smart enough to destroy any evidence that would leave a trail. They had talked about this before - what to do in case he was close to being caught. The Mercedes had already been reported stolen back in Chicago, the report would be back-dated by a few days by one of Paul's friends on the Chicago PD. Joey had ditched his cell phone in a trash bin at the gas station and he carried no valid ID on his person. If the trail led back to Chicago and Lapone Enterprises, Joey would be ID'd as a disgruntled ex-employee who was fired for his drinking and drug problems. One phone call and anything connecting Joey as a recent employee would disappear. His presence in Detroit would be explained as revenge against Paul by threatening his business associates. It could get sticky but he was confident that they could at least divert any investigation. Like Joey, he had a personal contingency plan to leave the country with a new identity. First there was the matter at hand. Charlie and Bob knew too much and he'd have to deal with them. After his call with The Boss he was certain what to do next. He called Bob the Banker.

"Yeah, Bob here."Answering in his familiar loud voice.

"We got more problems. We need to set up a meeting with Charlie ASAP. Tonight if possible. Tell him we want to work things out with him. Tell him we will help him stay out of this mess. I want Sam there too."

Surprised by the change in tone from their earlier meeting Bob was skeptical. "What problems? Why do you want to help him after you said he was screwing us?"

"I can't explain right now. Just get a hold of him and set up a meeting. Let me know where and when."

Bob was still skeptical but decided to go along. He already had a meeting scheduled with Sam Ford and knew that he'd be available. "I'll call you back as soon as I talk to him. What if he won't meet with us?"

"Make it happen Bob. Tell him the newspapers will receive some information about him that will end his political career if he doesn't."

Knowing that attacking Charlie's ego was the best way to persuade him to cooperate he agreed. "Yeah. I'll tell him. Any place special you want to meet?"

Paul was thinking ahead about what he'd have to do but he didn't want to scare either of them. "Let him pick the place. He'll feel safer."

"Good idea."

After finishing the call with Bob, he opened his briefcase and extracted a black leather binder with critical information regarding the next steps in his plan. The binder contained names and phone numbers of persons that would be able to provide necessary services. He had not called some of them in a long time but he knew he could count on their help, for a price of course. He was waiting for the location of the meeting before he could finalize details but he had people on stand-by waiting for his call. It was after one AM when Bob Called back.

"Day after tomorrow at the governor's summer home on Mackinac Island. Charlie wants to meet us at a little airport in Pelston at noon and we'll all fly up to the Island together. He says he's glad that you want to help him. He also said that he knows about Rita and he's afraid. He doesn't want anything to happen to him."

"Why not tomorrow? We really need to resolve this now."

Bob had tried to get Charlie's agreement on a meeting for the next day but Charlie refused saying he had to make some arrangements first. "He said that it'd take a day to get everything organized up there. We can't just drop in unannounced, he's telling his staff that it is just a part of his extended vacation."

A smile came to Paul, the first time all day. Things were going better that expected. "Good. That's the perfect place. We'll be away from the action down here. I heard it's quite nice up there this time of year."

"Yes. Yes. It's really nice and peaceful. When will you tell me what you are going to offer him? "Still a little skeptical.

"I'll tell you on the way. Pick me up Monday morning at the Troy Marriot. What time do we need to leave?"

"I'll pick you up at eight. It's about three, four hours to Pelston."

"I'll be ready."He almost hung up before remembering one more thing. "Oh before I forget. No assistants. Just the governor, us and Sam if you can get in touch with him.

"I am sure he'll be available. See you Monday at eight."

52

Charlie paced the room waiting for Karen's call. It was Sunday morning, six AM and he had not slept at all after talking to Bob the night before. Things had gone too far. Rita was dead and he knew that he could be next, even if he was the governor.

The Governors summer cottage is a magnificent old Victorian home built in nineteen hundred and two and sits on a bluff high over the Straits of Mackinac. The home was sold to the State by a Detroit Family in the nineteen forties. It features eleven bedrooms and nine bathrooms. Frequently used by governors over the years to entertain dignitaries and political friends the home was managed by a foundation, which also offered guided tours when the governor was not occupying the stately home. There would be no tours on Monday. But there would be a few guests and some surprises.

Unfolding the slip of paper he had retrieved from his wallet Charlie looked at the name and number. Something about this Hagan fellow made him think that he could help with his plan. Recalling the conversation on Thursday at the Big Beaver site, he got the sense that Mister Hagan was the right guy to act as a go-between with the police and possibly the FBI. He dialed the number.

After six rings he heard the somewhat familiar voice on the message. "This is Dick Hagan. Leave your message and a number. I'll get back to you."

After the annoying instruction and necessary beep, Charlie left his message. "Mister Hagan. This is Governor Vandenberg. I must speak with you right away. Please call me." After leaving his new cell phone number he added. "You cannot tell anyone that I called. I hope that I can trust you."

His next move required the help of Karen. He would avoid telling her all the details but it was up to her to make the arrangements on Mackinac Island. She arrived at the apartment with coffee and bagels shortly after eight AM.

"We are going to the island."He said before she even placed the coffee on the kitchen counter.

Looking at him with curiosity she replied. "When?"

"Monday morning. Me, Bob, Sam and Lapone."Approaching her as she handed him the coffee he continued. "You will go there tomorrow and make some arrangements. I want this kept low key and discreet."He was now standing very close and for a moment she felt her heart rate speed up and a warm sensation in her chest. She had felt this way before when he was near and she was confused and nervous. Their relationship was always professional except that one time but there was no way she could ignore the sexual tension of the moment and then he told her the shocking news. When he placed a hand on her shoulder she noticed the wetness in his eyes. "Rita is dead. They found her body on a beach in Mexico."

"Oh my God. No!"She exclaimed as she stepped away briefly. "No. No. It can't be true."

"I'm afraid so. I spoke with the hotel manager in Cozumel and they say it was diving accident."

Reaching out toward Charlie she drew him close to her and pressed her head against his chest as her own tears welled up. "I am so sorry for you. I don't understand how this could happen. First Walt and now Rita. What's going on? This is crazy."She stopped herself as he pushed her away gently so he could look at her face.

A single tear merged with his quivering lower lip as he began to explain to her as much as he could. "I believe Rita's death was no accident. This whole deal with Bob and Lapone has gotten out of control. She knew too much. I told her things and they worried about her talking."A long silence followed as Charlie just gazed out of the kitchen window. Thoughts of what might have been if this stupid deal hadn't blown up distracted him for the moment. The cabinet position, Washington social circles, the big political stage. It was going to be fun with Rita along and probably Karen too. Not any more. Now all he cared about was making sure he got even with Paul Lapone and Bob the Banker. They were going to pay. And now he needed Karen's help to pull it off.

She looked at him worriedly. "Are you alright?"

Returning from his distracted thoughts he said. "Yes. Yes. But I need your help. You are going on ahead to the cottage to make some arrangements. If anyone asks, I am still on a mini vacation and I will be meeting with some old friends for lunch. When you get there I expect that Mister Hagan will contact you. You should cooperate fully with him and give him the details of this meeting when he gets there. Understand?"

Confused for the moment she looked at him. "Hagan? Isn't that the guy who spoke to you at the ceremony last week?"

"Yup.Him. I am expecting a call back soon and I think he'll cooperate."

Karen didn't like the sound of this and she made it clear to Charlie. "Are you sure about this? I mean won't you be implicated as well? What about the media? You can't keep them away for long. As soon as the papers and TV gets wind of this they'll come after you."

"Let 'em come. I'm ready to take the hit. We're talking about murder here Karen. Lapone is a murderer. And Bob is now in it with him. I don't care how far we go back, he crossed the line. I'm done with him."

The reality of his plan had sunk in for her. It was probably over. The governorship. Washington. All of it. She felt angry and disgusted but she was still loyal to Charlie V. If this were the way he was going out, then she would help him. After all she liked Rita too. Maybe Charlie would be able to come out of this with minimal damage. She talked herself into believing somehow, someway things would still turn out. "I'll do whatever you need me to do."She reached out to him and wrapped her arms around his waist. "I'm still with you."

Charlie looked down at her face and returned the hug. "Thank you. I don't know how I'll repay you, but I will. I promise."

Michael Ripinski

53

Melissa heard the faint sound of Dick's cell phone from the living room. He had left it in his jacket which was hanging on the back of a chair .As she glanced at the red numbers on the clock radio next to the bed she saw that it was six thirty. *Too early to get up yet*, she thought, gazing at his face, his eyes closed and a breathing deeply. She decided to ignore the phone and placing her arm around his shoulder she closed her eyes and drifted back to sleep.

After making his way to the bathroom, splashing water on his face Dick looked in the mirror as he sorted through the events of the past few days. It was like he was working again and he now remembered why he retired. It sucked. The stress. The fatigue on his body. The pain in the ass criminals he had to deal with. At that moment he decided to tell Carson that his answer was "No."He just wanted to stay retired and play golf. As he stood there observing the lines on his face he heard the faint sound of his cell phone in his jacket pocket. He thought about not answering.

After listening to the message he returned to the bedroom where Melissa had awakened but was still laying in bed. "I just got a message from the governor. He wants me to call him right away."

"What do you think he wants?"

"Don't know. But I have a hunch this has something to do with last night."Walking over to the bed he sat on the edge and kissed her gently on the cheek. "I still want to look inside Rita's locker this morning. Why don't you get cleaned up while I make this call."

Doing as he requested, Melissa gathered her overnight bag and retreated to the bathroom. Dick went to the kitchen and started a pot of coffee before locating a pad of paper and dialed Charlie at the number he provided.

The governor answered on the second ring. "Hello. Who is this?"

"Governor, its Dick Hagan. You asked me to call you."

After a few seconds Charlie replied. "Yes I did. Thank you for calling back. Mister Hagan I don't know exactly how to say this but I'm going to get right to the point. I need your help."

The old adrenaline rush of being on the case replaced his thoughts of a few moments before. "Okay, sir. How can I help you?"

Charlie began by asking for his complete confidence, which Hagan reluctantly agreed to. There was something about this man. Call it the Charlie V charm or maybe it was just the fact that he was governor of Michigan. Charlie continued. "Tomorrow I am meeting with some men on Mackinac Island. I believe you have met one of them. Bob Banker. The others are Paul Lapone and Sam Ford."

Dick recalled his encounter with Bob the Banker. "I spoke with Banker at the funeral of Walt Jacob."

Rita's death had not yet been reported and Charlie felt that he needed to fill him in. "Mister Hagan, I know that you had also spoken with Rita Jacob. I am afraid that I have some disturbing news for you. She's dead."

"What? How? I thought she was in Mexico."

"She was."The governor continued. "I am being told it was a scuba diving accident. But…"He couldn't finish as his words became difficult.

"But what governor?"

After regaining his composure Charlie was able to explain. "What I am about to tell you could cost me my job and more. I can't really go to the police or FBI but I am going to ask you to act on my behalf. I can assure you that I have no desire to save my own ass. I want these other guys to pay for what they have done. Can I trust you Mister Hagan? Will you help me?"

This was an unfamiliar feeling. Having been involved in several big cases over the years in Detroit, Dick had been used to dealing with unexpected developments. Suspects who wanted to make a deal or victims that probably deserved what they had gotten. There was even a case that involved the top aide to a U. S. Congressman who Dick was sure had covered up for his boss but could never be proven. There was also the famous case of the ex-mayor of Detroit and a stripper but nothing like this. He had to remind himself that he was speaking to the Governor of Michigan. Not some common crook or thug in the city. "I'm listening."

"Please. I need to know that you will help me and be discreet, at least for now."His voice raised and more agitated.

Looking back toward the bathroom he could hear the water running and felt that Melissa was not able to hear. "Well Governor, you called me. You are putting me in an awkward position here. If you tell me something that involves criminal activity and I intentionally withhold the information, I could be breaking the law as well. But I am going to help you anyway."

"Good. Thanks. I assure you I want justice to be done here."

"Not so fast."Dick replied. "I want you to know that I will only help you as long as I am not asked to break any laws."

Charlie decided to proceed. He didn't have much time and he really had no other choices. There was something about this ex-cop who he had only met once. He remembered that Rita was friendly with his girlfriend and somehow there was a connection. "I want you to go to Mackinac Island as soon as possible. You will meet with one of my aides, Karen Bastow."

He remembered her as being difficult during their prior conversation but he assumed that she was doing her job. "I have spoken with Miss Bastow before."

"Yes. Yes. I guess you would have. Well when you get to the island she'll fill you in. There will be a meeting that I want you to hear. Karen is going to make arrangements to have the conversation taped. The others won't know."

"That's illegal governor."

"I know. I know. But only if it is used in a court of law. If you personally hear the conversation, you can be a witness. The tape will be my insurance. Once they know they can't beat this thing I am sure they will follow my lead. At least Bob and Sam anyway. Lapone, I am not so sure about."

Not sure where the governor was going with this Dick asked. "What do you mean?"

"I am fairly certain that Lapone had something to do with Rita's death and he was responsible for Walt's as well. That was no suicide."

Thinking about the prior evening and all the events of the past week, Dick began to put the pieces together. This Lapone seemed to be the missing link and quite possibly an associate of the guy he had killed in front of the church. But what did the Hodges kid have to do with it? Was he just in the wrong place at the wrong time? It looked that way. He could have stayed on the sidelines and let Carson handle this by himself but as it now developed he was right in the middle of probably the largest political scandal in the state's history.

As he was about to speak he noticed Melissa coming out of the bathroom. She had a curious expression and mouthed the words "Charlie?"

Holding up one finger toward her he spoke into the phone. "Just a moment sir."And then speaking to her. "You'd better sit down. I have something to tell you as soon as I am off the phone with the governor."

Holding her hand to her mouth she eased herself into the chair next to the sofa. Eyes wide and attentive she listened to the rest of the conversation.

Charlie asked. "Who is that with you?"

"My friend Melissa who is also a friend of Rita's as you might know. She is Rita's personal trainer."He was now most eager to retrieve the contents of Rita's locker at the health club remembering the voice mail.

Annoyed that Dick was not alone, Charlie sternly advised him of the seriousness of this matter and suggested that he keep things confidential for now. But he was not aware of what they had endured the previous night and was taken back by Dick's reply.

"Excuse me sir. Before you dictate what we can and cannot discuss, I think you should know that this lady and I narrowly escaped being harmed, even killed, by a man who I suspect is an associate of your Mister Lapone and Bob the Banker. Unfortunately this slime ball can't tell us anything because I had to put a few rounds into his worthless ass and he died before we could get any answers. So, with all due respect, I think you had better just back off."His lips pursed and his eyes squinted as he waited for the governor's reply.

"I...I...Had no idea. What happened? Are either of you hurt? "

Dick paused for a moment as he observed Melissa sitting there in disbelief at how he was speaking to the famous and powerful Charlie V, Governor of The Great State of Michigan. Gathering himself, Dick spoke calmly. "We are fine. I really don't want to discuss the details and as I said, I'm going to help you Governor. But I must tell you that Melissa is coming with me. And she is knowledgeable about this whole affair. If anything goes wrong, she will be able speak for me. This is not negotiable. Understand?"

"Understood. I didn't realize they had gotten to you. It is all the more important that we put a stop to this. I'm sorry if I offended you."

"It's okay. Now tell me what you want me to do once we get to Mackinac Island."Dick had a pen and pad ready to take notes.

After laying out his plan and giving Hagan instruction to meet with Karen once he arrived on the island, Charlie advised him of a place for accommodations. "I'll make sure you have a room at the Market Street Inn. It's a cozy B & B near the center of town. The owner is a long time supporter. He'll take care of you. Make sure that you and Karen get everything set up ahead of time. Once we get what we need I'll decide how to handle my resignation."Just saying those words made the blood empty from his head. Sitting down for the first time during the entire conversation, Charlie had one more thing to say. "Mister Hagan, I want you and Melissa to know that I really did love Rita Jacob. She was a wonderful woman. And she didn't deserve what happened to her."

Sensing the emotion and sincerity of the moment, Dick could only respond softly. "Yes sir. I believe you."

After reviewing the plan one more time Charlie thanked him for his help and promised to see him on the island the next day.

Placing the phone on the table, he moved to the sofa and motioned to Melissa to sit next to him. Placing his arm over her shoulder and pressing his lips to her forehead he held her tight as he disclosed the news of Rita's death. As expected she did not take it well. Angrily, she screamed. "No. No No." as she pounded her fist on the padded cushions. He just held her tight and let her release the anger. Later he would fill her in on the rest of the phone call and explain the reason for the sudden trip to Mackinac. They would need to leave before noon and it was now nine AM.

54

Besides being an accomplished sailor and yachtsman, Sam Ford was also a pretty good pilot. When Bob called about the meeting with the Governor he insisted on flying them all up to the Island in his Cesna. Instead of meeting in Pelston they would meet at Flint Bishop Airport. That slight change put a small wrench in Paul's plan. He had to scramble but the necessary calls were made and soon everything was back on target. He would meet Sam, Bob and Charlie in Flint and they would fly up to the island together. At least that was what he told them. Paul had other ideas.

As expected the Troy and Royal Oak police departments were inquiring about Joey Palzonian and his activities of the past few weeks. Paul had prearranged the cover up story back in Chicago before leaving. They were told that Joey was a part time security guard who had lied about his prison record and was subsequently fired from Lapone Enterprises about 3 weeks ago. They were unaware of his whereabouts and he had stolen the Mercedes. A statement issued by Paul through one of his secretaries said that they were shocked and saddened by the behavior of this ex-employee and would cooperate fully with the police in Michigan. A TV news report vaguely linked Lapone Enterprises to Walt Jacob and indirectly to Charlie V. Paul figured he could hold them off long enough to implement his plan and by the time anyone figured it out he'd be long gone out of the country. His only remaining loose end was the Boss. The last phone call was not pleasant but he didn't care any more. After Monday no one would be able to find him and all of the evidence would point to Bob the Banker and Charlie V.

Sitting in a webbed chair on his balcony, Paul watched the sun descend behind the adjacent building as he sipped a glass of Jack Daniels on the rocks. He wondered how it had gotten to this. After all the Big Beaver project wasn't the most significant deal he had ever manipulated. The only reason he got involved was because he was told that it mattered to the success of their business. Of course he knew about all the Michigan connections. That was how he met Sam Ford and later Bob the Banker. Sam was okay he thought but Mister Banker was a real scumbag. And he knew scumbags. He met enough of them in his time and most of them were crooks, thugs and low life fraud artists. Bob was just like all the rest only he had accumulated a lot more money. He'd seen everything from dishonest stockbrokers to shifty insurance agents. He even was familiar with a few morally bankrupt politicians and to him; Charlie V was just another rat in the pack. All of them smiling to your face while trying to squeeze the blood out of your hand and the money from your bank account. He had no use for politicians except when he needed to bribe one, which was never hard to do. Someday, he figured, one of his deals would fall apart and then he'd have to cover his tracks. That someday had arrived. The emergency getaway plan, which he'd developed a long time ago, was now ready to be implemented. Only a few more details.

After darkness enveloped the balcony, Paul returned to his living room, turned on the lamp and sat on the couch. A recent phone message from his assistant in Chicago, Mary Ann, confirmed the inquiries about Joey Palzonian. Mary Ann was a loyal employee and although she suspected that all of Paul's business ventures were not entirely legit, she did not ask too many questions. He rewarded her generously and she helped him maintain a low profile. She would be okay he thought, even after the police or Feds came looking for him. Even she would not know where he would be. Later on he planned to send her a substantial amount of money anonymously.

Finally, the call came. He answered on the second ring. "Hey Sam. Did you get things all arranged?"

Sam Ford replied confidently. "All set. We'll meet in Flint and fly up to the Island together. Bob wasn't happy about it and Charlie seemed to be annoyed but everyone agreed that this meeting is a good idea. Do you really think we can shut this project down with minimal damage?"

Paul had explained that he was sure they could put the blame on Bill Greening for not disclosing the biohazards at the site. "Yeah sure. We just need to get our stories straight." And then he added. "There is one more thing. There will be a UPS package at the airport with some important files on a laptop inside. I sent it there today. It is addressed to you. I called the desk at the executive terminal and they will hold it there until you arrive. If I am running late make sure it goes on the plane with you."

"No problem. Aren't you driving up with Bob in the morning?"

"Right now, that's the plan, but I could be delayed here for a bit and might have to meet you there." He lied knowing that he would be headed elsewhere. He had no intention of joining them on that flight.

Sam was not suspicious and decided that it was no big deal that Paul could be delayed. It never crossed his mind that he was being set up. "Good then. We'll see you tomorrow."

"Good night Sam. See you tomorrow." After he hung up, Paul poured another glass of Jack Daniels and turned on the TV. A redneck comedian was telling unfunny jokes on the Comedy Channel so he changed to a baseball game on cable. Ironically it was the Chicago Cubs playing at Wrigley Field. He'd been there many times and for the moment he was saddened by the realization that he'd probably never be able to see a game there again. He hoped that he could get the games on satellite TV once he got settled in Costa Rica. That was where he was headed as a retired Canadian real estate broker from Calgary. Entering Canada from the border at the north tip of Minnesota he had been planning this move for ten years but he didn't plan to go there so soon. But now that Joey was dead it was only a matter of time before they caught up to him.

Michael Ripinski

55

As they drove to the Health Club, Melissa at the wheel, Dick had made the decision to call Sean Carson and bring him into the loop. He wasn't sure what was going to happen on Mackinac Island but he knew that somehow this was going to be tied into the Hodges case, which was the only crime that involved Sean's jurisdiction. He wasn't even sure whom to call about Rita Jacob. The Feds? Probably, but he was going to let Sean handle that. And as far as Royal Oak was concerned they were wrapping up the shooting at the church. Now he found himself assisting the governor and he wasn't sure what he was doing was entire legal.

"Carson here." Sean answered with his usual reply even though he recognized the familiar name on his cell phone.

"Hi. It's Dick. How's the eye?" Thoughtfully he inquired about Sean's injury from shootout with Joey Palzonian.

"It's sore. Just a scratch though. Another inch higher and I'd be missing an eye .How are you and your girl doing?"

Melissa steered the Saab into a parking space at the club, which was already busy with the weekend workout regulars. Dick continued on his call. "I've got a lot to tell you and it's getting very interesting. I received a call from the Governor this morning."

Carson interrupted. "The one and only Charlie V?"

"Yep. And wait till I tell you what he said." He paused for a moment because he wasn't quite sure exactly how much he was going to tell Sean. "Melissa and I are going to Mackinac Island today. We are supposed to meet up with one of Charlie's aide's who is going to arrange for us to eavesdrop on a meeting. He says that we will find out about who killed Walt Jacob and a cover up that includes Bob Banker and another guy named Lapone who is connected to the guy I shot last night. And get this. Rita Jacob is dead."

"What? You kidding me?"Carson was stunned.

"Yeah, it seems she knew too much and they got her out of the way. Supposedly it was a diving accident in Mexico, but Charlie is convinced she was murdered. He has asked me to be a sort of go between for him and whomever I feel are the right authorities in this case. I guess we should contact the FBI and that's what I want you to do."

Thinking about what he had just heard, Sean was concerned about what his old friend was doing. "Are you sure that you are not being set up?"

"Pretty sure. Charlie was in love with Rita and now he wants to get the guys who are responsible including his old crony, Bob the Banker. I want to play this as he has requested but I think we should have some FBI presence on the island. Their jurisdiction is a conspiracy to cover up a murder and possible bribery of a government official. That should peak their interest."

Considering what he had just been told, Sean Carson was skeptical but decided to go along with Dick's request. He knew a few people at the Detroit office of the FBI and was certain they would want a piece of this. The challenge was getting everyone up to Mackinac Island in time for tomorrow's meeting. "I'll get in touch with Bill Tasker with the FBI. You remember him from the Carlissa Cummings investigation?"He was referring to a corrupt Detroit City Councilwomen who was part of a drug-money laundering ring. She died of a stroke before being brought to trial.

"Yeah. I remember Bill. Good man. Do you know him well enough and do you think he'd be able to get it together by tomorrow?"

"We play poker once a month with a few other guys from the old days. Johnny Rodgers, Ken Patterson, Eddie Marino and some guys from the FBI that Bill works with. He'll be creamin his jeans over this."

Dick felt relieved that his old friend would be able to come through. Now all he had to do was get his hands on the contents of Rita's locker and then they'd be on their way up north. "I'll be staying at the Market Street Inn on the island and you can give Bill my cell number. I think it'll be okay up there don't you?"

"You should be okay. I think by now they have all the latest technology. I think they even have indoor plumbing."Laughing sarcastically because everyone knew that they did not allow cars on Mackinac Island, only horses and bicycles for the most part. It was part of the charm and allure of the place – along with all the fudge shops, family style restaurants and quaint hotels.

"There's one more thing."Dick interrupted. "Melissa had a message from Rita Jacob before she left for Mexico. She has left something for me in her locker at the Health club; we are headed there right now. And before you say anything about an illegal search, I know what I am doing. Her voice message all but gives Melissa permission to open the locker. I believe Rita was trying to protect herself from these guys and also from Charlie. Even though she loved him, I don't think she entirely trusted him. She was worried for her safety and as it looks now, rightfully so."

Carson didn't have time to dissuade his friend from the search. He had to move fast if he was going to contact Bill Tasker and get things in place. "Alright. But be careful. We don't need any tainted evidence if this goes the way we both think it's going. Call me when you are on you way to the island."

Giving his assurance that he'd stay in touch Dick concluded. "I'll let you know what we find in her locker and I'll call as soon as we are on our way. Thanks again man."

"You got it. Talk to you later."After he hung up, Sean realized the magnitude of what they were dealing with. The Governor of major midwestern state was about to implicate some powerful people in a major criminal case, including possible murder, while exposing himself to certain impeachment or resignation. He knew that they had to dot the I's and cross the T's all the way.

Michael Ripinski

56

Arriving in Mackinaw City on the mainland, Dick parked near the Arnold Ferry docks in the area designated for those staying overnight on Mackinac Island. Most of the parking was reserved for the day tourists who went over on the large ferryboats staying for a few hours. Only enough time to take a horse drawn carriage ride and buy several pounds of overpriced famous Machinac Island Fudge. The locals called these people "Fudgies" and as soon as the six-oh-clock boat left with that last big throng, sunburned and carrying bags of souvenirs, the island settled into a calmness amid the occasional bicycle bell and rhythmic clapping of horse hooves. You could actually hear the wind blowing off the Straits as the sun dropped into the deep blueness of Lake Michigan just beyond the great Mackinac Bridge. Five miles in length connecting the lower and upper peninsulas of Michigan it is one of the engineering marvels of the twentieth century.

After a relatively smooth ride to the island they checked into the Market Street Inn, a cute B & B located at the bottom of the hill at the top of which was located the historic Fort Mackinac. Dick remembered working as a volunteer guide at the fort with the Boy Scouts when he was twelve years old. They got to spend a free week on the island as part of a summer camp project as long as they spent four hours a day as guides offering directions to the tourists. He had forgotten the hourly cannon shot that was part of the ceremonies associated with the tour of the fort. Two young men dressed as nineteenth century soldiers wearing triangle shaped hats, white knickers and red coats with shiny brass buttons loaded the cannon and set the charge as a puff of white smoke emerged from the barrel followed by a rumbling boom that could be heard all over the island. Melissa practically jumped into his arms as the noise startled them both. Dick glanced at his watch. It was three PM.

"I need to contact Miss Bastow."He said retrieving the cell phone from his pocket. "I want to let her know we have arrived."

Melissa frowned, hoping that they could check into the room first and decided to proceed inside leaving him standing on the porch to make the call. Karen Bastow answered on the first ring.

"Miss Bastow. This is Dick Hagan. I am at the Market Street Inn. How soon can we meet?"

Karen was awaiting this call and had made arrangements to have him picked up by a horse drawn taxi. "Someone will pick you up in a few minutes to bring you to the governor's cottage. We will discuss everything once you get here. Are you alone?"

"No. My friend Melissa is with me and you should know that she is aware of what is happening."

"You must come alone Mister Hagan. It is important that we contain the matter to as few people as possible. I am sure you understand."

Not wanting to get into an argument about containment, Dick agreed. "Okay. I'll be ready in five minutes."

"Good. We have a lot to go over. I'll be waiting for you here."

After hanging up Dick thought how naive she was to think that this could be contained. This can of shit had been opened and there was no putting the contents back inside, no matter what Karen Bastow thought. He wondered if Charlie had told her everything and if she knew that he had more or less resigned himself to no longer being governor. He would find out soon enough.

Joining Melissa in the room after she checked them in, he told her of his plans. "I am going to meet with her in a few minutes. She asked that you not come along. I think that would best for now anyway. I'll send for you as soon as I think it's okay."

She didn't argue. "I need to get some rest anyway."Flopping herself prone onto the queen size brass bed she told him to go ahead. "I already check my cell phone and I have service here. Call me as soon as you know more."

Reaching over the bed, he kissed her on the forehead and turned to leave. "If a guy named Tasker comes by looking for me, give him my cell number. He's the FBI contact."

As he stepped out onto the porch he noticed a red cariaidge pulled buy a single horse waiting in the street. The driver spoke. "Mister Hagan?"

"Yes."

"I am here to take you to the governor's cottage."

Dick stepped up into the back seating area as the drive cracked a buggy whip and the horse clopped ahead toward their destination. He wondered how all this was going to play out. Reaching into his coat pocket he retrieved the envelope that they had taken from Rita Jacob's locker examining the contents once more. Opening the carefully folded note he read Rita's instructions to Melissa.

Dear Melissa,

If you are reading this, something terrible has probably happened and I am sorry for dragging you into this mess. You have been very nice to me and there is no one else I truly can trust. Enclosed you will see the suicide note from Walt. I believe he was forced to sign it. He never used the name Walter as long as I knew him and I think he was trying to tell me something. You should also know that Bob Banker and his associates are blackmailing Charlie over a recent land deal. It is all connected. Please give this information to your friend Mister Hagan. He will know what to do next. Ask him to try and help Charlie. Thank you and God bless you.

Rita

The other folded piece of paper he left in the envelope. He had already examined the suicide note and he did not want to handle it any further knowing that forensics could possible find traces of evidence that would be useful later on. For a moment he thought about just handing this whole thing over to the FBI but after recalling the shoot out with Joey Palzonian he felt like he was personally invested.

Michael Ripinski

57

Sam Ford flew from Detroit City Airport up to Flint in the Cessna, arriving after only twenty minutes in the air. As promised the package from Paul Lapone was waiting for him at the executive terminal and without thinking twice he signed for it and placed it in the plane so he would not forget later. Taking a seat in a leather chair in the finely appointed lounge area, he glanced through a copy of the weekend edition of the Wall Street Journal and nodded to three other men wearing casual clothes seated around a coffee table. Sam guessed correctly that they were on their way to one of the golf resorts in upper Michigan. Treetops or perhaps Grand Traverse. Glancing at his watch he realized that he had an hour before the rest of the group would join him.

Charlie arrived first in the green Lincoln being driven by Don Stinson who was not thrilled that the governor was traveling on the plane without a bodyguard. Charlie explained that there was no room and that Don should drive on up and take the ferry over to the island. Karen would then make arrangements for him at the mansion. He was to be kept in the dark about the purpose and details of the meeting. Opening the glass door to the terminal all heads turned as the three golfers and the girl at the desk instantly recognized the governor.

Sam rose and walked directly over to the desk offering his hand. "Governor. It's great to see you again. We're just waiting for the others to arrive."

Shaking Sam's hand firmly he responded. "Good. The sooner we get up there the better." Then turning to Don he ordered him to proceed on the road. "You'd better get going. It will take few hours to get to the ferry docks and you know how busy it gets this time of year.

I'll see you at the cottage."

"All right sir. Are you sure you'll be alright on this trip?"Don was comfortable with Sam's flying but when he had been told that Bob the Banker and Paul Lapone were the other members of the party he had some reservations. He'd been around long enough to know that these guys were a little on the shady side and he just had an uneasy feeling.

"I'm okay Don. I'll see you later on the island."Holding the door he encouraged his aide to be on his way.

An awkward moment followed as Sam and Charlie stood watching the green car drive away and then faced each other without speaking. Finally Sam offered. "Can I get you anything Charlie? Coffee? Pop? Water?"

Looking around and noticing the three men staring, he smiled at them and nodded using the old Charlie V charm as all three nodded back and returned to their conversation discussing the newest technology in golf clubs. "Maybe a bottled water. Thanks."

Retrieving two Desani's from a vending machine, Sam motioned with his head for Charlie to join him at the far end of the terminal, which was really nothing more than a large room, about twenty by forty with dark Berber carpet and dark green walls. Recessed spotlights gave a soft glow among the leather chairs and glass top tables arranged in clusters of four. Sam and Charlie sat adjacent to each other in an area where their conversation would not be heard.

After taking a sip of his water, Charlie leaned toward Sam. "Are you aware of everything that's going on? I mean everything Sam? I need to know because I may want to keep you out of some parts of this meeting...."Looking back over his shoulder and lowering his voice even further. "For your own protection."

Narrowing his eyes and slanting his head slightly with a quizzical look, Sam replied. "I know that we are meeting to figure out what to do about the Big Beaver project. According to Bob it looks like our friend the late Mister Greening may have left a paper trail regarding our discussions with him last month."

Charlie tried to assess Sam's body language and the sincerity of his voice - two conversation skills that had served him well over the years. He usually knew if somebody was being less than forthright. Concluding that Sam really did not know all the details of Walt and Rita's deaths and probably didn't realize the extent of the cover up, he spared his friend any further involvement for now. "Listen. When we are meeting at the cottage I may ask you to leave the room. Don't be offended. There are some matters that only involve me, Paul and Bob. Are you okay with that?"

"Sure. Sure. I understand. But I need to know if the lid is going to blow on this land deal so I can have my own attorney protect my interest. You understand where I 'm coming from right?"

Sometimes Charlie was surprised by Sam's cleverness. He could come across, as a bit of a clown and not too bright but it was a pretty good act that had served him well over the years. Especially with the ladies. "Yeah I know." said the governor before taking another long sip from the plastic water bottle.

For the next fifteen minutes the two men sat mostly silent waiting for the other members of the group. Occasionally Charlie glanced over his shoulder back at the three golfers who were now in a heated debate about which course was the most challenging. Sam was leafing through a copy of Newsweek and had decided on a diet cola instead of the water, which sat on the table untouched. From time to time the roar of a jet engine could be heard from the runway, which was located only a few hundred yards from where they sat.

Bob entered through the glass door with a cell phone against his ear and was obviously upset about something. Sam rose and waved for him to join them at the other side of the room. Bob held up one finger suggesting that he'd join them in a minute. At this same time, a man in a green nylon jacket who seemed to be telling them to follow him out to a waiting plane joined the golfers. One of them, a short balding man wearing a bright yellow Nike shirt with matching blue cap came half way across the room to get Charlie's attention. "Keep up the good work Governor. Keep those tax cuts coming."

"Thank you, Thank you. We are working hard every day." Slipping into the Charlie V mode and flashing his famous smile.

The golfer turned and left, delighted that he just had a conversation with the famous Charlie V, Governor of The Great State of Michigan. By the time the story would be retold three or four times he would be giving advice on the economic policy for the entire state and the Governor would become his good friend Charlie V.

Standing with his hands on his hips looking very annoyed Bob shared what had made him upset. "Paul is not coming with us."

Together Sam and Charlie Shouted. "What?"

"He's not coming on the flight. He's going to meet us on the island. Something came up and he had to stay back in Detroit for a few hours. At first he said he'd meet us here when I went to pick him up this morning and now he just called and said he would make arrangements to fly up later today."

Charlie was skeptical. "Are you sure he's not up to something?"

"I don't know. He's the one who wanted this meeting. I don't think he's going to skip out on us."As both men stared at him with concerned expressions he continued. "I think he'll be there. Whatever he's dealing with seemed pretty important. He said something about an associate of his who has gotten into some trouble with the police. You know Paul. He's always working on some connections to help him gain an advantage."

"That's what worries me."Said Charlie. "I don't trust that guy one bit. And you should know better too."Jabbing his finger into the air directly in front of Bob's face.

Sam interjected. "Well we can still fly up to the Island and wait for him. As you said, he's the one who called for this meeting."

Looking at Sam and then at Charlie, Bob wondered how much he had told him. What did Sam know about regarding the cover up and especially the death of Rita Jacob? "I think he will be there. We have a serious problem here as you know. He said something about having an exit strategy but he wants to meet in private."Directly looking at Charlie he continued. "I need to have a word with you."Turning to Sam. "You won't mind?"

"Of course not."Sam replied. "But I would like to get in the air soon. Can you make it quick?"

Bob motioned for Charlie to follow him to the far end of the terminal near the restroom. Holding the door for the governor he followed making sure there was no one in the stalls.

Charlie spoke first. "How the hell do you think he's going to get us out of this? You know he'll save his own ass first. Somebody's going to take the fall and I think they are standing right here in this shitter."

"Wait a minute my friend."Bob responded angrily. "Do you think I am stupid or something? I have enough of a paper trail on him that if we go down he goes too. And he knows it."Walking over to the sink and splashing water on his face before reaching for a paper towel on the counter, "We will listen to his plan and then if I smell something rotten I'll play my hand."

Charlie joined him at the sink washing his hands and looked at both of their reflections in the mirror. "That bastard had Rita murdered. I can't prove it but you and I both know it. She didn't deserve that Bob. All she ever wanted…"

He interrupted. "Oh so now you're all broke up about Rita. You didn't seem all that upset when Walt died. That was okay huh? Walt's out of the way and you and Rita can play. Where's the feeling for old Walt Jacob? You phony son-of-a-bitch. Don't tell me about Rita. You're the one who said you could handle the problem at the Big Beaver Project and you didn't turn down the campaign contributions from Paul and his friends in Chicago."

Charlie knew he was right. As much as he hated to admit it, he was not all that sad that Walt was out of the way. Moving away from the sink and throwing the paper towel in a trash container near the door, he turned back to Bob. "Let's go. I want to hear what he has to say. But remember something, Paul Lapone is a lying, cheating, murdering asshole. He is going to try to screw us. You know it and I know it. We just don't know how. I am not agreeing to anything unless he is one hundred percent with us."Jabbing his finger toward the figure in the mirror. "Don't take me for granted Bob. I am not so sure we can all survive this without damage. And right now I really don't give a shit."Without waiting for a reply he opened the door and exited the bathroom leaving Bob the Banker alone with his thoughts. After a minute he joined Charlie and Sam in the terminal. Together they walked out the door and headed to the waiting airplane about fifty feet away.

Sam instructed them to place any bags in the storage compartment below the cockpit and motioned for Charlie to take the seat next to him in front. Bob sat directly behind Sam leaving the seat, which would have been Paul's, empty. Sam cranked up the engine and waited for clearance from the tower before taxing out to the main runway directly behind a ten-seat Lear jet that had just moved into take-off position. The rumble and whoosh of air shook the smaller plane slightly as the Lear rocketed down the runway and was airborne in seconds. Sam positioned the Cessna into the same space occupied moments before by the jet. After the okay from the tower he pushed the throttle forward gaining speed and soon the wheels were off the ground. Sam concentrated on flying the plane as Bob and Charlie stared out the window. No one said a word as Sam steered the plane on a northward track toward Mackinac Island.

58

Paul Lapone thought about events of the past few days as he drove the rented Jeep Grand Cherokee along I – 94 on his way back to Chicago. There was one loose end to tie up before he left the country and began his new life in anonymity. With Joey dead and it only being a matter of time before they connected him to Walt Jacob and the whole Big Beaver Project, he knew he'd have to act fast. The plane, he figured, was nearing the straits based on the phone call from the ground mechanic who was glad to accept the fifty dollars he paid to be informed of the time they departed the airport in Flint. Another phone call and the first part of his plan would be complete. No turning back after that. Once it's done, it's done.

Back in his office, he would gather the needed documents from a safe under his desk and then he'd pay a quick visit to the boss. Only a few minutes there and then he'd be on his way. No one would catch on until he was long gone and the truth about Charlie V and Bob the Banker was discovered. He had left a file in his office explaining how Charlie planned the whole Big Beaver cover up and was now trying to blame somebody else including his long time friend Bob Banker. They would eventually come up with his name in the deal but Paul Lapone would cease to exist in a few days. Not a trace. His new name was to be Garret Rolston, a Canadian, retiring to a life of leisure in Costa Rica. It was all arranged once he left Chicago, drove to Calgary stayed there for a few weeks and left on the plane to Mexico, then to Cuba and finally to his new home in the small Central American Country. If necessary, he was prepared to change identities a second or third time in order to avoid capture. The only person who could identify him as

Rolston was Joey Palzonian who helped him arrange the identity and Joey wasn't talking to anybody any more.

Glancing at the dashboard clock he figured it was time to make the call. He hit the speed dial number for Bob Bankers phone. After the fourth ring and the usual computerized female voice explaining his options to leave a message or page the subscriber, he anticipated the voice on the other end.

"Banker here."Bob announced just as the voice mail was about to begin. "Who is it."?

Paul knew that Bob would not recognize the new cell phone number and proceeded to get right to the point. "How's the flight going?"

"Oh, it's you. Speak a little louder. There is a lot of noise up here."Yelling over the rhythmic buzz of the Cessna. "I can hardly hear. Speak up."

What a jerk off. Paul thought. If only he knew. Then speaking as loud as he could without shouting. "I called to let you know that I am not coming to the island."

"What? What do you mean you're not coming?"

Charlie turned around in the seat after hearing these last few words. Surprised. "Tell him he'd better get his ass up here."

"What? What? "Bob yelled into the phone and the "Hello? Hello?"a short pause and the staring at the phone Bob said. "I lost him. The cell dropped."

"Well what did he say?"Charlie asked loudly.

Sam chimed in "Yeah what the hell's going on?"He said this as the twin towers of the great Mackinac Bridge came into view. He was about to make a banking turn to the west and begin his decent toward the small airport on the flattened out strip of land on the top of the island.

Bob had an ashen look on his face as he nervously replied. "I think he said 'Rot in Hell'."

At that moment, Sam remembered the package that he had stored on the plane after Paul told him it was his laptop. "Oh no."he screamed. "That asshole."

Bob and Charlie looked at Sam as he reached for his radio, the fear in his face apparent and his voice quivering. "He had me place a package on board before we left Flint."

"Oh shit."Screamed Bob.

Charlie was remarkably calm. *How could they have been so stupid?* He knew better than to trust Lapone. It was all a set up and now there was nothing he could do.

Standing on the deck of the Arnold Ferry as it transported a full load of tourists toward their destination on Mackinac Island, the ten-year old boy pointed at the small airplane approaching high above the bridge. "Look Dad. There's an airplane coming in."

His dad looked up just in time to witness the explosion. A bright yellow flash and a muffled boom accompanied pieces of the plane scattering in every direction. The main part of the fuselage descended in a ball of flame splashing into the turquoise water, briefly suspended on the surface before disappearing beneath the waves. The Ferry captain radioed to the port what he had witnessed and several cars on the bridge had also seen the fiery wreck hit the water below. In the control tower on the Island they tried for a minute to reach the plane but it was soon evident what had happened. In a matter of minutes word reached Karen Bastow and Dick Hagan at the Governor's cottage.

Back in his car, Paul Lapone folded his cell phone, placing it on the seat as he slowed to exit the freeway near Marshall Michigan. After dialing the number to the receiver located inside the fake laptop, the small burst of electricity was just enough to ignite the low voltage detonator and set off the charge inside the cargo hold of the Cessna. In a twisted sort of way, he was disappointed that he was not there to see it. The only regret was that Sam had to go. He actually liked the guy. Envied him in a way. Paul wished that he could be as easy going as Sam. Enjoying life and living from day to day, from party to party, from woman to woman. *Too bad.*

He pulled the Jeep into the drive-thru lane of a Burger King next to the menu sign. A voice crackled from a small speaker next to the picture of a whopper. It had been a long time since he ordered anything from one of these fast food joints so he just ordered a plain whopper and a Coke. After paying at the first window and receiving his drink and bag with the hamburger at the second window he drove around back pulling up next to a large green dumpster. Looking around to make sure he was unnoticed, he grabbed the cell phone, undid the seatbelt and quickly exited the car. He pushed open the side door to the dumpster and tossed the phone in with the whopper and then he flipped the bag in among the garbage from the restaurant. Driving away, sipping the coke, he thought only about his next move. He'd be in Chicago in couple of hours.

59

Karen Bastow dropped the phone and began screaming uncontrollably "They killed him! They killed him! The bastards! Fuckin' bastards!"

Dick came running from the porch where he was sipping an ice tea when he heard the screams. Karen was kneeling on the floor with her head in her hands, tears cascading from her cheeks onto the oriental carpet. "What happened? What's wrong?"

She threw her head back and with an angered expression gave him the news. "He's dead. The plane just crashed. They're all dead. I know he was murdered. Oh my God. They just killed the Governor."

Stooping to one knee as he placed his arm around her as a sick feeling came over him. Thinking back to the last few weeks and how he became involved in this case, Dick realized that something sinister, something evil was behind all of it. It appeared that somebody was willing to go to any length for a cover up. Or was it? It didn't make sense. His experience told him this was more than a cover up. His instincts, which had served him so well in Detroit, told him this was an act of revenge. There was more than just the illegal land deal. But what? He had more questions than answers and it seemed like the people who could provide those answers were dying fast. He needed to act fast so he motioned for one of the house staff, a maid who came running in when she heard the screams. "What's you name?"he asked the middle aged Hispanic looking woman.

"Imelda."

Motioning for her to take his place next to Karen he said. "Imelda. There has been a terrible tragedy. I need you to take care of Miss

Bastow and make sure someone contacts the rest of the Governor's staff."Using the limited Spanish he learned on the streets of Southwest Detroit. "Por Favor."

"Si. Si Senor."Imelda reached for Karen who was still sobbing heavily and guided her to a couch near the window.

"I have to leave now."He spoke to Karen. "I'll be in touch soon. There is something I need to look into. When Agent Tasker gets here tell him to call me right away."

He wasn't sure if she had heard him but he did not want to waste any time. Running from the scene at the governor's cottage, which was already being guarded by a team of island police and the FBI agents that were waiting nearby. One of them was probably Tasker but he didn't have time to find out. With no motor vehicles on the island and the horse drawn taxi's moving at a slow leisurely pace, Dick noticed a red coaster-brake bicycle propped against a fence. Thinking that he would have to make sure the bike was returned to the proper place after he borrowed it, he hopped on as he pushed off down the hill. It had been a long time since he rode a bike and for a moment it wobbled unsteadily as he gathered speed narrowly missing a boy and his mother who were slowly making their way down the hill on separate bikes. At the Market Street Inn, he let the bike slide off into a grassy area next to the porch as he leapt up the steps. Quickly he made his way up the stairs to the room, hoping that Melissa had not gone shopping. The door was unlocked and he found her reading a book while sitting in a blue wing back chair opposite the bed.

She noticed his sense of urgency. "What going on?"

"We gotta go. Now."Grabbing his few pieces of clothes that he had placed in a drawer and shoved them into his duffle. "Charlie's dead. The goddam plane blew up."

"My god! I heard some sirens out in the harbor and lots of noise down the street, but I had no idea."

"It's a hit. I am sure of it. I just don't know who yet but we are going to find out."

Melissa tossed the book onto the bed and reached for him. Grabbing his arm and turning him toward her she was trembling. "I'm scared."Making him look at her now. "First Walt and Rita and now

Charlie V. Who are these people? Who would do this? I don't want to be involved any more. This is Crazy. What the hell is happening Dick?"

Reaching his arms around her, he realized that he had taken her for granted. She was involved by accident because of Rita Jacob but she was not like him. She was not trained for this. She did not have the instincts and the energy for this. And he knew that in the moment as he held her close in the second floor room of the Market Street Inn on Mackinac Island, he would have to go on without her. It was going to get dangerous and she had been exposed too much already. "I'm sorry babe. You should not be here anyway. Let me go on ahead and you make your way back when you are ready. I think there is a bus from the mainland back to the Detroit area. I have to take your car, okay?"

Looking at him through tears she whispered. "Be careful. Call me and let me know what's going on."

"Yeah sure. I have to get back right away. I'll call Carson and let him know so he can check up on you when you get back. I may not be there though. I think this trail leads to someplace other than Michigan. That guy who kidnapped you, the one I had to shoot, was from Chicago. I have a feeling that's where I am going."Letting her sit back into the chair he sat on the bed facing her. "I just don't know who I am looking for yet."

"Why don't you get Sean Carson to help you? And what about the FBI?"

"I know. I know. I will bring them all up to date. But I think time is important here and both Sean and the FBI have too much procedure to follow."

They sat facing each other for a moment and both knew that this was a turning point in their relationship. He had to go and she would not go with him. When this was all over and they had time to sit down and talk it through, neither one was sure if they would be able to go on. Finally, Dick rose from the bed and reached for his bag, stopping at the door.

"I'm sorry you got involved. I know you won't understand, but I have to do this. Not for Rita or Charlie or even poor Walt. It's about the kid who was shot in front of my place. Tom Hodges. Someone has to answer for him. I know that the guy I killed probably killed Tom but there is somebody else behind it. Somebody who is calling the shots. And that somebody has to pay. Its justice. It's what I have been doing all my life and I have to see this through."

She looked at him through moist eyes and said. "Please be careful. Call me when you are ready. I'll be waiting."

Dick turned and took a few steps toward the door before retreating back to her chair. He knelt down at her side and kissed her gently on the cheek and then on the lips. "I will be back. I promise."He rose and without turning around walked out the door and down the stairs.

Main Street was filled with tourists gathered in small groups all obviously stunned by the news that had by now filtered through the island. The Governor's plane had crashed near the bridge. Charlie V was probably dead. No one could believe it. Dick hurriedly made his way to the boat docks and was just able to get onto the Shepler's Ferry back to the mainland. This was the high-speed, semi hydroplane, bi-hulled boat that was the fastest way off the island. Many of the passengers looked off to the west toward the area filled with small and large boats marking the spot where the Cessna went down. Some pointed and spoke in hushed words. Others just stared.

Dick contemplated what he was about to do. Realizing that he had no real authority he might be actually breaking some laws by going alone. This was the best way he thought. Once he got back to Detroit he'd obtain the information that he needed and go after his suspect. Pulling his cell phone from his coat pocket, he scrolled down the names until he came to the one he wanted. It was a good thing his cell service worked up here he thought as he pressed the green button on the phone and waited for an answer.

"Abernathy here."

"Rambo. It's Hagan. I need your help."

"I was going to call you pal. I just heard about the Governor. You all over this thing?"

"Yeah. You could say that. I was on the Island when it happened. I'm on my way back to Detroit now. Are you on Duty?"

"Yeah but I get off in an hour. What do ya need?"

Not sure exactly what he was going to ask his old friend he paused before continuing. "I need some information about Walt Jacob and his buddies." Another pause. "And I think your chief may be the one that can give it to me."

"Whoa. Wait a minute. The Chief? Mike Slattery?"

"Don't get excited .I know that you have to be careful. I just need to know where I might be able to, you know, sort of bump into him. Preferably alone. Do you know anything about his habits? Like what time he comes in or when and where he goes to lunch?"

Rambo thought for a moment and then said. "I'm not sure but I hear that he goes to lunch just about every day at Peabody's. He meets up with some old friends from the city. Lawyers. Doctors. A few Chamber of Commerce types. Maybe you can catch him coming or going."

"Great. That would be perfect. I know the place. Call me back as soon as you know for sure. I need to see him tomorrow."

"Too bad about Charlie V." Said Rambo. "I met him once. He was the kind of guy you 'd like to have a few beers with."

"Yeah too bad." Said Dick.

After giving it careful thought, Dick reached for his phone again and called Sean Carson. He explained his theory and what he thought they should do next. Sean was able to convince him to let the Fed's take the lead on this now. They really had no jurisdiction in the assassination of Charlie V but he was sure that his old friend Agent Bill Tasker would keep them in the loop. He got more than he expected.

Michael Ripinski

60

Dusk was settling in as the Chicago skyline came into view. Paul eased the Jeep into the right lane as the busy evening traffic merged into the local lanes of the Dan Ryan Expressway. Heading north, he exited onto Lake Shore Drive passing the convention center and the newly renovated Soldier Field. Glancing off to his right he made the popular observation that the shape of the stadium, home of the beloved Chicago Bears, reminded him of an oversized space ship. He liked the old stadium better as did many other Chicagoans. Approaching Navy Pier, he continued on toward the North Shore area and finally exited at Fullerton. After a series of turns to maneuver the one- way streets, he arrived at a newly renovated, three-story, brown-brick townhouse next to an alleyway. He pulled into an empty parking spot at the rear and made his way up a flight of stairs on the backside of the building. Once inside, he tossed his soft leather duffle bag on a glass table and walked over to a desk near the front window. He sat down and placed both hands on the desk and took a few, slow deep breadths. Looking at his hands. Steady. No nerves. Good. He was still under control. Paul had learned a form of a Zen meditation from a former girlfriend a few years back and he found it useful in high stress situations. This certainly qualified.

After ten more minutes of meditation, he rose from the desk and began gathering the things he would need for the trip. Actually there wasn't very much. Just a few changes of clothes and an envelope filled with his new identity papers. Driver's license, Birth certificate, bank account numbers in the Cayman Islands. A few thousand dollars in cash and a few ATM cards. All under his new name. The rest of his papers and documents didn't matter. They belonged to Paul Lapone and as of this moment he was Garret Rolston. There was nothing left behind that could connect the two names. He entered the bathroom off the kitchen and proceeded to use a throw away razor to shave off his mustache. Next he carefully placed two blue tinted contact lenses in his eyes covering his natural brown color. Using a trimmer he purchased just for this occasion, he gave himself a buzzcut leaving barely a half-inch of hair. Turning from side to side he admired his knew look before placing the razor, trimmer and hair clippings into a garbage bag. Wiping the sink clean he clicked off the light as he left. Opening the leather bag he had brought with him, he retrieved a Glock 9 millimeter, identical to Joey's, and proceeded to load the magazine from a box of Remington cartridges. Reaching back into the bag he took a short metal tube and screwed it onto the adapter on the end of his weapon. The silencer would be needed in case anyone was nearby. He hoped he would only need to fire one shot. He decided to do it quickly. Just walk in and shoot. Don't even let the Boss have a chance to say anything. He'd leave right away and ditch the gun along the way before he entered Canada. He checked his watch and saw that it was time to leave. After one last look around he closed the door as he left, not even bothering to lock it. It didn't make any difference. He figured they would be here to search the place pretty soon. Maybe even tomorrow. But by that time he'd be gone and he was certain they would not be able to find him. They would be looking for Paul Lapone and he no longer existed.

He took the Brown train, getting on at the Diversy Station, and headed toward downtown. The boss always worked late and on this day he was certain of that. Especially when word of the plane crash reached back here to Chicago and Paul was supposed to check in. It was approaching eight PM when he exited the train and made his way up to street level. Walking briskly toward the building he shared with the other businesses, he stopped suddenly as he noticed the flashing lights of the Chicago police cars parked in front. From a block away he watched as first one then another car pulled up and several uniformed cops emerged from their vehicles and took positions around the entrance and sides of the building. Then he noticed a few plain black cop-type cars parked across the street and one at the corner. A small crowd formed and the uniformed cops were pushing them back toward the corner. One of them was coming his way and he instinctively put his hand in his bag wrapping his fingers around the handle and trigger of his gun.

"Move on back."Ordered the cop.

"What's goin on?"asked a young woman wearing a tight blue sweater and jeans.

"None of your business. Now move back?"Yelled the cop.

He merged with the crowd retreating back across the next street and stood behind a row of people straining to see what was happening at the building where Paul Lapone had an office and where the Boss would be waiting for him. Change of plans No time now. He had to move fast if he was going to get out of Chicago. *Damn. I can't do it tonight. Got to get out of here. How did they find me so fast?*

Hailing a taxi, he slipped into the back seat without looking back and instructed the driver to take him to an address on Division in Bucktown. From there he walked a few blocks until he came to an alley where he walked a few hundred feet before ducking into the side door of an old garage. Tossing the canvas cover to the floor he ran his hands over the smooth finish of the sleek two thousand five BMW. The one he purchased as Garrett Rolston from a private owner a few months ago. Cash. Only twenty-two thousand miles on the odometer. The garage he rented on a six-month deal from an old widow. Paid in advance. Also in cash.

Taking the key from his pocket he punched the un-lock button and the doors clicked open. Moving around to the front of the garage he unlocked a deadbolt and slid a latch across the metal frame before reaching down and lifting the door to the open position. He returned to the car and it started immediately with a soft hum. Not loud like the American cars. Quiet. Just the way he liked it. He slowly maneuvered the BMW out of the garage and returned to close the door when a pair of African American men in dark clothing startled him. He noticed that they were moving to either side of him and one of them was reaching into his pocket for something. *What was that? Something shiny. A barrel.* Now the other one came up behind him and grabbed him around the throat with his forearm. He noticed a tattoo on the man's wrist. The word *Killer*.

Shit. They're robbing me. He thought. "Wait. What do you want"? The car? Go ahead take it."

Neither one of his attackers spoke right away but the one with the gun, a small caliber, a 22 maybe, lifted the barrel and placed it at an angel against his temple.

"Don't shoot. Don't. I have a lot of money. Just not on me. I can. I can get it for you."

The tattooed one said. "Pop the mutherfucker. We'll take the car."

The one with the gun said. "What chu mean a lot of money? How much you got?"

Had to think fast now. What did he have on him? A few thousand in the bag with his gun. They'd take that and shoot him anyway. "I got an ATM card that I can use to get as much as you want. Thousands. I can go to different machines."He lied.

"I said pop him Rodney "The one behind him speaking again.

Rodney said. "No I want to see if whitey here is fo real."

Tattoo man relaxed his grip and reached for the gun from his accomplice, wrapping his fingers around the handle. Paul saw the brief opportunity as the two men had their moment of disagreement and as Rodney raised the gun up in the air to keep it from his partner, he shoved his elbow into the ribs of his attacker causing a yelp of pain and turning, he shoved both men against the garage. The gun went flying into the air and landed a few feet in front of the BMW.

"Motherfuckin punk ass."Shouted Rodney as he dove for the gun. Paul dove to the open car door, reached into his bag, extracted his own weapon and came out firing, hitting Rodney in the forehead dropping him to the ground. In the next second he saw the other one coming toward him. He fired twice into his body and the second man fell back against the garage.

He looked around and saw that no one had witnessed the attack. Calmly easing himself behind the wheel he closed the door, put the car into gear and sped off out onto Division leaving two bodies in the dark alley. As he drove along in a daze, the realization of what happened hit him. He observed his left hand gripping the wheel tightly; his right hand was resting on the console and it was shaking. *Deep breaths Deep breaths*.

He drove on through the night. The plan was to head on to north of Great Falls and then on up to Calgary. Crossing the border should be no problem in this part of the country. After a rest in a motel west of Duluth, he would be ready to move on. One thing kept nagging on him though. He really wanted to finish off the Boss. No way could he do it now. But maybe some day he would sneak back into the country. Maybe someday, but not now, he had to keep going. After a few withdrawals from ATMs located along the way, he had enough cash for the next few weeks. Of course he carried less than the ten thousand in US currency allowed to travel across the border. The rest of his money was in a Cayman bank waiting for the call from Garret Rolston in Costa Rica.

Michael Ripinski

61

When the state police and the FBI learned the names of the passengers on-board the Cessna, one name was clearly missing – Paul Lapone. Karen Bastow had told them that they were on their way to the island for a private meeting and that it was her understanding that Lapone was to be on the plane and part of the meeting. She explained that she did not know him very well but she believed he was from Chicago. After Agent Tasker shared this information with Dick and Sean, it didn't take long to connect the dots from Walt Jacob to Joey Palzonian to Paul Laopne. The Chicago Police were notified and immediately charged off to the office Building on State Street despite the request from the FBI to wait for further instructions. Their over zealousness saved Paul Lapone- now known as Rolston the Canadian, from walking into an ambush.

The BMW was further distancing Paul from Chicago. He briefly thought about turning back in order to finish it. Leaving The Boss alive meant further risk but he was confident they would never catch up to him. Not as Rolston. It was a name they would never find in any of his records or through any of his connections now that Joey was dead. He kept driving.

As news of the assassination reached the public, further details of the Big Beaver land deal began to leak out to the news media. At the local FBI office in Detroit, Agent Tasker, now the lead investigator on the Charlie V case, was speaking to a select group of five men and one woman from the state police, FBI and local law enforcement. Invited to attend this meeting were Dick Hagan and Sean Carson.

Standing at the head of a long conference table, Agent Bill Tasker spoke first. "I have invited these two gentlemen here to assist in our investigation."Nodding in the direction of the two men seated at his left. "Sean Carson is with Troy Police and Dick Hagan here is formerly with Detroit PD. You may have heard that he was the one who took down the suspect in front of the church in Royal Oak."

He got their attention as all those at the table immediately looked in Dick's direction. The woman, Betty Malkowicz from the state police crime lab, knew Dick from Detroit where she worked before moving to Lansing. She gave him a subtle wave with her fingers without lifting her hand from the table. Tasker continued. "Sean and Dick are going to fill us in on what they have which I think is going to lead us in the right direction. Sean, why don't you start?"

Rising from his chair and taking Tasker's place, Carson cleared his throat. "We first became involved with this case during a murder investigation in Troy that just coincidently took place in front of Mister Hagan's condo. Dick and I worked together back here in the D and he was agreeable to assisting us. That led us to one Mister Walter Jacob. A reported suicide in Birmingham on the same day. Our victim, Thomas Hodges, was the Jacob's landscaper."

One of the FBI agents, a middle aged white man in a rumpled gray suit interrupted. "We knew about Walt Jacobs. Birmingham PD confirmed it was a suicide. You telling us they lied to us?"

"Not exactly. It depends on whom you talked to. Dick why don't you fill us in here."

Hagan rose and joined Sean at the front of the table. He was used to this scene during many investigations over the years, bringing together combined groups of law enforcement personnel in order to share their findings. The trick was to not step on anyone's toes. "I can't tell you how we received this information."He began by protecting Melissa's identity for now. "Rita Jacob never believed her husband took his own life. I used some sources to dig into the matter and we discovered that Rita and the late Charlie V were having an affair for some time. You all know that the Jacob's were major backers of the Governor. Rita was more than just a financial supporter."At this point Sean produced a ten by twelve, brownish envelope placing it on the table. Dick removed the sheet of paper clearly showing the fold lines from being hidden in Rita's jacket. "This is the suicide note left by Walter Jacob. The signature matches."Sliding the note around the table, everyone gazed at the typed message.

"I thought you said you don't believe it was suicide?"Betty asked as the others nodded in agreement with her question. "He must have been upset to discover the infidelity of his wife and Charlie V."

"Before she mysteriously died in Mexico, Misses Jacob told a friend about the note and stated that she felt he was forced to sign it. He never used the name Walter in the entire time they were married. She believed that he was sending a message."

"Okay. So you have a suspicion of foul play. I don't understand how this involves your landscape guy?"asked Lieutenant Bill Haupman from the State Police investigative unit. A middle aged man wearing a perfectly tailored, black, Brooks Brothers suit, crisp white shirt and red tie. He was rumored to be next in line for the top State Police job in Lansing.

"We believe that Tom Hodges heard or saw something that day while he was at the Jacob's house. The same people who killed Walt took out Tom. It happened in front of my condo where he was scheduled to meet with a new client. The meeting never took place."

Sean Carson spoke next. "We have a match on the gun used to kill Hodges and a weapon found on Anthony Palzonian, the guy who Dick shot by the church in Royal Oak."

Haupman asked "What about Birmingham Police? I met Mike Slattery at a few conventions and I would be surprised that they missed this one as a murder. I mean there must have been other clues right?"

At this point Dick and Sean exchanged glances and as previously agreed, decided to keep it purposely vague. Before speaking, Dick recalled the meeting he had with Chief Slattery only two days before. The Chief invited Dick back to his office where he confided the details of the investigation under the condition it was - off the record. After all, Dick was not an official officer of any jurisdiction and had no legal authority in the matter. He explained how things are handled in Birmingham among the close-knit, upper crust, residents and that Rita and Walt were his friends as was Charlie V. He knew about the affair and decided to avoid any prolonged investigation in order to spare any embarrassment. Dick was satisfied that Slattery knew nothing of the note and the other murders. By expediting the crime scene at the Jacob's house on that day, he did nothing legally wrong. It was completely in his jurisdiction and he acted as many others would have in his position. It was sloppy police work. That's all. He recalled that this was nothing compared to the many cases of police using discretion involving prominent citizens and elected officials in Detroit. Sometimes you just looked the other way.

Sean said. "They had no reason to believe anything other than suicide."

"I spoke with Chief Slattery myself."Said Tasker backing them up. "It looked like suicide all the way."

A few moments passed as everyone digested the information laid out so far. They continued by reviewing the leads and the documents produced regarding the Big Beaver land deal. Betty was reading the DEQ approval letter and then looked up at Agent Tasker. "Has anyone spoken to this William Greening guy from DEQ? It looks like he signed off on a possible contaminated site without proper testing. "

"I'm afraid that's not possible. He's dead also."Said Haupman as all heads turned in his direction at the other end of the table. "We started looking into this right after the plane crash and we found out he died in Las Vegas a few weeks ago. He was mugged but died of a heart attack before he could get help. What is starting to fit in is the fact that he lost thousands of dollars at the gaming tables before he died. Money he just didn't have from his salary in Lansing. We think he was bought."

"By whom?"asked FBI agent Daniel Wansted, a former CPA and white collar crime expert

Dick said. "By Bob Banker and friends I believe. I met Mister Banker and we now know that he was the moneyman behind Charlie V. He probably leaned on the governor to get the DEQ to rubber stamp his project."

Tasker once again took over. "All evidence leads to this land deal on Big Beaver in Troy. Banker, Sam Ford, Walt Jacob and the one guy we can't find, Paul Lapone, were the principal investors. I found out this morning that the former landowner, Edna Norris, was related to Charlie V. and he knew the site was a former landfill. It is possible there is major contamination from Mercury and PCB's. If the site were bad, the investors would have lost many millions of dollars. There is your motive. Our suspect is one Paul Lapone of Chicago. We believe he is responsible for the death of Governor Vandenberg and the others."

"Do we know where he might have gone?"Betty once again chimed in.

"We have our agents in Chicago looking for him now. He had an office there under the name of a company he controlled. Unfortunately the Chicago PD misunderstood our request and went in like the Marines on Iwo Jima. If he was anywhere nearby, they scared him off. We have located his condo and it looks like he was recently there. He can't be too far ahead of us. I have been in touch with the Federal Prosecutor here in Detroit. He is ready with a capital charge on the assassination when we find Lapone."

After further discussions, Bill Tasker gave each person an assignment regarding the investigation and asked Sean and Dick to stick around. They waited in the conference room for about five minutes before the FBI agent returned carrying a file folder. He needed their further help.

Michael Ripinski

62

Carson dropped Dick off at Melissa's condo before heading back to his Troy Office. He had not expected the request from Tasker but then he never expected to be involved in a major case like the assassination of the Governor. The FBI had already received permission from Troy PD to temporarily assign him to this case. He knew Tasker had connections but this was Big Time. At the meeting with he and Dick after the others left, Tasker informed them of a secret investigation being conducted by the Department of Justice. The name of Paul Lapone had come up in this other case and now they were being asked to coordinate their information. Tasker didn't like it. There was something else going on in Chicago and he needed to send somebody on an independent mission. He was authorized to use other resources if necessary. Dick and Sean were to leave for the Windy City in the morning. They were to find out as much as possible about Paul Lapone and Joey Palzonian without running into the other agents and report back to him directly. They hesitantly agreed after a long discussion about jurisdictions and suspect rights.

Melissa was waiting in the living room when Dick arrived. "How did it go downtown?"

"You're not gonna believe this. I am going to Chicago tomorrow with Sean. Agent Tasker needs us to do some type of covert thing. I can't tell you too much but just know that I will be careful."

She frowned at hearing the news that he was still on the case. She thought it was all over since the FBI had taken over the investigation. She expected they would be called as witnesses at some point but not that he was still doing police work. "You can't say No can you?"

"Look babe, I probably know more about this case than anybody. If I can help catch Lapone, I want to be there. Don't you think Rita Jacob deserves some justice?"

It was the one angle that made it all right. For poor Rita. She thought about her often in the past few days. Remembering that she really thought of her as arrogant and aloof when they first met but in the end she felt like a friend. Certainly Rita considered her a friend trusting her with custody of the letter and suicide note. And then there were all the coincidences. Tom Hodges being killed in her boyfriends front yard and Rita's husband Walt being murdered - not a suicide. "I guess for Rita. If you can help find this guy."

"I think we may find more than that."He surprised her.

"What do you mean?"

"I can't say right now but Lapone could not have been doing this all by himself. It doesn't add up. He doesn't appear to have the kind of money and power to pull this thing off alone. That's what Tasker wants us to check out."

Melissa reached out for him without standing and he eagerly moved over to the couch easing himself next her. They kissed and held each other close for a moment before she took the lead guiding him to the bedroom. He felt lucky to have her close at this moment. She was sure that she loved him. Neither one wanted the morning to come any time soon.

63

On the way to the airport they stopped at a Starbucks for coffee and they just re-entered the car when Sean Carson's phone buzzed in his pocket.

It was Agent Tasker. "We got a break guys."

Switching the phone on speaker and placing it on the console between them. "Okay Dick can hear you now too."

"Chicago police found two black guys shot in alley a few days ago. One was in a coma for a few days but he came out. He says a white guy shot them as he was coming out of a rented garage. He says they were minding their business when they were attacked. Police think they were probably mugging the guy and it went wrong. Here's the break. Fingerprints on the garage door match to Paul Lapone. According to the victim, it looks like our guy has changed his look. Cut his hair and shaved his 'stache. He's driving a late model BMW and we think he headed out of town."

"Are you sure it's him?"Sean inquired.

"Yeah. We confirmed with the lady who owned the garage. The guy who paid cash for the rent, looked like Lapone before he shaved. We'll find him if he has not left the country. If he has, we have the Canadians on alert. White guy, traveling alone, in a late model BMW. He'll show up someplace. I want you two guys to continue as we discussed. When you get to Chicago, contact my friend Joe Barzinski with Chicago PD. Joe knows what's going on. Remember, if you come across any Department of Justice people, you are on your own."

"We got it."Said Dick. "Just one more thing. Do you have a name yet?"He was referring to a possible suspect that would be the source of the money behind Paul Lapone and all of his activity.

"No. No name, but you are looking for somebody he had a business relationship with. A partner on a previous deal or an investor. He wrote checks from an account with Chase. Follow the money. Joe has all the subpoenas if you need them. Good luck guys."

"Thanks. We'll call as soon as we get something."Sean replied before closing the cover on the phone.

"I'm still not quite sure why he wants us to handle this?"Dick said before taking as sip of his coffee.

"I spoke to him after our meeting and he told me that the Justice people are trying to get something squashed before we find out. He has a hunch that the same person or people we are looking for may be on some serious campaign donor lists in Washington. Somebody is afraid they will be indirectly connected to this whole mess. After nine eleven everyone in government knows what each other are doing. That's why we are on our own. Tasker knows we won't be on their radar screen for a while and it may be time enough for us to find out who is behind it all. This is going to be an interesting trip."

"No shit."Dick took another sip of his drink. "Let's get to Chicago."

After the one-hour flight on Southwest, they touched down at Midway and rented a car before heading into the city. Their first stop was at the building on Rush where Lapone had his office. It was one block from the offices of Griffin and Childress. A uniformed police officer was stationed at the door and inside only one employee remained. Kathy Dobbs, his secretary for more than five years was still there to answer phone calls and e-mails – all monitored by the FBI and Department of Justice.

Kathy was a single mom with two boys, nine and seven, who was trying to make a life for her family. Her job with Lapone Enterprises required that she take a lot of messages and be very discreet when it came to the activities of her boss. She often suspected that he was involved in some kind of illegal activity but she avoided the details and stuck to her basic job description. She became very good at being a conduit for his communication without knowing the details and

Paul paid her well. Last year she made forty five thousand dollars with bonuses. Her boys had new clothes and they never wanted for the basic necessities. Now it seemed her whole world would come crashing down. The Feds told her they would pay her normal salary as long as she stayed on the job while they sorted through his records and computer files. She told them everything she knew except the one thing that Paul always told her never to talk about. The one thing that the FBI and Justice would like to know- and that was the name of the mysterious person that he met with once a month at Griffin and Childress. He told her that if anyone ever asked, she should never give out that information. Her life and the safety of her boys depended on it. She kept to the deal in spite of an intense interrogation by the FBI. She agreed to the arrangement of answering messages, which turned out to be mostly solicitors and clients looking for answers regarding leases and over due bills. She spent most of her day reading books and practicing her computer skills on Excel and Office Suite knowing that she'd bee looking for a new job pretty soon. The rent had not been paid on the office for two months and the landlord was threatening eviction. She worried the same thing would happen to her at her apartment.

The entry to the building was a plain glass door on Rush with a common hallway shared by a talent agency and a dentist. Two other offices remained vacant. Lapone Enterprises occupied a three-room suite including the reception area where Kathy kept her desk. Sean and Dick entered after talking their way past the uniformed cop at the door by telling them they were doing follow up on the Palzonian case. By this time it was known that Joey had worked for Lapone Enterprises.

"Excuse me miss." Sean leaned over the counter in front of Kathy's desk. "My name is Detective Carson from Detroit. I was wondering if I could ask you some questions."

Kathy Dobbs looked up from her book grabbing a pen and paper. "Excuse me. I didn't get your name."

"Carson. From Detroit."

After writing down his name so that she would be able to give the information to the FBI she asked. "And what can I do for you

Mister Carson?"

"We are investigating a murder in Detroit that may involve a former employee of this company. Is there somebody we can talk to about this matter?"

"I don't think so. I am the only employee left. There was a bookkeeper and another secretary but they quit when everything happened last week. I don't know if I can help you."

Dick had remained in the background until now. "Does the name Joey Palzonian mean anything to you?"

She hesitated for only a second but it told them she knew. "I'm afraid the name doesn't ring a bell."And then to Dick with pen in hand. "I....I ..Did not get your name."

"Hagan. I am detective Carson's driver."He said sarcastically.

"Well Mister Hagan. I can't help you .I never heard that name."In fact she had told the FBI and Justice people that she indeed knew Joey and that he was a frequent visitor to these very offices. They had instructed her to talk to no one without their approval. Dick and Sean already had this information but they were trying to gauge her level of cooperation.

"Well Miss. Uh. Uh I didn't get your name."Said Sean

"I didn't give it to you."She replied coldly. "But it is Dobbs. Kathy Dobbs."Deciding to be professional about it.

"Thank you Kathy."Dick said. "We don't want to cause any more problems than you already have. We know about Mister Lapone and why they are looking for him. It's just that we are trying to solve a murder of an innocent man back in Detroit. A young man named Tom Hodges who was murdered, we believe, by Joey Palzonian who appears to have been an employee of this company. The victim, Mister Hodges was murdered because he saw or heard something by accident while doing his landscape job for a prominent client in Detroit. He was killed by these ruthless bastards for no reason - other than they thought he could identify them."

Shaken by the comment she pulled a tissue from the box on her desk and dabbed at her eyes. "If you already know who killed him, then why are you here?"

"Because."Dick said "His family could be entitled to some

monetary compensation if we can connect him to Mister Lapone. We understand he may have some assets that can be in play during a trial if we can connect him to Joey Palzonian.

"You said Joey killed this Hodges fellow. "The way she said his name convinced them that she knew him.

"Yes. We are certain. His gun matched as the one in the killing."

"I'm...I'm so sorry."She began to sob. "This has all been so stressful. I was told not to talk to anyone except the local authorities."

"Thank you Kathy."Sean said "So you knew him then?"

"Yes. Joey came around here about once a month. He called more often. He and Mister Lapone would meet occasionally but not here. They went to a bar called the Five Fifty Five Tavern. That's about all I know."

"That will be a big help Kathy. Don't worry. We won't tell anyone that you gave us this information."

"It's okay. I have had enough of all this. I'm done. Tomorrow I'll tell the officers here that I'm through. I need to move on and find a new job."After a pause. "Did Mister Hodges have a big family? "

"No. He had an elderly mother and a girlfriend who is pretty broken up though."

"I feel so bad for her. I hope you can help them."

"We are trying. You have been a big help. Thanks. "Dick patted her hand before turning toward the door.

Carson left his business card with a cell phone number. "Call me if you think of anything else that might help us."

"Okay."she said, placing the card in her purse.

After they walked out the door, she sat there thinking about the poor innocent man in Detroit. On top of the plane crash, which she still could not accept as something her boss was behind, she received this news. Only this time it was not hard to believe. She always thought of Joey as a creep. He once showed her his gun inside his waistband. As if that would impress her. It was the first time she started to have doubts about her employer, Paul Lapone. As she drove home that night she decided that she would leave the next day – with or without a new job.

Michael Ripinski

64

The 555 tavern was filled with the after work crowd. Young professionals, lawyers, advertising execs and managers all trying to look good while telling stories of their accomplishments, conquests and exploits. Standing two deep at the bar and crowded around the small, round, high top tables, the place overflowed with liquor and lies while the bartenders kept the glasses filled. As the evening wore on, the power ties were loosened and the white silk blouses offered a bit more skin. A few heads turned as Dick and Sean entered clearly looking underdressed and out of place having twenty years on most of the patrons. They squeezed their way into a space at the near corner of the bar next to the fold down section where the wait staff placed and retrieved the orders for the tables.

The young bartender with a slightly spiked haircut and black tee shirt highlighting toned biceps waved one finger and said "Be with ya in a minute guys."Keeping his word, he approached while placing two square white napkins on the table with the red numbers 555 in the lower right corner."What can I get ya guys?"

"Two Sam Adams. Bottles."Said Sean.

Dick leaned toward his friend and whispered. "I don't drink that crap."

"It's what the kids in here drink. Shows that we're cool"

"We couldn't be cool in this place if we were wearing ice cube hats."

Both men laughed as the bartender brought the beers setting them on the napkins and after telling them that he'd run them a tab, "Anything else? If you're hungry we make a pretty good burger and the nachos are a big portion. I'm Doug."

"Thanks Doug. There is something else when you have a second. No hurry though."Dick replied as the bartender moved on to his next customer, a cute brunette with sparkling eyes and breasts that literally extended over the bar. Sean was staring. "Hey partner. Put those eyes back in your head. She could be your daughter."Laughing, they clanked bottles while watching the action unfold around the room. It seemed that there were three guys for every girl and each took turns trying their best lines and moves while most often being rejected. The girls could be selective, after all. Even the least attractive of the herd, a slightly overweight red head wearing an unflattering too-tight Saint John suit, had two intoxicated rookie lawyers pawing her shoulders. She seemed to be enjoying the attention.

During a short lull at the bar Doug returned to the corner spot. "What was it you needed?"wiping the bar with a damp rag while lifting each bottle.

"We were told that a guy we know comes in here often and we have been trying to locate him. An old frat buddy of ours."

Looking skeptical at the two older men. "What's the name "?

"Joey. Joey Palzonian. He might go by the name Joe."Said Dick.

"Don't ring a bell with me but maybe he comes in during the day. I come on at five. The regular daytime bartender is Todd. He gets off when I come in. "

"Thanks man."Sean took a full sip of his beer before adding. "We'll stop back tomorrow."

"No problem. Anything else?"

"Well."Dick said. "If I was twenty years younger …"Nodding at the large breasted girl three chairs to his right.

Doug shook his head and smiled as the two men turned to leave.

The next day at three PM, the bar was virtually empty except for three men at a square table near the back and one obviously drunk, skinny, scruffy looking middle aged man barely lifting his head off the bar.

The bartender was overheard talking to the drunk. "Let me get you a cab. Bones. You've had enough."

The drunk looked up, his wobbling from side to side. "Okey Dokey."He smiled and then. "Where am I going?"

"Home. He'll take you home. I'll pay and put it on your tab. You can catch up with me on Friday."

"Uh Huh."His head drooped back down to the bar.

Sean and Dick took up there same post from the night before. It was unnecessary but they felt it was the best [place for a quiet conversation, though the only person who could hear them was the drunk.

"Hi guys. What can I get ya?"The bartender approached wiping the bar.

"Are you Todd?"Sean asked.

"Yeah. Why?"cautiously sizing them up.

"Well we were told that you might know a guy we're looking for. A guy named Joe or Joey Palzonian. We heard he comes in here."

"You cops?"speaking the obvious.

"How'd you guess? "Dick replied. "Is it the steely looking eyes or the cheap suits from JC Penney's that give us away."

Todd laughed, feeling at ease with his two patrons who seemed to be a little different from the other plainclothes cops he had met. In Chicago they seldom had a sense of humor. One or two times they had come in looking for a suspected drug dealer selling coke to the regulars. He knew the guy, but he felt it was better to keep out of it. "Not from around here, huh?"

"Nope. Detroit. Actually a city called Troy just north of the D."Said Sean.

"Long way from home. Anything to drink?"

"Maybe later. Do you know the guy?"

"There's a guy named Joey that comes in here. Don't know his last name and come to think of it I haven't seen him in a few weeks. Was in here with another guy. They sat at the other end of the bar. The other guy's name is Paul, I think."

They looked at each other with a slight smile and then with a bit more confidence they told Todd of the situation back in Michigan and the connection to the death of Charlie V. They explained that they needed to get as much information on these two guys as possible.

Todd said "Geez. I heard about the plane crash and how it looks suspicious but."

"I'm afraid so Todd. There's one more thing. Joey's dead. Was killed in a shoot out. We need to know if he ever met with anyone else in here besides Paul. Can you help us out?"

A little shaken by the news of the crimes committed by his customers, he leaned back against the bar rubbing his forehead. "I remember something about two months ago. Joey was here for a few hours and had a pretty good buzz going on. He left an envelope on the stool next to his and I held it for him till the next day. He came in all hyped up asking if anyone turned it in."

"Did he say what was in it or anything else? "Dick inquired.

"No but he gave me twenty bucks and seemed real happy to get it back. I remember the name on the letterhead for the return address. It was Griffin and Church or Griffin and Childs. Something like that."He snapped his finger remembering. "Griffin and Childress. That's it. I know the name because they have an office just down the street. One of the secretaries used to come in here. Haven't seen her in quite a while."

Putting a twenty on the bar along with his business card Sean thanked him for the information and turned to Dick. "We are going to see some people down the street."

"Huh?"

"I saw the name on the building about half a block from Lapone's office. A large nameplate in brass letters. Griffin and Childress. I remember thinking how cool the entrance looked with marble floors and dark tinted glass in the doors."

They thanked the bartender again and walked out of the bar heading west on Adams.

65

Knowing that subpoenas would take time – time they just didn't have – Detective Carson and Dick Hagan hurried back to Paul Lapone's office where they found Kathy cleaning out her desk. As promised she had decided to leave against the advice of the local cops and her own lawyer and get on with her life. An interview with a major property management company scheduled for the next morning sounded promising.

"Looks like somebody decided to pack it in."said Dick

She had hardly noticed them enter. "Oh it's you two again. Any luck at the five fifty five?"

"Actually something new has come up. Yeah, we were able to come up with a new lead."Sean announced. "But we need your help again."

Looking at them warily and shaking her head. "I'm sorry guys but I've told everything I know to the FBI and the guy from Justice. You can go ask them."

Dick blurted out "We can't."as Sean stared at him. "I mean we don't have time. I think we need to act fast on this and they may not even have the information we need."

Sighing and shrugging her shoulders as she stopped packing the last box. "Oh alright. What are you looking for?"

"A name."said Sean "Somebody at the company down the street. Griffin and Childress. We think that maybe Joey and Paul had some connection to them."

Running her hands through her hair she turned away from them for a minute. When she faced them again a tear was visible and her lip was quivering. "Griffin and Childress. Huh?"She looked away and then at them again. "I already told the Justice guy, Ballinger is his name, that Griffin and Childress are our landlords here. They manage our building and several others here in downtown. They have been harassing me for the past few days about the rent and asking when we were leaving the space. I told them to contact the FBI."

"Is that all?"

Hesitating she added. "No. That's not all. This is something I haven't even told the others. Mister Lapone had a girlfriend that worked there. I don't know her last name but her first name was Susan."

Taking his memo pad from his coat pocket Dick asked as he wrote. "How do you know she was his girlfriend?"

"One time, she called asking for him and he was out of town. She said her name was Susan but to tell him his girlfriend is looking for him. I think she was serious."

"No last name huh?"

"Nope. But I know he saw her often. He would leave here a couple of times a week and he would say that he was going down the street and he would wink at me. You know like it was a big secret."

"Is your computer still hooked up?"Sean asked.

"Yes but I think it is being monitored by the Feds."

"Well it wouldn't hurt to look something up for me would it?"

"Hey I'm done here."Pointing to the box she was now lifting. "Help yourself."Nodding to the computer as she stepped from behind the desk.

Dick sat in her chair and began typing into the computer after clicking on the Internet button. A few more screens and a fancy home page for the investment and venture capital company – Griffin and Childress – came into view. After a quick click on the People button, a few faces with names attached came into view. The picture of an older white haired man was next to the name Steven Griffin and then the dates 1925 –2004. Next was the picture of a mostly bald man with wire-rimmed glasses and the name James Childress, CEO. The third picture was a woman. A pretty, forty-something, blonde and the name-Susan Blackburn, President.

"Wait a minute."Said Sean "I've seen her before."

"Where?"

Scratching his head he tried to remember but no luck. "I can't say but I just know it. She is somebody I've seen before. Maybe with a different hair color."Closing his eyes he tried to imagine her picture with dark hair. "I'm calling Tasker."Taking the cell phone from his pocket.

Kathy Dobbs was leaving the office. "Good luck. I hope you find what you are looking for. I feel bad for that young man's family in Detroit."

"Thank you Kathy."Dick replied. "Good luck to you too."

Sean moved to the corner of the room and began speaking as Agent Tasker answered promptly. "Hey me Carson. I want you to run a name for me."

"Okay. What's this about?"

"We have a lead at a company down the street from Lapone's office. Griffin and Childress. There's a woman named Susan Blackburn. She's the President of the company."

"Give me a minute."He could hear Bill Tasker giving the name to one of his other agents at a computer desk back in Detroit. And then he could hear someone say, "Are you sure?"

Tasker came back on the phone. "You are not going to believe this. Are you sitting down?"

"Wait let me put this on speaker so Dick can hear."He placed the phone on the desk next to the keyboard and mouse. "Go ahead."

"Susan Blackburn is… or should I say was…Susan Vandenberg. She was Charlie V's wife until they were divorced right after he was elected. I remember it was a minor scandal but she quickly disappeared. Blackburn is her maiden name."

They just stared at the cell phone and then looked at each other like two bums who just found a twenty-dollar bill.

"Oh and here's one more thing. She was married before. Not too many people knew that before Charlie she was married to a Chicago man named Anthony Mancini for about six months. He was serving time for bank fraud and died of a stroke before he got out. Pretty interesting stuff huh?"

"Now what?" Asked Dick

"Now you go talk to Susan Blackburn." Tasker replied. "But be careful."

Before ending the call, they discussed the impending meeting with Charlie V's ex-wife. Tasker was taking a big risk sending these two in without notifying his counterparts in Chicago. He had his reasons. He had heard about a possible cover up due to a connection between a United States Senator and people close to the Charlie V case. Nothing concrete but he was aware of other cases that mysteriously dissolved due to lack of evidence after a prominent name surfaced in the investigation. He was not going to let that happen this time.

66

The BMW made a left turn on to North Avenue after exiting the expressway. He had not expected to be back in the city but after a week in Calgary his anger and desire for revenge got the best of him. Paul Lapone, also known as the Canadian, Garret Rolston, drove toward Lake Michigan took a right on North Lasalle before luckily finding a parking place after only a few blocks. He locked the car after taking his small Nike gym bag, placed a Chicago Cubs cap on his head as he began walking the four blocks toward Lake Shore Drive and East Schiller and entered the high-rise condo building using his own passkey that the Boss had given him. Inside the familiar surroundings he poured himself a glass of scotch and sat in a chair with the lights off and the shades drawn. It was almost five PM and he would wait as long as necessary.

Susan Blackburn entered the elevator not suspecting that anyone might be waiting for her in the lobby. She had been extra cautious these past few days, but no one came to talk to her. Of course she sent flowers to the memorial service for her former husband but used the name Susan Vandenberg. Most observers felt that she had acted properly by staying away from the service and paid her respects from afar. Confident that she was able to maintain a low profile by using her maiden name, she continued with her normal routine without attracting attention. Stopping at the security desk to bid her customary 'good night' to Peter, the night guard, she was surprised to learn that the two gentleman sitting in the leather sofas near the window wished to speak with her if she had a minute and discarded the urge to bolt for the door leading to the parking garage deciding that would be too obvious. She would handle these two cops or whoever they were.

Sean rose to greet the lady even before she reached the sitting area and was impressed by her walk, her looks and her wardrobe a dark pin striped Halston suit with a beige silk Calvin Klein blouse buttoned all the way up to the neck. She was stunning. "Excuse me. Miss Blackburn?"

"Yes. Peter said you wished to meet me. What can I do for you gentlemen?"

Dick had also risen from the sofa but let Sean do the talking. "My name is Detective Carson and this is Mister Hagan. I hope we are not bothering you but we're here from Detroit as part of an investigation that leads us to a man named Paul Lapone. We were wondering if you know him."

With out hesitation she replied. "I know the name. I think he is one of our clients here but I do not know him personally."

A quick look at Dick to acknowledge the lie before continuing. "Are you sure? Because we were hoping you could give us some information on him. Anything at all."

"I'm afraid I just don't have anything for you right now but if you want to come back tomorrow I'll have one of our staff see if they can help you out. Would that be okay?"

"Yes. Of course." Sean said before adding. "You may be interested to know that Mister Lapone seems to be an acquaintance of your late ex-husband Governor Charles Vandenberg."

For a moment Dick thought he noticed her knees buckle but she quickly recovered. "Well you obviously have done your homework on me Detective Carson. I try very hard to keep my privacy and I am deeply saddened by the death of my former husband but any relationship he had with one of our clients here at Griffin and Childress would be purely coincidental. Now if you'll excuse me, I have to leave now or I'll be late for an appointment."

"Very well then. We'll be back tomorrow."

She looked at each of them sternly the added. "I assume you'll have a search warrant. If not, I'll have you speak with our attorneys. Good evening gentlemen."

They watched as she walked away without looking back. She stopped again at the guard desk and said something to Peter before leaving through the plain door to the garage area. Dick walked over to the guard desk and asked Peter "Did the lady say anything to you about us?"

Smiling he said. "Yeah she did. She said if you guys come back or try to enter the elevator I should shoot you."

It took a moment to realize that Peter was just being a smart ass before Dick smiled back at him. "I don't think that would be good idea Peter. It would be kind of messy and the lady would probably make you clean it up."

As they headed for the front door Dick poked Sean in the arm and said sarcastically. "That went well now didn't it?"

Michael Ripinski

67

After parking the Lexus in the garage under her building, Susan entered the elevator and pressed the key to the penthouse on the twentieth floor. Unnerved from the conversation with the two detectives from Detroit, she planned to make a few phone calls thinking that she would need some help on this. Maybe even protection. She had not heard form Lapone and something made her uneasy about his absence. Their last conversation did not go well because they argued about the way things were going and her decision to eliminate Charlie and the others.

She closed the door behind her and dropped her soft leather bag onto the narrow table without noticing the figure sitting in the chair.

"Hello Boss."

Startled, she grabbed the back of a dining table chair. "Oh my God! What the fuck are you doing here? And what did you do to yourself? You look like shit."

He thought about just shooting her right then and there but decided that he needed answers first, having had a lot of time to think these past few weeks. Concluding that the whole thing was a set up to bring down Charlie, Bob and friends by getting them involved in the Big Beaver project he figured that killing them was not part of the original plan but became necessary in the end. Or maybe not. He needed to know. "I want some answers Susan."

Still standing by the chair she replied. "For what? You screwed up and we had to do what was necessary. Charlie was ready to give himself up and take us down with him."

"I screwed up?"He roared. Standing now she could see the

gun pointed at her and took a step back. "I don't think so. I think you had this whole thing planned from the beginning. Only you never expected to have to kill Charlie. But I'm guessing that it was not a difficult decision. You really hated his guts that bad didn't you?"

"You don't know what you're talking about. We had a nice deal going and we stood to make twenty, maybe thirty million. You and your boy Joey screwed up. After we took care of Walt that should have been the end. But Joey got careless."

He took another step forward and raised the gun at her head about five feet away. "You know I thought we had something special. I didn't even mind calling you 'Boss' because you liked it that way, especially in bed. That's all over now Susan. You underestimated me."

The portable phone on the coffee table rang which distracted him just enough for her to make a move. Susan Blackburn was a highly skilled in martial arts and possessed cat like quickness and reflexes. Dropping to the floor and pushing the chair at him she rolled to her right and grabbed the leather bag off the table while the phone continued ringing. He fired but missed as she continued sliding along the floor extracting her own weapon, a 38 Smith and Wesson, from the bag. With the light still off he could not see where she went and thought he saw a movement near the door but it was only her shadow. He fired another round into the floor and turned just in time to hear a click behind him. She stood holding the gun at his head.

"Drop it asshole."

The gun hit the hardwood floor and she kicked it away with her foot. "Sit your ass down over there."Motioning to the sofa. "I have to figure this out. I should just kill you right now but then I'd have to deal with your slimy carcass."

They remained in silence for a few minutes as she calmly sat across from him still pointing the 38 at his head. "Why did you come back? I had you figured to leave the country. You had told me once that if it ever got too hot, you'd just disappear and no one would find you."

"I don't know why. Maybe I had to know if it was all a set up. Was it?"

She didn't answer right away instead kept pointing the gun at him as a smile came upon her lips. Shaking her head from side to side she stood and motioned for him to stand up as well.

"Are we going somewhere?" he asked.

Still silent as they walked toward the door. "I don't know why I am doing this Paul. But I am letting you leave. But only if you promise to keep going and not come back. Don't think about going to Vegas. Dominic will be watching for you. I already spoke to him. Just leave and disappear like you always said you would. Do we have a deal?"

"Deal." He whispered realizing he had caught a break.

As he walked out the door she said. "Yeah. It was all a set up. Only you were not supposed to be included. It just worked out that way."

Michael Ripinski

68

"It took some digging but we have an address for Susan Blackburn. She lives in a high rise off Lake Shore just north of the Golden Mile or whatever it's called. I think it would be good idea for you guys to check it out, see if you can learn anything or see if she leaves. Follow her."Tasker was speaking to them again on Sean's cell phone.

Dick was thinking that it was time they turned this thing over to the Feds and headed back to Detroit. The whole thing was a little weird for him with the secrecy and all. "Miss Blackburn is a pretty sharp lady and I get the feeling that she would expect to be followed. She'll be watching out for us. Can't you get somebody else to handle it?"

"I wish I could give you guys the whole story but for now I ask that you just trust me. We can't let her slip away."

Sean said. "I agree with Dick but we'll go anyway. When this is all over. I expect some answers."

"We'll talk."Said Tasker.

They drove to the address provided and circled the block maneuvering the one-way streets with some confusion. Along one narrow side street they noticed a uniformed cop standing next to a black BMW looking inside and writing down the license plate. When the cop returned to his vehicle they could observe him on the radio calling in the plate and talking to someone on the other end. Lucky enough to spot a vacant space in front of a driveway about a half a block away, Sean parked knowing they would move if anybody came along to enter and the cop didn't seem to notice them as he sat in his vehicle waiting for further instructions.

"Didn't the APB on Lapone say something about him driving a BMW?" asked Dick

"Yeah but there are only about ten thousand black BMW's in Chicago." As Sean said this they noticed the man wearing a Cubs baseball cap and sunglasses walking briskly toward the BMW and slowed up as he noticed the cop exiting his vehicle. A conversation was taking place as the man reached into his pocket to extract his wallet presumably to show his ID to the cop who asked him to take it out and hand it to him. Without turning around the cop walked backwards to his car and reached in for the radio reading the information to his dispatch while the man in the Cubs cap stood looking around nervously. The cop returned and it appeared that he was asking more questions and Dick noticed that he had unclipped his holster placing his hand on the handle of his service weapon.

"Something's going down." Dick whispered.

"Yeah. Let's stay cool for a minute."

The Cubs guy was pointing to the trunk of his car and seemed to be telling the cop that he wanted to have him look at something inside. After a short discussion the cop took a step back and pointed for the man to open his trunk. As agreed the man popped the lid and stood aside as the cop came closer to peer into the space.

"Bad idea." Sean observed as they witnessed the man point to something toward the back of the trunk. Swiftly the Cubs guys reached over, slammed the lid down onto the cop's head, knocking him to the ground and began kicking him.

"Let's go." They said in unison as the man in the BMW reached down to retrieve the officer's weapon but they were on him before he could lift it out. Sean, directly in front of him standing in the street and Dick to the side, both had their weapons drawn.

"Don't even think about it." Said Sean with his gun aimed at the Cubs cap.

The man in the cap stood tensed and motionless, removing his hand from the officer's gun A few seconds later he raised his hands above his head as Dick moved in to check on the status of the cop.

"He's out cold but alive. I'll call it in on his radio."

"No wait. I can explain. This is a case of mistaken identity. They're looking for a local man and I am a Canadian citizen. I have a lot of money in my trunk and the cop was trying to make me pay him off to let me go."

"Nuh, Uh. I don't think so."Dick spoke as he raised his gun and moved closer to the man. "I think your name is Paul Lapone and you are going to answer for the murder of Charles Vandenberg among others."

Suddenly, Lapone lowered his head and barreled into Dick, wrestling him to the ground before he could get a shot off. The two men rolled into the space behind another parked car as Sean moved in closer waiting until the tangle of arms and legs could be sorted out. He saw that Lapone had escaped Dick's headlock and had begun running toward a fence near the alley where they had parked. Tempted to shoot for his head, he lowered his aim and squeezed off one round which entered the right thigh of his target sending him tumbling to the ground as another Chicago police car came speeding around the corner followed by a black unmarked detective's car. Uniformed and plain clothes cops had guns drawn and pointed at everyone including Dick who had risen from behind the parked car.

"I'm a cop"Shouted Sean Carson. "This bag of shit on the ground is wanted for the murder of the Governor of Michigan."

In a few minutes the whole thing was explained and the Chicago police took Lapone into custody while Dick and Sean were detained and questioned extensively on the scene. An ambulance was called for the original cop who had enough sense to call for back up in the first place. He had a concussion but nothing more serious. After several calls to Tasker in Detroit and the local FBI office, they were driven to the Chicago Police Headquarters where they answered more questions for the next few hours.

Michael Ripinski

69

Bill Tasker caught the next plane to Chicago as soon as he was notified of the capture. With authority in the case against Lapone for the murder of Charlie as well as the conspiracy in the Big Beaver land deal, he was able to move quickly against Susan Blackburn. Paul Lapone tried to cut a deal for life in prison in exchange for giving them enough information to arrest her. Knowing that she was being investigated, Susan Blackburn made an attempt to leave the country but was apprehended at O'Hare Airport after she was already seated on a flight to Montreal. She was fifteen minutes from getting away although the FBI was confident she would be caught on the other end. Of course she lawyered up and the trial would be months away. She tried to blame it all on Lapone.

As key witnesses in the investigation, both Sean Carson and Dick Hagan became somewhat famous as the two Detroit cops who apprehended Lapone; whom the newspapers began calling the *Ruthless Killer of Charlie V*. Dick was already being called a Super Cop for his taking down Joey Palzonian and capture of Charlie V's killer. Interview requests were numerous but he declined them all preferring to deflect attention to the case, which started it all in the first place. He had gotten justice for poor Tom Hodges and that was what meant the most to him.

As the preparation began for the trial of Susan Blackburn, Dick, Sean and Tasker sat in a private meeting room adjacent to the federal prosecutor's office in Detroit.

"I told you guys I would let you know why I sent you to Chicago."

Dick folded his arms and leaned back in the padded swivel

chair."We've been waiting for this."

"Alright."He began. "You guys recall the people you found on the website of Griffin and Childress?"

"Yeah. I remember. We were in Lapone's office."replied Sean.

"There was a picture of a distinguished white haired man named Steven Griffin. He was the founder of the firm and he died in two thousand four. Now does the name Barbara Griffin Williams ring a bell?"

"You mean Attorney General Williams?"asked Dick.

"Yep. Steven Griffin was her dad. She was from Chicago but after attending Harvard Law School she stayed on the east coast where she met her husband Stanley Williams of the Newport Rhode Island Williams family and heir to the Williams and Borland retail chain. Barbara Griffin Williams became a Federal District Judge before being appointed Attorney General three years ago.

Dick unfolded his arms and cocked his head to one side with a curious look. "Okay so what does this have to do with Susan Blackburn?"

Knowing that he was teasing them just a little bit it was time to fill them in. "Susan Blackburn's mother's name was Margaret Griffin Blackburn. She was Steven Griffin's older sister and she died in nineteen ninety five."

"So..."

Tasker did not let Sean finish. "Yup. Susan is a first cousin to our Attorney General. That's why the Department of Justice guys have been snooping around. They got a tip that Lapone was a client of Griffin and Childress and they were trying to do some pre-emptive damage control. We found him first. Thanks to you guys."

Placing his hands flat open on the table Sean asked. "Now what happens?"

"The news will break tomorrow about Susan's relationship to Barbara Williams and the Attorney General will issue a statement declaring her shock that a distant cousin, whom she hasn't spoken to in years, could be involved in such a horrific crime. She will distance herself so far they'll think Susan was an adopted orphan from a tribe of gypsies."

Standing and moving to the window facing Woodward Avenue in Downtown Detroit, Dick Hagan shook his head. "It still doesn't make sense. I mean I don't see the motive. Would Susan Blackburn have her ex-husband killed just for being a philandering jerk? Why did she go to the effort of the complex scheme on the Big Beaver land deal?"

As a light rain left droplets sliding down the pane, Tasker and Carson joined him at the window. Carson pointed to a plain black Crown Vic cruising down below. "You remember those days? We did a lot of good work in this city man."

"Yeah and we came out of it alive."Dick replied.

Tasker let them have their moment before adding. "Here's the motive. Susan Blackburn was bought out by Bob the Banker. He paid her off to leave Charlie. He wanted her out of the picture because he felt she had too much influence on the Governor. Bob and Susan disagreed fundamentally on just about everything especially the way state money was spent for private development. Bob also encouraged Charlie's little encounters, which eventually led to Rita Jacob. Obviously Susan hated her for stealing her husband but mostly for the way she flaunted it. So the plan to get them involved in the ill-fated Big Beaver project was her idea and she had Lapone to help her carry it out. I don't think she expected the screwups by Lapone and Joey Palzonian when he killed Walt Jacob and then the Hodges kid. Once it started she could not stop the wheels from turning and she eventually had to have them killed. Lapone was just a pawn. It was Susan Blackburn's game from the beginning. She's one ruthless broad."

After a few minutes of further discussion about all the details and confirmation of their meetings with the Federal Prosecutor, the three men stood by the door shaking hands.

"One more thing."Agent Tasker paused. Then added. "Lapone is going to sing. He will testify against Susan Blackburn if the deal is right. You'll like this one. He says that she made him call her 'Boss' even when they were in bed together. That's the real interesting part. She used him in more ways than one."

Michael Ripinski

70

The trial of Susan Blackburn was national front-page news for several weeks. All the dirty laundry from the administration of Charlie V was aired and cable TV enjoyed their highest ratings since the OJ trial. Eventually a jury took three days to convict her on three counts of conspiracy to commit murder and the assassination of an elected official. She received the death sentence but the appeals would take years. All the sleazy details from the trail were exposed and her lawyers made her look like somewhat of a sympathetic character who let her emotions get in the way. Lapone was also convicted as his deal with the government fell apart and he would keep the lawyers busy with the appeals process.

On a cool autumn evening as they walked together among the restaurants and shops of downtown Royal Oak, Dick and Melissa hardly spoke. He had finished testifying and needed some time away from the spotlight. He squeezed her hand gently. "I want to leave town for a while. I looked on-line and found a place in Key West that I can get cheap for a week or two."

Melissa had been on an emotional roller coaster herself and since he was all wrapped up in the trial, she had felt him becoming distant. She thought she was losing him. Now he was leaving. Maybe for good. "Do you have a ticket yet?"

He stopped and looked in her eyes, holding both hands in his. She thought that this was it. The big let down. *Thanks Melissa. You've been real sweet but I have to move on.* She could read his mind.

Reaching into the pocket on the inside of his sport jacket, he produced an envelope and held it for her to see the emblem of American Airlines. "I have my ticket right here. The plane leaves on

Saturday."

Her heart sank and she began to tear up.

"I also have a ticket for you. It'll be just the two of us."

He surprised her. What did he just say? He wanted her to join him in Florida. In an instant she jumped into his arms and they embraced as another couple passed by and smiled. "You bet your ass I'll go with you Dick Hagan."

They were somewhere over Kentucky as the jet cruised along at twenty eight thousand feet. Dick was looking out the window and Melissa was leafing through the in-flight magazine, reading the occasional article about attractions in one of the destination cities for American Airlines. Mostly she glanced at the ads for air purifying machines and cheap luggage as well as the latest in travel amenities like inflatable pillows and gel filled eye shields to help relive the stress for the hurried and harried business travelers.

"I forgot to tell you something."He mumbled.

"Did you say something? "she replied without looking up.

Reaching over and pushing the magazine down to her lap he spoke again. "I forgot to mention something before we left."Sounding serious as he continued. "Sean Carson and his chief in Troy called this morning before we left. They offered me the job as a detective in Troy again. Want me to start right after we get back."

Her forehead wrinkled, her lips quivered and she let out a sigh as she anticipated his next statement. She had seen him in action during the past few months and she knew that this work was in his blood. She loved him and she decided to stick with him no matter what. "How's the pay?"she asked for no apparent reason.

"I don't know. I didn't ask."grinning with teeth showing. "I turned them down. I'm done with all that. Hell I'm not sure we're even coming back from Key West. From what I hear I can get a job on a shrimp boat or learn to be a bone-fishing guide. That sounds a lot better than chasing scum bag killers."

"Oh you stinker."She exclaimed while smacking him lovingly on the arm. Then she leaned over and kissed him, holding on, running her hands through his hair as a smiling flight attendant reached over and turned out the overhead light.

70

The Fed Ex driver stopped in front of the house on Palmer Avenue in Madison Heights Michigan, taking a few minutes to check the address on the cardboard envelope in his hand. Stepping quickly from his truck and hopped up the steps to the modest, three- bedroom ranch, he did not even have to ring the doorbell as the stooped shouldered, white haired woman had already opened the door.

"What do you want?"with a gravel whisper.

"Are you Mrs. Josephine Hodges?"

"Yes."

"This package is for you. Can you sign here please?"Holding a signature device, he pointed to the square next to her name on the LED screen.

Confused for a moment by the instructions, she took the small pencil and scribbled her name.

"Have a nice evening."He said politely as he bounced back down to his truck leaving her standing on the porch looking at the envelope. After a moment she went inside and sat on the well-worn sofa in the small living room. She had spent most of her time in recent months just like this. Sitting alone in her house. Crying. Rarely going out except for necessities and worrying about how she would make ends meet now that her son was gone. Josephine Hodges opened the envelope and extracted a letter while leaving another smaller piece of paper inside. She noticed the letterhead from Griffin and Childress in Chicago Illinois and began to read:

Dear Mrs. Hodges,

As we became aware of the very sad and tragic death of your son, Thomas Hodges, at the hand of a former employee of this firm, we felt compelled to do the right thing. No amount of money can ever compensate for your loss but as a gesture of our deep sense of compassion and sympathy, please accept this check in his memory. You are under no obligation to end any legal proceedings against this firm or any of our current or former employees. We wish you only health and happiness in your future.

Sincerely

James Childress
CEO

Josephine Hodges slowly reached inside the envelope with a trembling hand and extracted the blue and white piece of paper. It was a check for five hundred thousand dollars.

ABOUT THE AUTHOR

Michael Ripinski has been developing his writing skills for many years while achieving success in various business management positions. He is currently a real estate agent in Royal Oak Michigan. Drawing on these experiences he enjoys creating interesting characters and colorful dialogue while telling a good story. He writes an occasional blog for the Royal Oak Patch, on-line newspaper, is a devoted and loyal fan of all the major Detroit sports teams and an avid golfer.

Michael lives in Royal Oak with his wife of thirty six years Dawne, and their two cats Geno and Lucie.